# THE MAN WHO
# LOST HIMSELF

Borgo Press Books by ANDRÉ BEAUNIER

*The Man Who Lost Himself: A Symbolist Novel*

# THE MAN WHO LOST HIMSELF

## A SYMBOLIST NOVEL

## ANDRÉ BEAUNIER

Translated by Brian Stableford

THE BORGO PRESS

MMXIII

CLASSICS OF
FANTASTIC LITERATURE
NUMBER EIGHT

THE MAN WHO LOST HIMSELF

FIRST EDITION

Published by Wildside Press LLC

www.wildsidebooks.com

# THE MAN WHO
# LOST HIMSELF

# CONTENTS

# INTRODUCTION

*L'Homme qui a perdu son moi* by André Beaunier, here translated as *The Man Who Lost Himself*, was originally published
in Paris by Librairie Plon in 1911. That translation of the titular
phrase is a trifle oversimplified because English cannot quite
reproduce the ambiguity of the French "L'Homme," which can
be construed as "the man" with reference to an individual or
"Man" in the sense of humankind. The "a" in the title derives
from the second significance, suggesting that the story of the
particular individual whose "loss" of himself is described and
analyzed can be seen as emblematic of the entire race having,
in a sense, lost its "self."

André Beaunier was born in Evreux in 1869 and educated
at the Lycée Henri IV and the École Normale Supérieure. His
literary ambitions took time to bear their first fruit, but eventually made him one of the most respected critics of literature and
drama in Paris, working in the former capacity for the *Revue
des Deux Mondes* and in the latter for the *Écho de Paris*. He was
the literary critic most esteemed by Marcel Proust, who regularly sought his advice about his works in progress, and he was
also a close friend of Paul Bourget—the dedicatee of *L'Homme
qui a perdu son moi*—with whom he wrote a comedy drama
in collaboration. After publishing his first novel, *Les Dupont-
Leterrier* in 1900—a reaction to the Dreyfus affair—Beaunier
maintained a prolific level of publication until his death in 1925,
averaging more than two volumes a year. Although many of
those volumes were collections or extensions of his journalistic

work, he also produced numerous novels and extended biographies.

In general, Beaunier's career trajectory seems to have been uncommonly untroubled; he was sufficiently well off while serving his long "apprenticeship" never to have to endure the financial hardships suffered by many would-be writers, and he was not only old enough to avoid conscription during the Great War of 1914-18 but had the rare privilege of being able to keep on working and publishing throughout the conflict. That lack of conspicuous misfortune and strife, as well as a hostility to political radicalism that was not unconnected with it, has undoubtedly contributed to the relative lack of attention paid by literary historians to his life and works, but it is doubtful that he would have considered his life to have been free of difficulty. His fiction strives hard to suggest—presumably sincerely—that he was by no means unfamiliar with suffering, albeit of a strictly cerebral variety, and that he had endured the torments that writers are supposed to undergo in order to fuel their inspiration.

Before his career got off the ground Beaunier had a strong interest in art criticism, and once planned to write an encyclopedic history of art, but eventually reduced his ambition to a more realistic scale, producing a theoretical work on *L'Art de regarder les tableaux* [The Art of Looking at Paintings] (1906), published in the same year as *Souvenirs d'un peintre* [A Painter's Memoirs], based on the life of Georges Clairin. His sweeping general interest in esthetics also embraced music, and his principal claim to fame in the Parisian literary community at the outset of his career was that he was Isadora Duncan's lover—or one of them, at least—during the interval she spent in Paris in 1900-02; a remarkable circumstance that the dancer felt obliged to explain in her autobiography, where she observed that although he was short, fat and bespectacled, she loved his intelligence.

Given that *L'Homme qui a perdu son moi* features a spectacular improvisatory dancer in a key symbolic role, it is probably worth noting that Beaunier almost certainly saw performances by the other two famous exponents of that art who were contemporary with Isadora Duncan, and were subsequently reckoned to be her great rivals: Loie Fuller, who had her own tent at the 1900 Paris Exposition and took Duncan away from Paris to tour with her in 1902; and Maud Allan, who was also resident in Paris in the early 1900s, and whose notorious "Vision of Salomé" he would undoubtedly have made the effort to see. (Isadora Duncan remarked that the only time she saw ever Beaunier in tears was when he heard news of the death of Oscar Wilde).

It might also be relevant to a reading of *L'Homme qui a perdu son moi* that approximately two years before he began writing it, in 1908, Beaunier had married another famously beautiful artiste, the opera singer Jeanne Raunay (1868-1942). She was the daughter of the historical painter Jules Richomme—Raunay was a stage name—and she promptly retired from performance following her marriage and was known thereafter as "Madame Beaunier." After her husband's death she took up writing herself, signing herself Jeanne André-Beaunier.

The direction that Beaunier's career would eventually take was effectively fixed when he obtained his first notable success with his fourth book, *La Poésie nouvelle* [The New Poetry] (1902), a detailed study of the Symbolist school that was described by Stuart Merrill as the best book on that topic. Although he was only a little younger than many of the Symbolist poets who comprised the school between 1885 and 1900, by the time Beaunier began publishing prolifically himself the bandwagon had passed, and his name is usually associated with Symbolism as that of an observer rather than a practitioner. He was, however, strongly influenced by the school and applied its methods conscientiously in many of his novels, including and especially *L'Homme qui a perdu son moi*.

Symbolism was primarily a school of poetry, although its philosophy and techniques overflowed prodigally into short fiction via prose-poetry, but the ornate and highly-structured prose favored by the Symbolist method is difficult to accommodate to the novel, whose fundamental narrative technique is naturalistic; wholeheartedly Symbolist novels are scarce and often somewhat misshapen. Many of the leading figures in the field never attempted a novel, and those who did often produced bizarre patchworks like Gustave Kahn's *Le Conte de l'or et silence* (1898; tr. as *The Tale of Gold and Silence*), but symbolism as a device rather than an overriding esthetic philosophy had always featured significantly in serious novels, including those of the most determined Naturalists, and although Symbolism and Naturalism were often regarded as rival Schools in the 1890s there was no real opposition between them. Paul Bourget had also been one of the prominent literary critics to analyze and praise the "*poésie nouvelle*," and his novels routinely used symbolic devices, although he became the central figure of a new school of "Neo-Naturalism," characterized by the intensity and supposed sophistication of its focus on the psychology of its protagonists. The first three chapters of *L'Homme qui a perdu son moi* have strong affinities with Bourget's narrative method, and it is only in the concluding chapter IV—which begins, tellingly, with an interpolated fabular narrative—that Symbolist technique takes over, corresponding with a watershed in the protagonist's descent into madness.

Beaunier's previous novels had used similar strategies of hybridization, the fabular element being most pronounced in his fourth novel, *Le Roi Tobol* [King Tobol] (1905), in which the protagonist is commissioned to find the secret of happiness, and is forced by a series of exemplary adventures to conclude that both individual and collective human happiness are impossible of attainment, although parrots might be better situated because of the limitation of their desires. *L'Homme qui a perdu son moi* is, however, more ambitious than his previous works in its scope and, even more conspicuously, in its passion. Although the protagonist is ostensibly presented as a horrible warning rather than a shining example, only gradually repenting ideas that the narrative voice ostentatiously represents as abhorrent, every sympathy is claimed for him, and the novel has admitted autobiographical elements that confuse its supposed moral and give rise to serious doubts about the narrative voice's reliability.

Even as an account of a particular individual who "loses" himself, the story of *L'Homme qui a perdu son moi* has intriguing paradoxicalities, but in vaguely attempting to make that story emblematic of a historical mis-step on the part of the human race (or, at least, its French lapsed Catholic component) the paradoxicality moves so close to manifest absurdity as to become an interesting specimen of psychological eccentricity. The means by which the novel's protagonist contrives to drive himself to madness and despair is becoming a scientist, and thus forsaking the religious faith of his childhood, gradually retreating from all rewarding human contact into a cold and lonely condition of pure cerebration, from which return eventually proves impossible. That was a story that had been told before, and might even be reckoned to have become something of a cliché, but Beaunier's attempt to use it as a diagnosis of a more general social malaise, and to make science itself, rather than excessive individual devotion to it, into a dire threat essentially inimical to human life, was much more extravagant than the argument's routine course.

As a devout Catholic—and, more particularly, as a Catholic whose belief had wavered in adolescence and young adulthood before being reaffirmed, all more zealously in consequence— Beaunier was far from being alone in his resentment of the manner in which propaganda in favor of science had generally been closely interlinked in France with a particular hostility to Catholicism. From Voltaire's scathing satires through August Comte's philosophical championship of "positivism" to Ernest Renan's skeptical analyses of Scriptural history, the two campaigns had marched in step. Renan's book *L'Avenir de la science: pensées de 1848* (1890; tr. as *The Future of Science*), which is cited as a significant negative inspiration in Beaunier's dedicatory preface, was so widely considered as an anti-Clerical text that its proto-futurological aspects were largely ignored; the notion that future history would be shaped by progressive developments in science rather than by the moralistic authority of religion was debated as a blasphemy rather than an empirical hypothesis. Most of the defenders of the faith were, however, consciously handicapped by their awareness that the empirical hypothesis did have a good deal of persuasive evidence in its favor. Beaunier was exceptional in being willing to try, at least as an experiment, to reject that evidence and argue that, in fact, science was not only not progressive but not even relevant to human life, and that insofar as it was thought to be progressive and relevant, it was inimical.

It is difficult to believe that Beaunier actually believed that, or even that the narrative voice he adopted in *L'Homme qui a perdu son moi* really believes it, in spite of its insistent protests, but at the very least he tried it out for size. He was, at least temporarily, prepared to consider seriously the argument that because science calls religious faith into question, it is therefore completely "inhuman," and thus intrinsically evil. His novel can be seen as a personal thought-experiment conducted to test that proposition, and from that viewpoint, its method and its result are interestingly confused.

What the novel calls "science" it represents as a relatively recent invention, and is, in fact, closely connected with the evolution of the idea of a "scientist": a specialist professional practitioner of "science." That notion had emerged along with the idea and evidence of the profession; in English the word "scientist" was coined in the 1820s by William Whewell, but it is arguable that the coinage was slightly belated, the idea dating back to the latter decades of the eighteenth century, when experimental chemistry conclusively replaced mystical alchemy and the modern theory of the chemical elements replaced Classical elementary theory. As soon as there were "scientists," however, in reality and in literary representation, they quickly acquired a set of supposedly-typical characteristics, partly borrowed from traditional images of wizardy (all the great proto-scientists of the Renaissance tended to be stigmatized as sorcerers and suspected of having made real or metaphorical Faustian pacts with the Devil) but mostly based on wry empirical observation.

The supposedly typical psychology of the scientist was analyzed in France by early proto-psychologists, especially the pioneers of "retrospective diagnosis" François Lélut and François Leuret, who were keenly interested in the supposed relationship between genius and madness, and by scientists themselves, notably Henri Poincaré, another writer cited in Beaunier's preface and footnotes. It was also, however, a key element of the early development of the French *roman scientifique*, which rapidly established a kind of standard portrait of "the scientist." That stereotype is explicitly and carefully delineated in Samuel Henri Berthoud's "Voyage au ciel" (1841; tr. as "A Heavenward Voyage") and "Le Second soleil" (c1860; tr. as "The Second Sun"), which are essentially psychological case-studies cast as allegorical fiction, but it was given more relaxed and popular representation in the works of Jules Verne, notably in the characterization of Professor Lidenbrock in *Voyage au centre de la terre* (1864; rev. 1867; tr. as *Journey to the Center of the Earth*) and Professor Aronnax in *Vingt mille lieues sous les mers* (1870; tr. as *Twenty Thousand Leagues Under the Sea*).

There is a remarkable unanimity about such fictional images, which represent scientists as people at least distracted and often completed isolated from the cares of social and domestic life by their cerebration, as obsessive in their quotidian habits as in their tireless research endeavors, so inattentive to formal etiquette that everyone around them is liable to regard them as eccentric, if not mad. Such characters are usually well-meaning, and often philanthropic, sometimes even beloved, but they are also seen as dangerous, to others as well as themselves, because of their negligence and lack of "common sense"—and they are seen as sadly vulnerable to more extreme forms of anti-sociality, as exemplified by Professor Aronnax's bizarre counterpart, Captain Nemo.

Real scientists are, of course, very variable as individuals, and this image is a caricature, but like all caricatures, it does exaggerate something real and fairly typical. Enough actual scientists bear enough resemblance to the stereotype to support it. The literary image of the scientist that became standardized with remarkable rapidity, however, did not assert that the alleged psychological peculiarities of the scientist polluted his science—quite the contrary. Much is frequently made in *romans scientifiques* of the fact that these strange, inept, rather quaint individuals, who cannot button their waistcoats properly, nevertheless produce something sublime, magnificent and useful, sometimes without meaning to or even being conscious of it. Insofar as the nineteenth-century *roman scientifique* began to build a myth of science as well as an image of the scientist, that myth is one of beautiful order emerging out of droll confusion, and great boons out of side-effects, the cardinal historical examples being the applications of mechanics, optics and electromagnetism to locomotion, work and both literal and figurative illumination.

In the twentieth century, that dichotomy came to seem less manifest, especially during the Great War, when the applications of science to mass murder became very obvious indeed, and the supposed intrinsic vulnerability of scientists to moral oblivion and outright madness much more dangerous, but in 1911, that tide had not yet turned, and Beaunier was exceptional. His stance was unusual not so much because he was skeptical of the assumption that technological and social progress went hand in hand, but because he made no use whatsoever of the best argument available to support that case: the proposition that, in giving humans more power, the technological applications of science were enhancing the destructive potential of political oppression and conflict. Indeed, he did not even take advantage of the argument that the contributions so far made by science to medical efficacy were largely illusory, which would have seemed far more plausible in 1911 than it does now. Instead, he not only conceded but emphasized the claim that applied science can not only produce effective medical treatments but is potentially capable of producing quasi-miraculous cures.

This concession creates tremendous difficulties for the narrative voice of *L'Homme qui a perdu son moi* in its apparent assertion that the attempts by the protagonist's mentor to argue that such effects are irrelevant—a position not even supported by the protagonist while he retains some semblance of sanity—are more than a mere psychological quirk, but somehow reflective of science itself and thus of a threat to the collective sanity of humankind. It is that strange confusion and conflict of ideas that makes the novel uniquely interesting as a specimen of the thought of its era.

Just as he was born a few years too late to participate in the heyday of Symbolism, Beaunier came into salon society a little too late to catch the days when scientists and littérateurs routinely mingled freely in Parisian salons. Even so, it is perhaps slightly surprising that his enormous list of acquaintances does not seem to have included Gustave Le Bon, who was a familiar face in several notable salons in the early 1900s and whose book *L'Évolution de la matière* (1905; tr. as *The Evolution of Matter*) is strikingly relevant to the theme of *L'Homme qui a perdu son moi*; its consultation might have enabled Beaunier to make his account of Michel's theoretical development of the properties of sirium far less vague and considerable more interesting. Indeed, for a novel that is supposedly about science, in a determinedly serious fashion, *L'Homme qui a perdu son moi* manifests a remarkable near-total ignorance of what scientific work actually involves, what contemporary scientific theories actually contained, and what the potential scientific implications of the discovery that functions as a pivot of the plot might be. So complete is that ignorance, in fact, that sirium not only becomes a purely symbolic scientific discovery but a symbol devoid of any real significance, and hence of any real force or meaning.

Beaunier's non-fiction includes several essays on what he was wont to describe as "the Darwinian crisis"—by which he meant the shudder provoked in religious believers by Darwin's publication of the theory of the origin of species by natural selection. In one of his articles on the topic in the *Revue des Deux Mondes* he complimented Darwin for saying that what had had advanced was a scientific hypothesis and not a "philosophy," and then went on to lambast Ernst Haeckel and, more particularly, Félix Le Dantec—not without justice—for trying to elevate "Darwinism" into a philosophy of life. In *L'Homme qui a perdu on moi*, however, the one thing that is crystal clear about the theoretical edifice that the protagonist builds on the basis of his experiments with sirium is that it is not a scientific hypothesis but a philosophy—an exercise in metaphysics rather than physics. In the same way, the protagonist's mentor, "the Alchemist," makes "science" itself into a philosophy of life instead of a compendium of hypotheses—and even though the narrative voice and author are both utterly antipathetic to the Alchemist, to the point of refusing even to give him a name, it seems that they do exactly the same, insisting on considering "science" as a philosophy—merely as a species of atheism—rather than as testable knowledge capable of material application.

If that is a flaw in the novel's schema, however—and from a purely intellectual viewpoint, it undoubtedly is—it is a flaw that has some interesting results, certainly in an artistic sense, and perhaps in a philosophical sense too. Although the finest exercise in Symbolism featured in the novel—the development of the allegory of Brigitte, and its complication by the introduction of her symbolic counterpart La Métienka, in chapter IV—is actually irrelevant to the argument about science, the earlier symbolic interludes, which are much more closely connected to that argument, are almost as striking. The psychoanalytical allegory of music developed while the protagonist is listening to the organ in the cathedral in chapter I is interesting in this regard, but the real heart of the novel's symbolism, as it regards science, is the exceedingly strange representation in chapter III of scientific theorizing as the building of solitary towers.

It is the representation of theory-building as essentially isolating—and thus productive of insanity—that would doubtless seem oddest of all to scientists, who imagine successful theorization as means of unification and the creation of productive communal endeavors; and precisely because it is so strange, one is tempted to wonder whether it might be more revealing than intended. Although it is clearly not an accurate symbolic representation of scientific endeavor, it might still be an accurate symbolic representation of something else, wearing scientific theorization as a disguise—something of which even the writer might only have subliminally aware. Given that the protagonist has such obvious affinities with the author, one is tempted to wonder how much of his own bitter experience is being trans-figured in the character. Writing is, by necessity, a lonelier busi-ness than scientific research, and its obsessive quality can be at least as disruptive of intimate relationships and as conducive to depression and despair. That puzzle, whether it has a solution or not, is what makes the novel fascinating in spite of its seeming absurdity, fueling its undoubted force and verve.

\* \* \* \* \* \* \*

This translation was made from the London Library's copy of the 1911 Plon edition, which is advertised on its cover as the "fourth edition," although that only means that it was the fourth printing of the first edition—each printing probably being a thousand copies. In the context of the time, that would have make the book a moderate commercial success, reflecting the solid reputation Beaunier had built by then.

# DEDICATION:
# TO PAUL BOURGET

My dear master and friend,

You have been kind enough to accept the dedication of this novel. I offer it to you as evidence of my deferential and affectionate admiration, and also in memory of hours, unforgettable for me, of common toil in which I have sensed your mastery and your amity.

As in my previous writings—but this time, perhaps a little more clearly—I have tried to make contact here between pure ideas and the souls that receive them, who make them the rule of their life, and, in so doing, cannot help but alter them. If I had an exegete or a commentator, and if I merited it, he would doubtless indicate that such, moreover, is the object of all my works: the encounter of ideas and souls.

As a historian, I would have shown how humanity has been occupied, throughout the centuries, in diverting from their true significance the ideas that the princes of intelligence find, spread and thus deliver to troubling tribulations.

This novel is merely an anecdote, but an emblematic one. I have utilized it for the purpose I had of comparing science and religion, which are the two ideological compendia between which the epochs hesitate. The argument between scientists and the faithful goes back a long way, and it is ongoing. Where is the truth? It is not my prerogative to say. If I had had the audacity to claim that, I would certainly not have produced a novel but a dogmatic tract—and I would, for preference, have written in Latin, in order immediately to deter a reader who has good reason to be frivolous.

Whatever the dialectical conflict is in which scientists and the faithful are caught up, what I think I have perceived, having arrived at the end of my youth, is this: that one is wrong to count on science for the organization of societies and individuals.

In spite of the cherished individualism to which I remember having consecrated all my adolescent fervor, I can see today that we are not simply locations where ideas are brought into logical connection. My protagonist tries to do that, and he loses himself; I mean to say that science does not favor the happy and normal development of our individuality. It is abstract, and we are alive.

If my protagonist seems bizarre, that it because he takes his project to its conclusion, whereas, in reality, even the most scientific do not live entirely scientifically. They are scientists; that is their profession; but the essential principle of their life they have borrowed from other disciplines.

Michel Bedée proves, to his detriment, that science is inhuman. That word is not intended to denigrate it, but I observe that admirable science is something very different from us and, in brief, has almost nothing to do with us.

In 1890, when men of my generation spent their twenties, we were strongly influenced by a book that dated from 1848 but had just appeared, *The Future of Science* by Ernest Renan. We imagined then, with a prompt certainty, that science alone was going to govern our minds and guide our lives. We ardently read the preface to *Ten Years of Historical Studies* in which old Augustin Thierry, ill and blind by virtue of having worked incessantly, composed the sublime gospel of devotion to science.[1] And I had for a teacher the great Gaston Paris, who

1. Author's Note: "Here are a few lines from the preface of *Ten Years of Historical Studies*. This preface is dated Vesoul, 10 November 1834. 'If, as I am inclined to believe, the interest of science is counted among the number of great national interests, I have given my country all that a useful soldier

resembled Charlemagne and whom I loved respectfully. In 1870, at the Collège de France, he affirmed tragically that the quest for the exact truth is paramount, and did so with patriotic fervor. He was animated by an immense love of France; and, when he announced those noble formulae in the midst of war, he offered to his scientific faith a magnificent and paradoxical sacrifice.[2]

Such imposing doctrines stirred me; my entire generation

---

does on the field of battle. Whatever the destiny of my works might be, that example, I hope, will not go to waste. I would like it to serve to combat the kind of moral collapse that is the malady of the young generation; that it might bring back to the straight road of life some of those enervated souls who complain of lacking faith, who do not know where to go and search everywhere without finding anywhere an object of worship and devotion. Why say with so much bitterness that, in the world constituted as it is, there is no air for lungs, no employment for intelligences? Is there not serious and calm study? And is it not a refuge, a hope, a career within the range of everyone? With it, one gets through bad days without feeling their weight; one makes one's own destiny; one uses one's life nobly. That is what I have done, and would do again if I had to begin again; I would take the route that has led me to where I am. Blind and suffering, without hope and almost without release, I can render this testimony, which cannot be suspect on my part: there is something in the world worth more than material enjoyments; better than fortune; better than health itself; which is devotion to science.' In 1890, some of us recited that page like a gospel."

2. Author's Note: "The lecture by Gaston Paris to which I make allusion was given on 8 December 1870 at the Collège de France; it was entitled 'The Chanson de Roland and French Nationality.' Gaston Paris was substituting for his father, Paulin Paris. The 1870 lecture was not published until 1885 by Hachette in the first volume of La Poésie du moyen âge. Gaston Paris delivered his lecture in the middle of the 'circle of steel' that the German armies made around him, in 'terrible circumstances from which every moment that distracts us in patriotic preoccupations almost seems an illegitimate self-indulgence.' He declared: "I profess absolutely and without reserve this doctrine, that science has no other object than the truth, and the truth for its own sake, without any concern for the good or bad, regrettable or fortunate consequences that the truth might have in practice. Anyone who, for patriotic, religious or even moral motives, permits himself, in the facts he studies and the conclusions he draws therefrom, the slightest dissimulation or alteration, is not worthy of his place in the great laboratory, in which probity is a more indispensable entitlement for admission than skill.' The entire lesson is magnificent."

was aware of their prestige; they produced scientists, scholars and philosophers who made good use of science and served it well.

Those philosophers, scholars and scientists did not, however, go as far as my protagonist in the absolute abandonment of everything that is not pure idea. They did not, like him, make the sacrifice of their selves. They were, therefore, able to endure, and so I think that their example is illusory, if it is a question of establishing that science is sufficient in itself to constitute an ethic.

How much more human and better adapted to our needs is a very ancient belief, which has accompanied, through many ups and downs, our families, our ancestors, and which had gradually, even before our birth, prepared our souls and the conditions of their natural blossoming!

That is what I have attempted to say, in the form of a persuasive allegory, in this novelistic account of *The Man Who Lost Himself*. Will it be understood? I hope so. And will it be understood, as I desire, that I have examined, with tremulous sincerity, a fact about which nothing can be done, a poignant fact: the necessity of having, in the final account, fortified reasoning only to submit to it? It was at the time when I was reaching the middle of what is a very long life that I experienced a grave tenderness for my childhood, from which I once hastened to escape.

In sum, my dear Paul Bourget, here is this novel. I fear for it, but I have placed it under the tutelary protection of your name.

—André Beaunier

# CHAPTER ONE

*The tree of knowledge is not the tree of life.*
Lord Byron

"Michel! Michel!"

A loud voice resounded in the silence of the provincial dawn. Michel Bedée, who was coming from the railway station with a valise in his hand, raised his head and recognized the face of his old professor in the frame of a high window.

"Oh! Bonjour, Master!"

The other continued: "Is it really you? But what are you doing here, man of genius? Maman isn't ill?"

Michel shivered. "I hope not...I don't think so...."

"But no, no...I'd know that. Come in for a while, so that we can chat."

"Later, Master. I've just arrived—I haven't been to the house yet."

"To the house! You said that like little Michel Bedée, who was so sweet, gentle and namby-pamby. But it's not yet five o'clock. Are they expecting you? No? Maman's asleep—don't wake her. Come in here, until a reasonable hour."

Michel hesitated. He looked at his mother's house the end of the avenue: an old, quiet house with its shutters closed; a house asleep.

"That's true," he said. "I'll come in."

"Good—I'll open the door. Wait two minutes for me—I have to get dressed."

The other disappeared. Michel examined the window from which the cry of "Michel! Michel!" had come—and he remembered having heard, a second before that, without paying any heed to it, the sound of a window-catch grating, a sash opening, and two shutters, briskly pushed, clicking against a wall. He imagined the cheerful awakening of his master, greeting the dawn and the day that was recommencing with the quotidian cock-crow.

Five o'clock chimed at the cathedral. The first stroke caught Michel unawares, scaring him. Then he was astonished by the strangeness that the most familiar impressions of his childhood had for him. The five strokes succeeded one another at such long intervals, and such was their beautiful gravity, that one might have thought that the clock was bringing a certain emphasis to marking the phases of time. A sudden din; then a vibration that diminished toward silence; but then the din burst forth again. In the depths of his memory, Michel rediscovered the sounds and their rhythm. After the fifth stroke of the hour, he waited for another: the silence spread and flourished, an invisible marvel that reached the entire extent and tried to fill it.

The old man's house and its neighbors extended the top of the fortified bank of the old town, a sort of acropolis around which life had spread over the ages. For its lower story it utilized an old rampart that emerged from the ground like a natural rock. That centuries-old architecture was surmounted by walls that were not much younger, and just as solid, pierced by narrow windows; they did not stand entirely straight, but were slightly slanted back, forming a large truncated pyramid.

By virtue of that fact, the buildings of the avenue gave the impression of resting on naked foundations. Their irregular file, viewed from a distance, resembled a gigantic jaw whose incomplete dentition had bare roots.

On the other sides of the avenue, at a lower level, there were the gardens of the bishop's palace, the foliage of their beautiful trees shining with cheerful morning light.

While Michel waited, in front of a wooden door fortified

with iron, as low as an entrance to catacombs, and contemplated the deserted avenue and locked houses, he thought that sleep, in which the misfortunes of life are eased, had its most tranquil refuge in this part of the world.

The old man arrived.

"One second! One second!" he announced through the door.

The key turned in the lock, awkwardly—and then the loud voice cried: "Come in, Michel, man of genius!"

\* \* \* \* \* \*

The old man whom Michel Bedée called his mater was known in the little Breton town as the Alchemist. That nickname summarized the displeasure and alarm that his person inspired.

He was a man of seventy, tall, thin and vigorous, his bushy white hair cut short, his white beard sharply pointed, with small restless eyes and remarkably delicate features—save for the nose, which had once been damaged by an exploding retort. Swollen, scarred and pimply, that nose gave the face a comical aspect. One imagined that the local children would have made fun of it, multiplying facile gibes, if the habit of seeing it had not long abolished, in successive generations, the aptitude of noticing it. It was like the gargoyles on the buttresses of the cathedral, ridiculous and grimacing, which one went past without noticing, and which did not prevent the monument from being consecrated to a sublime fervor. If one observed the Alchemist's face in the right way, that nose no longer seemed to be the result of an accident; on the contrary, it became indispensable, adding a character of disdainful bonhomie and deliberate wit to the physiognomy. The soul that reigned in the little eyes reigned over heavy and ugly matter.

The old man had been the professor of chemistry at the college, but he had soon given up teaching. Devoid of all ambition, refusing the positions that were offered to him to, as he put it "perform his tricks," he dreamed of nothing but a quiet life and perpetual work. A small income permitted him to realize his ideal of solitary existence.

One day, he had been formally accused of atheism. That was nothing: he was suspected of devoted himself to diabolical works. Was he not trying to create life chemically? Had he not shown his pupils test-tubes in which bizarre arborescences were ramifying in a pale gelatin, born at his behest from as sulfate of calcium, like that plant that climbed from the loins of Jesse on church windows bearing saintly genealogies? From then on, he had been viewed with a suspicious eye. Devotees made the sign of the cross when he went past. The parents of pupils would not allow their sons to be exposed for a minute longer to the contagion of his skepticism. Pusillanimous and judicious, the principal had asked his colleague to deny the nasty rumors that were circulating: no, he was not trying to create life; no, he did not desire to rival God....

"The question can't be put in those terms," the Alchemist had replied, simply, and added: "Besides, I have better things to do than argue with such blockheads." And he had handed in his resignation.

Then he had lived in seclusion at home. From time to time, he went for walks—but not, like the philosopher Kant of Koeningsberg, at regular hours; docile to his experiments, he awaited their pleasure, and did not want any other liberty than they would grant him. As he no longer had the college laboratory at his disposal, he transformed his kitchen for that purpose, and sent his old housekeeper elsewhere, even though she protested against that invasion of diabolical cookery.

* * * * * * *

"Come in, my boy, come in," said the Alchemist to his former pupil.

He had taken him by the hand like a child, and led him along dark and winding corridors; then he took him into the laboratory.

It was a large room, poorly lit, which resembled the guard-room of an ancient castle or, even more so, the crypt of a church. Hollowed out in the bank against which its back wall rested, it only had one window looking out on to the avenue, barred with iron. The ceiling, with arched cavities, descended at regular intervals on to strong, stout pillars, crushing with motionless effort the sculpted capitals on which could be seen, among the faces of angels, a preacher with a fox's head throwing little women into his hood, and Aristotle on all fours with a prostitute astride him. All of that was covered and plastered by a thick layer of paint, worn away in places, allowing the sight of sharp corners of smoke-blacked stone.

In dark corners, furniture could be seen: a credenza, a sideboard and tables laden with books, flasks, mugs and pans. The floor was formed by granite slabs. An immense fireplace took up almost all of one wall and seemed capable of sheltering a shivering family under its mantel, like Saint Ursula in the most ample folds of her robe.

The Alchemist no longer made use of the fireplace; he threw old utensils and debris into it. He had installed a beautiful modern stove for coal, gas and electricity under the window; it was there that he worked; and, substituting his scientific labors for the alimentary labors of his housekeeper, it was there that he did all his conclusive or chimerical chemical cookery.

He led Michel Bedée into the light that entered through the green-tinted windows; he put his hands on his shoulders, looked into his eyes and said, gravely: "Greetings, Michel, man of genius!"

"No," Michel stammered. "Don't say that, I beg you, Master."

"And you, don't call me *Master* any longer. You seem to be mocking me. I known full well that I'm not...but after all, you are a man of genius, and I'm an old fool."

"Is that so?" said Michel, forcing himself to laugh for want of a better reply.

"Don't laugh. It's the exact truth!" replied the old man. Then he went on: "Now let's sit down, and you can tell me a little about your discovery."

There was an expression of lassitude on Michel's face, as if he were having difficulty searching his memory for the tedious details of an old adventure that no longer interested him.

The old man noticed that. "I'm annoying you—but that doesn't matter. Come on, tell me: your sirium, you first found it in Sirius?"[3]

"Yes, in sum, yes...or rather, in Sirius, but it wasn't me who found it. It was known that among the substances making up Sirius, revealed by the prism, there was one that was unknown, and singular, whose spectrum could not be confused with any other. Then, while studying the rare earths, I found a substance that had exactly the same spectrum. It was the same substance. I called it sirium. It's infinitely less abundant here than in the

---

3. Author's Note: "It is obvious that I have invented sirium on the model of radium. Today, it is no longer believed that radium emits electricity or transmits motion without any diminution of its own volume and substance. It is probable that the diminution is extremely slow and almost imperceptible, but nevertheless real. Thus disappeared the strangest characteristic of radioactive substances. However, on 17 December 1906 at the annual session of the Académie des Sciences, Henri Poincaré said with regard to radium: 'The more one studies the new substance, the more unexpected facts one finds, which seem to give the lie to everything we thought we knew about matter. Mysterious emanations have been observed whose successive transformations appear to be the cause of the heat produced and which, ultimately, conclude with helium, a very light gas found in the sun well before being encountered on earth. Was the dream of the old alchemists thus realized? Were we in the presence of the transmutation of elements? Those who are frightened by novelties are wrong to be alarmed so rapidly. It is probable that chemists will succeed in bringing these strange phenomena into the frames that are familiar to them. Everything is always settled, in fact; and if an element is, by definition, that which remains constant in all transformations, it is necessary that it be immutable. Even so, these are reactions very different from those we know, and bring into play extraordinary quantities of energy. Perhaps we have been too hasty, but of that which has been dreamed, enough still remains for the entirety of physics to have been subject to an upheaval'."
Marie and Pierre Curie discovered radium with the aid of a spectroscope in 1898, but it was not isolated as a pure metal until 1910.

star. I only have small quantities of it, but it exhibits strange properties."

"Which will revolutionize chemistry?"

"Possibly."

"Which is to say...?"

The old man pressed Michel with urgent questions, and so keen was his curiosity that Michel could no longer think of putting him off.

"Well, this is it: sirium emits heat, light and electricity. It's a source of perpetual energy. It never ceases to be active, and without any loss of substance—without any diminution of its volume or its mass."

*"Sacré bleu!"* murmured the Alchemist.

"At least, I believe so," Michel added. "I'm not certain...."

The Alchemist, however, neglected that final weakening of an affirmation that he found overwhelming.

"So?" he said, bluntly. When Michel did not reply, he continued: "So, the law of conservation of energy, the unique and absolute dogma on which, since antiquity, we've based all our hypotheses and directed all our research...?"

Michel Bedée raised his arms and let them fall back again. He opened his eyes wide, pursed his lips and said nothing. There were a few seconds of silence between the two scientists. Immobile, they looked at one another, not seeing one another, each lost in his own dream.

"That's stupid!" said the Alchemist, finally, standing up— and he burst out laughing, but without gaiety, with a kind of sarcastic wonder. Then he started pacing back and forth in his laboratory, meditatively, while Michel did not budge from his stool. Again, he exclaimed: "That's tragic—and magnificent!"

Folding his arms, he came to stand in front of his pupil, and said: "I've been laboring at my stove for half a century now, Michel, as if the conservation of energy were the primary truth—and I might as well, fool that I am, have spent the time playing marbles, like a child, or having a life, taking advantage of the beauty of women and chasing after them. Anyway, I have no regrets...."

He emphasized the last words with a kind of stoic violence. Then he went on: "It's ridiculous, ridiculous. Anyway, what does it matter to me? I'm only one worker among thousands in the laboratory of science. But think of the great scientists there have been in the last three thousand years! It's them, the sublime and efficacious portion of humankind, that you have to see leaning over the stoves where they were cooking nothing but error, with a glorious zeal. What an adventure, Michel, my boy! You, you arrive, you're young; we took you for a child last year. And you discover that we've been saying nothing but stupidities from the very start! I repeat that it's tragic and magnificent."

Michel Bedée wanted to put things in perspective. "Wait, Master. It's not yet proven. I've only formulated hypotheses...."

The old man continued to stride back and forth. From time to time he asked Michel a question, paused momentarily to listen to the reply, and set off again. And he was thinking, with a stubborn ardor. When he had come to a conclusion, he came back to Michel and said, softly: "My boy, you have work to do. And in order that we, the old, can get back to work, you have to demonstrate our error to us, once and for all, and give us another doctrine—or else you have to be mistaken. Until then, we're in a state of stagnation." Laughing, he added: "You're a redoubtable lad, you know? When I think that my imbecile neighbors are afraid of me! It's you who are the Devil, Michel. It's you!"

A little later, he perceived that Michel was not following him, remaining apart from his excitement and occupied with other ideas. He asked: "But given all that, what are you doing here, instead of working and making haste, while we're hanging on your research? What are you doing here, in this stupid little town?"

To that question, so squarely posed, Michel sensed that he would not be able to reply in a sentence, and that he might not be able to reply at all. He remained silent.

The old man was peering at him like a doctor at his patient. He sat down beside him and said, softly: "You have troubles,

Michel?"

Michel would have like to run away, without saying a word, without saying a single one of the countless words that would be required to indicate the extravagant misery of his heart and mind. Amid all those words, he went astray, and was only able to murmur: "Yes, troubles...big troubles...."

He hoped, for a moment, that that might suffice—but the old man seized him by the wrist. "What?" he said.

Michel tried to evade the question again: "Oh, nothing...it's nothing...."

But the old man shook him, sternly. "I asked you: *what?*"

Michel was confused.

"Come on, what?" repeated the old man.

"If I told you, it would take forever...."

"Ah! And you've come here, Michel, to sort it all out?"

"Sort it out? Oh, no—I don't expect to do that."

"So?"

"So, I've come...I don't know really why. I haven't come; I've run away. And since I was running away, where could I go, except here—home, to my childhood?"

"Eh?"

"What do you expect? It's instinctive. Little children in distress take refuge with their mother."

"Yes, but you're no longer a child...."

"Yes I am!"

The old man became annoyed. "You're mad, Michel. How long are you going to stay here?"

"I don't know. All my life, perhaps...."

These fragments of sentences made a discordant noise in the Alchemist's head. It was as if, in the idle of a smoothly-running experiment, an absurdity had become manifest. He did not admit absurdity; it shocked and frightened him. Hurriedly, he resolved to get rid of it.

"Come on, Michel, this won't do. You have to tell me what's wrong, and right away. I've had enough. What is it?"

"Well, my wife...but it isn't only my wife, it's...everything!"

"Your wife is being unfaithful to you?"

Michel went pale, and he exclaimed: "No, no, no...what are you thinking?" And he shivered.

"So?"

"So, no, she hasn't been unfaithful to me. But she's bored...."

The Alchemist nearly burst out laughing, but he was furious as well, and, in a tone of mocking commiseration, he growled: "She's bored? What a shame!"

Such was the misunderstanding, which lent itself to joking, that Michel could not longer stand it. Crestfallen and discontented, he explained, and the words did not come quickly enough for his liking.

"Yes, yes, she's bored. It's my fault; I don't pay any attention to her. The days weigh upon her, and I sense that she no longer loves me...."

The Alchemist interrupted him.

"What do you mean, she no longer loves you?"

"You know full well what it means," Michel replied, impatiently, "to love a woman who loved you, and is beginning not to love you any more...."

"No, I don't know. And you ought not to know either, since you've devoted yourself to science."

Michel only shook his head.

"Come on, my lad, come and see." He took Michel Bedée by the arm and led him to the capital of Aristotle.

"You see? That humiliated blockhead is Aristotle our forefather: the greatest mind of old. Look at him. On all fours! Look—a naked woman is riding on his back. Its sensuality that has brought him low, has degraded him. This old emblem is rich in significance.... You're not saying anything?"

Michel was, indeed, not saying a word. The Alchemist, by way of conclusion, demanded a confession.

"You're in love with your wife, Michel?"

"Yes." Michel felt his heart swell, and he also felt a tremulous memory of sensuality run through him.

"Oh, Michel, my little Michel, the old story! When you

came to tell me, two years ago, that you were getting married, I foresaw it all, divined it all. I said to you: 'Michel, don't get married!' You were caught, I could see. You were in love...."

"I still am!" Michel declared.

The Alchemist looked him up and down. "Shut up, Michel—you disgust me. Once one has consecrated oneself to science, one has obligations to science; and when one is a man of genius, one has more imperious duties. A scientist is a chaste man; that is the first duty of a scientist. Chaste in mind, I mean! The rest is a matter of physiology, and lust only shocks me when it undermines the intelligence. One makes arrangements, damn it! One adopts regular habits, in order...do you understand?... in order not to think about it in the meantime. But it's necessary for the mind—or the heart, or the soul, as you wish—to be above such things. The mind of a scientist is a place where facts and ideas come together and combine logically. Catholics who go to communion fast, in order to receive the body of their God appropriately at the tabernacle. It's necessary that the mind of a scientist should be clear and pure, in order that ideas and facts aren't polluted there, and can operate here by themselves, all alone, in accordance with unblemished logic. A scientist, Michel, is a kind of monk, who imposes a severe rule upon himself. He renounces being himself in order to be the sanctuary of science. You're a monk who has sinned...you're a bad monk!"

Michael groaned. "I can't do anything about it. Too bad!"

"You can't do anything about it? Oh, two years ago, I didn't know that you were a man of genius. Otherwise, I wouldn't have let you do what you did. I would have begged you to do better! I would have nipped your sin in the bud! I would have cured you...or I would have had you locked up."

"I'm not a man of genius!" Michel murmured. "I'm only a poor creature who asks to be permitted to live, in his own way, as best he can—yes, in his own way, as maladroit as all the ways of life that find creatures down here for their particular usage, one after another...."

The Alchemist cut him off. "Shut up! You're not a poor creature. Science needs you. You've taken it to a critical point at which it can't languish, and you don't have the right to leave it there, if you're...if you're simply an honest man."

Michel jibbed. "Well, I am leaving it there! Too bad!"

Michel and the Alchemist were both standing, face to face—and Michel, for the moment, had the upper hand. He surrendered to his excitement, and spoke loudly. "Oh, it's too demanding, at the end of the day! I've given it too much, sacrificed too much. I've had enough! I'm rebelling!"

"Michel!"

"Now I'm reclaiming the happiness that it stole from me—or, rather, that I surrendered to it, foolishly. You're looking at me angrily, Master, and are scornful of me? All the same, it's because of science that I lost the affection of a woman I adored. I've neglected that woman, in order to work. If you knew! That work doesn't only take over the mind, but the body, the senses... oh, how can I put it? One is possessed, one no longer exists....

"So I made life impossible for that woman. Between her and me, even by night, there was an intruder: science. I didn't understand that until now, and it's too late! When one takes a woman for one's wife, one has to enable her to flourish. Science put an unbreathable atmosphere around us, an atmosphere in which I gradually allowed myself to asphyxiate, without perceiving it. Abruptly brought into that atmosphere, she perceived the peril she was in, and she protested. She opened the windows wide to let in light and air, and while I remained stupidly at work, I thought she was getting drunk on the effluvia that arrived from outside with marvelous abundance...."

Michel was getting carried away and taking advantage of the facility of metaphors. The Alchemist summoned him back to concrete realities.

"So?"

"So, she'll leave...."

"Through the windows? Yes! Close the windows!"

That brutality of expression did not trouble Michel. He

replied, softly "No, I don't want to kill her; I won't oblige her, or invite her, to die with me."

"Let her go, then. And you, work."

"No, no. She'll leave, I can tell. She's already left me, in imagination. Except that I won't work any more...."

There was a moment's silence. The Alchemist seemed to be contemplating a disaster, and he said nothing.

Michel continued, vehemently: "Before sacrificing my wife to science, I sacrificed my mother to it. Perhaps you haven't forgotten that? Perhaps you haven't forgotten the frightful days when my mother wept all the tears that an already long life had left her, because I, the child she had pampered, left the house of my birth, the shadow of the church and the faith that she had given me."

"Your mother wanted to keep you tied to her apron strings. I'm the one who rescued you from a puerile servitude."

"I don't hold it against you, Master, you did it for my own good."

"Not at all! No, I didn't do it for your good, I did it for the good of science. I did it because I saw that you had a curious, intelligent mind...and in that, I wasn't mistaken...and because I thought that you would be a good servant of science...in which, it appears, I was mistaken."

"You were mistaken," Michel retorted, resolutely. "Since then I've distanced myself from the existence that my antecedents had prepared for me here, and since then, the gentlest, most attentive and most affectionate of them all, my mother, has almost ceased living. She prays for me. She associates my sister with her prayers and her continual grief. I've come to ask forgiveness, from both of them."

"You're mad."

"I'll ask forgiveness for an escapade that took me away from them, and from which I've come back, but of which they'll die all the same."

Michel fell silent. The Alchemist looked at him in amazement. Suddenly, as if he were concluding rapid and urgent meditations he said: "Listen, Michel. If you go to your mother's house in your current state of mind, you're doomed. She's the one who has rendered you as sentimental as you are—she and your sister! Both of them have alarmed you, day after day, by means of affection, Catholicism and tearful caresses. They want to get you back, I tell you. Listen: it's them or science. Choose!"

"The choice is made."

"Michel, you're a coward!"

Several seconds went by, in a silence like a sea, a silence that seemed agitated by profound and violent undercurrents. The Alchemist, sitting on a stool with his elbows on his knees, his cheeks applied to his palms and his eyes lowered toward the floor, pronounced his words slowly.

"When I think, Michel, that it's you who have genius, and not me! More than forty years I've been working, without interruption. At dawn, or even before dawn, I get up, go into my laboratory and get to work. That lasts until dusk. I have experiments in progress that I began five years ago. I'm old. One day, I'll be picked up, dead, from beside my stoves, like an imbecile and like a brave man. I haven't made one significant discovery, and I won't...but I stay, and I shall continue to stay at my post, beside my stoves. It's necessary to have a moral impetus in life. Well, personally, all my moral impetus is in a phrase of Claude Bernard's, a simple phrase that exhorts people 'to experiment, in order to see.' Yes, multiply experiments; there are hundreds of thousands of them to do, in order to see whether something unexpected might suddenly be revealed.

"So, there it is. I do experiments, and I look—except that I've seen nothing, or almost nothing. However, it isn't possible that, in the number of my experiments, no admirable phenomena have been produced. I must have had all their mystery before my eyes, in the depths of my pans...except that I've looked hard, but haven't seen, because I don't have genius. That's a pity—oh, not for me, but for science. Yes, Michel, it's a pity that it's you, and not me, who has genius, because I have the character of a scientist, while you...."

He abandoned himself momentarily to his melancholy. Then, as if he did not want to participate in a frightful disaster, he got up, and said to Michel, imploringly: "There's still time, my boy. Pick up your valise. Go back to Paris, right away, without going to your mother's house. Explain to your wife...." He warmed up as he spoke. "Explain to you that you're setting her free. If she hesitates, send her away. Yes, throw her out. It's not possible, otherwise. It has to be done! And then, as soon as she's gone, Michel, get back to work. You've wasted too much time already. To work—good God, to work!"

Michel said nothing.

"Well? Don't you have anything to say?"

Michel replied: "I'm sorry to have troubled you.."

"Get out! You're a coward!"

Michel left, valise in hand. The old man listened to him walking along the corridor, the door to the avenue opening, and then closing again. Then, by way of a chair, he climbed up on to his stove, and through the window he shouted: "Michel! Michel! Not that way! No, no...do as I said.... Michel!"

Michel did not turn back.

And the old Alchemist, in a dull voice, moaned: "Adieu, Michel!"

The he got down again, passed his hand over his forehead, struck a match on the wall, lit the gas of his stove and started work, as he did every morning.

* * * * * *

When Michel Bedée found himself on the avenue again, he did not hesitate and headed for his mother's house. He did not raise his head to look at the Alchemist, but he marched swiftly, like a man tormented by a singular confusion of ideas but guided by a firm resolution.

In spite of the Alchemist, the railway station and an immediate return to Paris did not represent duty to him; it was, on the contrary, temptation; he wanted to see his wife again. Internally, he appealed to her: "Geneviève! Darling Geneviève!" But he continued on his way.

The sight of the family home at the end of the avenue saddened him and drew him on reluctantly. He went forward, his eyes fixed on the brown-painted door, the wrought iron bell-pull that was hanging down and which, when he seized it, would activate a complex system of quivering iron wires before resounding the grave ring that he was already imagining.

He trembled as he drew nearer.

He feared the affection that was about to greet him with a melancholy urgency. He divined the joy that the two sad women, his mother and sister, would feel on seeing him again: a very gentle and subtle joy; a joy that would immediately ask how long it would be granted to them; a joy afraid of departure that would be spoiled by the thought of its brevity.

And he arrived with a mortal chagrin in his heart, afraid of having to hide a secret, of having to deceive, with difficulty, the demanding intimacy of amicable souls; perceived, his dolor would be further intensified.

As he pulled the bell-cord, he no longer knew why he had come; he regretted the absurd and imprudent journey. At the same time, he felt that he could not elude the peril—and when the familiar racket that he had anticipated resounded in the corridor, he was invaded by a flood of tenderness.

*Here I am, Maman!* he thought.

The word *Maman* echoed in his mind in a seductive, dolorous and delightful fashion. It seemed to him that he had just awakened the sleeping soul of the old dwelling. The ringing of the bell became more frantic; now it was stammering like a senile plaint. From outside, Michel heard doors opening along the corridor: that of the kitchen and that of the small drawing-room. Footsteps sounded.

Finally, Michel saw, on the shade, limned in shadow against the light, that came in through the glazed garden door, his sister and the faithful maidservant Melanie coming into the corridor.

"Oh! Bonjour, Michel!"

"Bonjour, Monsieur Michel!"

"Bonjour."

And from the drawing-room, weak and glad, urgent with difficulty, another voice called: "Oh! Michel , Michel...is it you? Kiss me first!"

She insisted: "Michel, Michel, your Maman first!"

Marie had already placed her hands on her brother's shoulders and was offering her lips to him; she moved aside, obedient and scrupulous, and let her arms hang down—and Michel saw a confused resignation in the young woman's eyes. He seized her fingers and led her away; he smiled nervously.

"Dear Maman!"

From her impotent armchair, Madame Bedée stretched out her arms, waving them. She took possession of the beloved head that leaned toward her and covered it with kisses and tears. Michel, his eyelids closed, abandoned himself; and thought he had become a child again, but with a terrible anguish.

"How long are you staying?"

Michel no longer knew. At hazard, he replied "One day."

"Is that all?"

"For now, yes."

And all three of them had said it all, the essence of their common adoration, in the first kiss. They fell silent, all sitting close together, involuntarily, and looked at one another. Michel saw his mother, a few months older—but for the first time, he perceived that his sister was aging. His noticed her finer lips, her thinner nose and her paler cheeks, the skin of which was less glossy. He kissed her eyes. For a second, he thought that the silence would be rent by a triple sob.

"Where's your luggage?" asked Madame Bedée.

It was not ambiguously that Michel replied: "There's only a valise. I put it down in the hall."

Madame Bedée was not asking for information; she was simply interrupting the excessively poignant silence. The futile question, asked in time, affected the rescue of one of those help-less souls about to drown in silence. A vain chatter commenced:

Michel detested luggage; he had never been able to tolerate dragging trunks after him, waiting for them when the train arrived, negotiating with porters. A constrained laughter was born of that poor conversation, which was merely an alibi for alarmed affection.

Melanie brought a cup of hot chocolate, roast meat and a glass of fresh water on a tray. Michel ate breakfast. He recognized the dented silver spoon, the cup with gold thread and pink flowers. All that, all the details of the past, moved him; he experienced a sentiment mingling painful nostalgia and quiet joy.

Suddenly, Madame Bedée asked: "And your wife? Is she well?"

"Very well."

They were both content that the question had been asked and the answer given. Madame Bedée did not know Michel's wife very well and did not like her at all. To begin with, she was displeased that her son had married a Parisienne, who was doubtless frivolous; and secondly, she was jealous of this Geneviève, whom Michel adored and who had him all the time—as jealous as mothers are, who are also women.

Then Marie asked her brother: "By which train did you arrive?"

Michel confessed that he had arrived on the five o'clock train and that, in order not to wake his mother, he had gone into the Alchemist's house.

Madame Bedée was discontented. "Oh, you've seen him? Already?" She added: "I detest him."

Michel was well aware of that. The quarrel went back several years, but he knew that his mother's rancor was long-lasting.

"He's the Devil, that man!" she said.

"No," said Michel, "he's a simple and innocent man who works hard; he's a kind of lay saint, almost sublime...."

"They are no lay saints!" declared Madame Bedéee.

In the violence of that assertion, Michel recognized the character of every kind of dogmatism. He had found the Alchemist no less impetuous. And he reflected, silently: *Every kind of dogmatism expresses itself and acts as if it were the only one in the world—but there are several; all the misunderstanding stems from that. They remain, therefore, marvelously irreconcilable. What a joke it would be if all of them are wrong!*

Madame Bedée went on: "God will judge him, and I don't want to commit in his regard the sin of the Pharisees who, proud of their piety, conclude too quickly the imperfections of their neighbors. I forgive him, since it's written: 'Forgive us our trespasses, as we forgive them who trespass against us.' Except, Michel, that what I have to forgive him is having deprived me of your daily company. He has taken you away from me. He has put his scandalous mania for science into your head. It's his fault that you haven't remained my pious little Michel, submissive to God and faithful to the teachings of the Church. He's the one who launched you into an imprudent research, by which you were dragged away from belief in the verities of Scripture. Oh, Michel, if I did not command myself to forgive him, I would hate him—and my most frequent sin, the most difficult temptation for me to avoid, is that of hatred.

When she yielded like that to the vehemence of her faith, Madame Bedée's face lost its maternal softness. Anger marked her features rudely; her wrinkles seemed to freeze, to harden, to compose a primitive physiognomy of marble sculpted long ago and captive of its form forever.

"Are you scolding me?" asked Michel, in a tone of childish timidity.

"No, no, I'm not scolding you, Michel; even when you were small, I never scolded you—remember that! It's no time to start, now that I no longer have, before God, the burden and responsibility of your soul, and now that I'm old...old....Do you see how much older I am than last time you came?"

"No!" replied Michel, anguished.

Madame Bedée smiled sadly, and in a surge of tenderness that rejuvenated her, she cried: "Come and kiss me again. You've hardly kissed me at all. Come!"

Michel drew closer to her, and she coaxed him, petted him,

playing with his head as she had once, when he was a baby almost devoid of weight, played with his entire being. As she cradled that dear head against her cheek, she even started singing to him:

> Knock, knock! Who's there?
> It's Polchinelle, Mam'selle.
> Knock knock! Who's there?
> Oh look, it's Polchinelle!

Then Michel hid his eyes against his mother's shoulder, in order that the tears rising to his eyes would not be visible— warm and abundant tears that were multiplied, note after note, by the nursery rhyme and his despair.

The song, which he had forgotten, he suddenly remembered, with such exactitude that his memory anticipated the words and the tune, every detail of the inflection into which the rhythm drew the quavering voice, which was trying to be sprightly and light. Between the voice of yesteryear, still intact in his memory, and the voice of today, however, he perceived a difference in every line of the song: the poignant measure of the years gone by, evidence of fatigue and debility.

That song, which he had forgotten, which had been dead and was reborn all-but-dying again, awoke with it a variously distant past. Michel's thoughts went back through the years, one after another, until they were lost in the mystery of original consciousness. It seemed to him that he remembered, obscurely, facts that he had not known and sensations that he had scarcely felt. He recognized them and believed, in spite of the vague shadow in which the new apparition was manifest, that he had never known them as clearly as he did now. His early infancy was there, and surrounded him, a soft, soothing and harmonious singer of dormant and seductive refrains, intent on holding him in a state of ignorant bliss.

For a few seconds, Michel savored that forgetfulness—but suddenly, the excessively beautiful fiction fell apart, and the more the dream had enchanted him, the more the reality would now torture him.

He dared not straighten up. He divined that his mother, like him, was docile to the prestige of the renascent past, and he was afraid of showing her a consternated face.

Gradually the song about Polchinelle became less lively, and softer. The voice became weary, the intakes for breath more frequent, interrupting the monotonous flow of the words. The song was no more than an idle babble; the cradling arms relaxed. The song and the cradling ceased at the same time.

Michel felt a tear fall on to his ear.

He straightened up. He gave his mother a long kiss, and, to excuse both their tears, he laughed, saying: "Your baby is no longer small enough."

"Your Maman is no longer young enough!" retorted Madame Bedée.

They both fell silent, grave and emotional.

Michel observed that Marie was moving back and forth, pretending to rearrange, here and there, various trivial objects on a shelf or reels of threat in a sewing-basket. She was trying to distract herself from the melancholy that was taking hold of her.

"Shall we go for a little walk soon, Marinette?" Michel asked her, with a false cheerfulness.

"Oh, how nice!" she replied. And she clapped her hands, momentarily younger. "How nice!" she repeated.

"The word "nice" echoed strangely in the midst of the sadness that had taken up residence in the room so many years before that it seemed impossible to get rid of it. And Michel reflected silently on the misery supposed by the joy that welcomes a little charity. Marie, at the offer of a walk, had had the expression of gratitude one sees on the faces of genuinely poor beggars when one gives them a sou.

Involuntarily led to make himself suffer, Michel persisted in such images, which dressed the soulful distress in which he had left his mother and his sister. He pitied them, and he repented bitterly of not having devoted all the fervor of his life to them.

Marie and Michel sat down by their mother's armchair, facing one another, a little in advance of her, and she extended a hand to each of them. Michel and Marie, similarly, held hands, all three of them thus forming a closed circle. There was an old game, which they all remembered, and they said "Friends! Friends! Friends!" while waving the chain of their arms. Then they fell silent again; every memory they revived afflicted them.

As they were still emotional, Madame Bedée looked Michel in the eyes and said to him: "Today's Sunday—will you go to mass with your sister?"

"Yes," said Michel. "I'd like that."

He had recognized, in his mother's voice, the tone of imperious supplication that she had always put into her requests, and which rendered them, for him, more compelling than orders. Her words, softly spoken, and their tone of tremulous anxiety, already contained the threat of the grief that Michel would be bound to see in his mother if he neglected to say yes. That affectionate strategy had ruled, enslaved and oppressed his adolescence and then his early adulthood. Michel rediscovered it, docile as of old, with impatience.

Madame Bedée went on: "It's sad, for me, no longer to be able to go to Church with you."

They said nothing; Michael knew full well where his mother was trying to go. Indeed, she said: "It would be kind of you, then, to recite with your old mother, who no longer has her legs, a dozen rosary-beads before mass. Would that upset you, Michel? No? I see that it doesn't. You're very kind. Thank you. Kiss me."

Marie knelt down, and swiftly took a shiny steel rosary from her pocket, made the sign of the cross and began to recite the prayers in Latin. Michel had stood up. He observed that his mother had closed her eyes, pretending not to watch whether he made the sign of the cross. He stood there, his arms extended and his hands together. Then it seemed to him that that attitude of deferential protest was futile and stupid, and he knelt down.

The *Aves* succeeded one another, one by one, and Michel,

with his mother, punctuated them with the mysterious *amen*, which has come from the Orient to the souls and lips of all Christian countries, and which devotedly repeats the quiet ignorance faithful to those two unintelligible syllables.

*In principio erat verbum*, Michel said to himself. *In the beginning was the word; and significance is no longer necessary, once the word is charged with hazardous and touching memories....*

*"....Nunc et in hora mortis nostrae."* Marie concluded her recitation.

"Amen," replied Madame Bedée and Michel.

As he got to his feet, Michel made the sign of the cross.

"You're good children," murmured Madame Bedée.

The cathedral bells began to ring. Their magnificent sound spread out in long and quivering waves.

"There are the first chimes of high mass," said Madame Bedée. "Get ready—it's time."

Michel had heard that phrase every Sunday in days gone by. He looked out of the window at the garden full of sunlight and the beautiful tumult of flowers. Roses and geraniums were in bloom there, in regular beds bordered by round bricks, and a virgin vine was climbing the back wall, mingled with ivy. Michael remembered Easter mornings, when he had thought he saw miraculous bells pass by in the splendid sky, which dropped divine and prodigious gifts of sugar eggs among the flowers of the family garden.

\* \* \* \* \* \*

To go to the cathedral, Marie and Michel followed the avenue bordered and shaded by old trees. The ground was worn; the pebbles comprising it seemed sharp and worn themselves.

Afterwards they went into a back-street so tightly contained between the hunchbacked and unequal houses that carriages could not get through it. In any case, it was blocked by two boundary-markers that ought to have been attached by a chain;

the first links could still be seen, sealed into the stone, rusty and polished at the same time, the stone having become as shiny as marble by virtue of the friction of passers-by.

The brother and sister walked at the same slow and distracted pace. Occupied with parallel thoughts, which variously tinted their reveries, they said nothing, as if they were afraid of the words that might escape them.

Finally, Marie asked: "Do you find Maman much changed?"

"Yes," Michel replied, in a tone of painful confession. "Yes, even more nervous and anxious." After a pause, he added: "You have such a sad existence!"

Marie raised astonished eyes to look at her brother, and said, with a despairing smile: "No; I'm used to living like this. I don't think about any other existence. I'm neither happy nor unhappy."

When they went into the cathedral, Michel initially had a sensation of soft and moist coolness. The immense nave, where immense pillars surged forth like stalagmites, put him in mind of a marine grotto, where the same atmosphere persists in spite of the changing of the seasons and the warmth of the sun. The half-light was ornamented at intervals by lamps, but they did not spread their light very far; their gleam only served to render the diurnal gloom enclosed there more sensible and agreeable to the eye.

And the silence!

One might have thought that all the silence of the ages and all the silence of the earth, expelled from everywhere, had taken refuge between the walls of the cathedral, filling it with its sovereign presence. It reigned there, incontestable and intangible, in such a way that the usual noises of the comings and goings of people, did not offend it. If the scrape of a prie-dieu on the flagstones or the hacking cough of a devotee sometimes scratched it, the scar was soon formed. In the same way, the fall of a leaf does not long disturb the water of a pool; the ripples draw away gradually, and disappear; the depths have not been reached and the surface, momentarily tremulous, resumes its eternal immobility.

Michel and Marie went along the central aisle and then through the narrow pathways between seats to reach their places beside the bench, facing the pulpit. On copper plates nailed to the supports of the prie-dieus names were engraved in black: Madame Bedée, Mademoiselle Marie Bedée, Monsieur Michel Bedée. Michel verified that his place was waiting for him, as of old. Year after year, Madame Bedée continued to pay for that triple location. Only Marie took advantage of it; but while the impotent mother and the prodigal son did not come to pray before the sanctuary, their faithful names subsisted, to attest that they were still counted among the parochial community.

Marie knelt down and covered her eyes and ears with her ungloved hands, blocking the senses through which the superfluity of the external world penetrates the soul, gathering herself in divine contemplation. One of her hands was only liberated for the time require to beat on her breast the *mea culpa* of scrupulous sinners; the eye it uncovered remained closed, the ear evidently deaf.

Michel, standing up, gazed at the rose-window flowering at the end of the transept, where the morning light of the sun was broken into shafts of light. Angels whose wings were red shone there, the petals of the blooming rose—and those angels held lyres, viols, trumpets and cymbals, in such a way that it seemed that their concert was that of the beautiful radiant colors, and that supernatural music emanated from the mystic flower instead of a perfume.

The mass began. Michel hardly noticed it—as if, in spite of the time passed, habit had suddenly gripped him and he was continuing an uninterrupted practice, he witnessed without surprise, and without his attention being solicited, the various episodes of the office. The Oriental emphasis of the worship that made such a striking contrast with the habits and customs of the little town did not strike him with wonder; nor did the simple familiarity of those good folk who were at home in God's house as in their own astonish him. Nor, finally, did the discipline that required him to get up and sit down again at fixed points importune him. He was tired; the nocturnal hours spent on the train and the confused emotions to which he had been subject since his early morning arrival left him in a state of bleak numbness. The calm of the place and the compassed slowness of the divine protocols drew him into a kind of torpor. He was no longer gazing at the faithful who surrounded him, and who were watching him; it was as if he saw them every day; besides, he knew them, as they knew themselves, fixed in the habits of a morose and docile life.

He did not even hear the organ, at first—but he suddenly did, and was carried away by its imperious violence.

There was a sudden release, a tempest of exasperated forces. Michel thought that a terrible wind was rushing past, destroying everything, and with its continuous whistling was mingled the din of collapses and ruinations. Such was its vehemence that its haste sometimes relented and, sure of its calamitous effects, it became playful, affecting a false nonchalance; then, over the universal disaster, with a sovereign ferocity, it scattered the persiflage of its irony. Michel approved. His despair, which the racket had stirred up, loved that nihilism.

He looked around at the devotees of both sexes, the worthy people of the town and the surrounding countryside, and young boys and girls, their placid faces certifying that the tempest was passing over them without affecting them.

The organ relented and fell silent. The officiating priest proceeded with the divine sacrifice. A bell signaled the poignant moment when the host and wine became the flesh and blood of the redemption. All those in attendance bowed. Michel, who had omitted to lower his eyes, and who was following the symbolic gestures of the priest distractedly, was frightened by feeling that he alone was indemnified of the prestige, exempted from the grace offered to everyone else.

Longer than anyone else, Marie remained confined within herself, entirely given to her God—and Michel, next to her, was as distant from her as if they had been separated by the entire diameter of the earth.

The organ multiplied its beautiful tumults again. Michel, who was not following the stages of the mass, abandoned himself to the tormented will of the symphony. It no longer suggested to him, as it once had, the religious sentiments that were supposed to accompany the course of the liturgy, but it still uplifted him, exciting within him, instead of the pieties of old, an ideological fervor. Involuntarily, he turned it away from its real significance; he accorded it an alternative metaphysics and put it in the service of a scientific dream....

Was not that voice, as powerful as a natural energy, which seemed disordered but was nevertheless obedient to a profound rhythm—which had its ebbs and its flows, unequal waves, some rising high, others round and turbulent, others delicate and fragile, bearers of fine and crystalline droplets, similar to the sea, shaken in its heavy masses and free in its superficial fantasies—the very voice of the subconscious, the fertile matter of souls, the secret substance of our thoughts, of our contradictory, crazy and countless impulses?

Michel meditated on that, and thought, led by the indefinite caprices of the organ:

*Subconscious, prodigious reserve, ocean full of elementary life, primary swarming of all ulterior spirituality! To go from the darkness of absolute unconsciousness to the light of clear consciousness, is a long and perilous journey. Our souls, our souls, many of you get lost in the course of that journey—and how poor you are, on arrival, indigent and yet so vain! You attract pity, like ladies who were once rich but, having experienced reversals of fortune, still wear the last jewels and baubles that remain to them, and simper!*

*About the unconscious, we have nothing to say; silence, which is no more nothing than everything, is its formidable and mysterious symbol. For consciousness, the paradoxical masterpiece of human individuality, there are words, beacons, and one can arrange them as one wishes—but for the subconscious, the only language is music, and, marvelously, that of the organ.*

*O music, indeterminate and, for that reason, chaste speech, you do not pretend to recount the vain anecdotes of our life, but you are a poignant allusion to the profound verity of ours souls!*

The sonorities of the organ filled the nave and collided with the walls of the chapels. Sometimes, a melody was detached from its hectic multiplicities, and, timid at first, anxious in its audacity, frail in the disorder of the accompaniment, was like a flower growing on a slender stem amid the frenzy of a storm. Michel sympathized with it, was afraid for it, and thought:

*Thus is born a thought in the troubled depths of the subconscious; it rises above the redoubtable turbulence to which it owes its origin; against so many threats, it has nothing but its virgin pride. There it is; it emerges and, the higher it rises, the more fragile it becomes. Often, it is broken before coming entirely into bloom, and then it falls back into the abyss in which it germinated; it is caught and drowned, annihilated....*

The melody played, as if disdainful or unaware of the din; it played, and amused itself, as if divinely distracted and a trifle puerile. Sometimes it became more cheerful, without knowing whence its pleasure came; sometimes it had a charming grace, laughter that it rendered melancholy with a languorous coquetry; sometimes it saddened, requesting and soliciting pity; and, mournful, was very artful in awakening a chagrin similar to the one of which it complained. Swoons and jeremiads alternated, while the surroundings thundered, amid the squalls and the gusts, with victorious fatality.

It was deployed with so much impetuosity that no obstacle could have stopped it; it broke everything in its passage; whatever subsisted in its surroundings it had disdained. When the tempest blows over the forest, the trees are destroyed, but after their fall, blades of grass and flowers survive. In the same way, the furies of the subconscious spare small ideas, which dart their uncertain stems high enough to blossom in the regions of clear consciousness.

It was as if, in the extravagant torment that whistled through trees, raced over mountains and reverberated in echoes, oboes and flutes were obstinate in singing and threading their tenuous, pretty, delightful sounds beneath the menace of natural clamors. Sometimes their delicate music was impossible to hear; one thought that it was lost; one regretted it—and then, at the first favorable occasion, it returned, subtly; it took advantage of the slightest space in which to insinuate itself, like a vivacious plant growing in a fissure in rocks; and then one was glad that it was not dead.

By the end of the office, Michel had built a system of ideas on which the religious influence of the place imposed a theological form.

"Yes," he said to himself, internally, "there are three hypostases, in accordance with the wish of ancient dreamers. The unconscious is the Father, the subconscious is the Son and the conscious is the Spirit.

"*Spiritus domini ferebatur super aquas*...the Spirit of God moved upon the face of the waters. That means that clear ideas float upon the profound ocean of the subconscious, which is the first realization of total unconsciousness.

"The Spirit is only the third hypostasis. Like the first two, from which it results, it merits the name of God, thanks to their efficacy. But the Father is only God, the Son is made human, the Spirit is human: the hypostasis the most distant from God and the closest to us, it is us divinely. Divine power is weakened in passing from the Father to the Son. God diminishes all the way to the human mind, which is his ultimate reality. The prodigious abundance of the unconscious is impoverished in the subconscious, and it is impoverished further in order to conclude with clear and distinct ideas.

"And we, the earthly reasoners, who try to put those ideas in a logical and necessary order, are committing the same methodological sin as if, neglecting the roots of a tree and only looking at the flowers, we tried to explain the flowers by means of one another. The work of our dialectics is like a bouquet of wallflowers, lilies and daisies. Their stems having been cut, one can arrange them as one wishes, but it is only an artificial assemblage.

"Just as all truth is in silence, all error is in the dialectical speech. But that is all we have! Lord, since, by the fact of our individual birth, we are expelled forever from the paradise of your silence, where all truth is, permit us sometimes to avoid the cruel suffering of the Spirit. Individuality is the original sin. All the redemption of which we are capable is in the subconscious, where much truth still subsists. Yes, the Son is the sole redeemer offered to humankind.

"Lord, since your silence is unreachable for us, preserve us from the words of the Spirit, and give us, if not magnificent peace, at least repose and release in music!

"While waiting to reenter your silence, when the crime of our individuality is suppressed by expiatory death, allow us to enjoy the subconscious, which is like a purgatory between your paradise and our inferno.

"The organ sings the glory of the Son!"

The mass had finished. The prie-dieus and the chairs pushed back over the tiles grated. After long constraint, the crowd stirred gladly. On arriving at the axis of the nave, the women bowed toward the tabernacle, and then went to join one or other of the groups that were already forming in order to go out and go home together, chatting dominically.

Marie was still praying, indifferent to those departures. Michel waited for her. When she took her fervent hands away from her face, she seemed to be waking up with difficulty from a dream; and one might have thought that earthly light offended her eyes.

She got up. Politely, as if she were coming back from a long way away, she said to her brother: "Bonjour, Michel. It's nice that you're here!" And she added: "Would you like to go to the Chapel of Dolors?"

It was, in fact, a custom to go after mass on Sunday to that chapel, which nestled between two of the cathedral's buttresses behind the choir. Innumerable candles burned in that mystic corner and filed it with an acrid odor.

At the back, amid that swarm of smoky yellow glimmers,

between paper flowers framed by golden foliage, upright on a stone pillar, stood the statue of the suffering Virgin: a bizarre, semi-barbaric statue which dated from problematic eras and must, in the course of centuries, have changed its significance. The town's archeologists affirmed that, before having been installed in that Catholic shrine, a very long time ago, it had belonged to a Druidic temple, where it depicted some divinity the memory of whom was lost. Her face was grim, with terrible eyes and thick, grave lips, its dark coloration intermediate between red and ocher. She was not smiling; she did not have the ineffable expression of more recent madonnas; she was not carrying the divine Child in her arms; she was not holding out to the world the redeemer that her maternity sacrificed. Devoid of gentleness, she was nothing but a heavy stone, crudely carved in human form.

The new piety that had fallen to her accorded her moving virtues and the renown of the Virgin Mother and dressed her in golden garments. That small robe, of thick rich cloth, did not suit her, fitting her badly and not finding any means to grip her arms, scarcely sketched in the stone and engaged in the opulent block of the body. The head bore, awkwardly, a diadem of gems. At the height of her left breast, a large metal heart had been attached, in which seven blades were stuck.

Michel recognized it, such as he had always seen it, without surprise, and he followed his sister meekly, to the extent of placing his lips on the pillar of the statue, in a place which a cleric wiped with a cloth as soon as a devotee appeared. He recognized the chill that the stone imparted to his mouth.

Then both of them, the brother and the sister, among the other people accustomed to that devotion, settled down a short distance from the Virgin. Marie began to pray again; Michel gazed at the narrow and pathetic sanctuary.

He thought about the tribulations to which the statue had been subjected before being immobilized there, and he thought about the tribulations that awaited it when its worship had fallen into the neglect into which the fervors of human anxiety inevitably fall. He gazed at the unequal candles, which were consuming themselves patiently before the beautiful idol, and he thought about the last candle that would eventually—a long time hence—be lit for her. Would it be left there, to burn down the last fragment of its wick, its soul, and its tallow, its body— or would some fanatic, hasty to conclude, snatch it from its herse, scintillating today like a morsel of nocturnal sky fallen to earth with its stars, and extinguish it beneath a republican heel? Michel imagined, in the former hypothesis, the ultimate ardor of the candle, its final gleam, decreasing, hesitant and moribund, reanimating momentarily, but ever more feeble—and suddenly dead.

He looked at the gilded copper hearts suspended from the ceiling of the chapel, forming a triumphal arch over the statue, over which dozens of little gleams were reflected. He look at the ex-votos that rendered thanks for temporal benefits, perils avoided, cures obtained; he noticed, ranged on the wall, crutches that attested to the medical efficacy of the Virgin. And, as before, he loved that so-human sanctuary, which, not far from the choir where divine metaphysics were exalted, lent itself better to the quotidian and humble pleas of a suffering clientele.

He said to himself: "The three hypostases, by means of which I was about, just now, to constitute a heresy, are insufficient. Souls need chapels that resemble hospital rooms. What they require is not a mystical certainty, but the sticking-plaster of good consolation. All souls are like that, not only those of poor people, but also mine, which is not content with science. I have locked myself in a laboratory where the crutches of miracle cures have been hung up in the guise of incontestable evidence. Inhuman science is nothing to me. O third hypostasis, O Spirit, I would abandon you for the Virgin of the Seven Dolors, if your audacious follies had not distanced me from the meek chapel where a human dream coddles human suffering and puts it to sleep!"

In being there in the credulous company of his sister, Michel savored a kind of appeasement. It seemed to him that things around him were disposed as he wished, and were inviting him to the life for which his mother had brought him into the world and educated him.

When Marie got up, having finished her prayers, he regretted going away. Neither the sign of the cross nor the genuflection was an effort of voluntary submission. He felt habit reborn within him; the gestures came to him first, and perhaps the prayer would come later.

* * * * * *

When they emerged from the cathedral, still pained by penetrating religion, Michel and Marie saw the Alchemist from the portal, walking at a rapid pace toward the post office. He was holding his letters in one hand and his hat in the other. He was well-known for that mania of going bare-headed; he loved to feel the freshness of the air on his brow. He saw them, but pretended not to have seen them. Michel was bewildered: science was passing by, calling to him, scornful of him, reclaiming him.

As she did every Sunday, Marie acknowledged friends and greeted them. Michel had to endure a certain amount of chatter, and maneuvered in order to avoid more.

On the parvis, groups had formed, which were looking at the brother and the sister, waiting for them, watching out for their passage.

"Let's go home," said Michel.

Marie knew full well that he did not have provincial patience or politeness.

"You're always so savage!" she said, laughing. And she hastened her pace to match his, guiding him, a skillful pilot, through the dangers of ready conversations, avoiding the alluring gossips and accepting her share of the susceptibilities excited by that evident refusal of affability.

The mass had lasted a long time. The little town had been transformed during that hour and a half; its matinal appearance of hasty and incomplete awakening had been replaced by the true Sunday, idle and flirtatious. Townspeople and tradesmen, petty rentiers and soldiers, had put on their best clothes. Bright ribbons and flowers decorated the women's hats. And the people who had to devote themselves to leisure that day were moving at a slow, weary pace under the burden of ennui. On seeing them, Michel remembered Sundays of old, dragged through the streets in summer with new shoes that the pavements scuffed, or in the silence, traversed by the hum of bees, of enclosed gardens, a book of tempting voyages on his knees.

Behind his window, beside giant yellow, red and green bottles that reflected the sunlight, the stupid pharmacist, who had been a classmate of Michel's, was doing nothing. In his Sunday best, he remained faithful to his post, because pharmacists do not take days off, any more than disease does; he was, however, idle without wanting to be, beside his languishing remedies. At the sight of Michel, he became animated.

"Let's run!" said Michel.

Marie, amused, related: "He's a municipal councilor, you know—and a rabid radical socialist.

"That's natural," Michel remarked. "If a pharmacist weren't a radical socialist, who would be?"

They both laughed.

Afterwards they went past an open window through which emerged, like effluvia of exalted torpor, the repetitive strains of a piano. Michel recognized the house, and immediately imagined a childhood friend, clad in silk, who, that Sunday, as before, and interminably, was carrying out with a ridiculous zeal her vain exercises. playing her scales, her "Prayer to a Vigin" and all of her repertoire. Alas, alas she was still there, the demoiselle de Trémément, so distinguished, upright and faithful to her imperious ancestors! She had not finished unwinding the series of her similar days, and even the piano, jerky and chirping, had not cheered up!

"She's only thirty-two!" Marie objected.

"But every one of her years," Michel replied, "is exactly the same as all the rest!" And it seemed to him, quite sincerely, that

Mademoiselle de Trémément might have done better to save herself the bother of such futile repetition.

The thin melody, scattered in the already-warm air, had an infantile or senile gentility. Sometimes it hurried on in vertiginous trills; sometimes it languished—and that alternation of anticipated effects, always the same, was so poor in invention, so naively pretentious and nonsensical, that Michel pitied both the artiste and the melody. But the music made such an effort, in the silence of the street where the shops were closed and the passers-by were morose, that it conquered all of the space. It was the very voice of a soul that that inhabited that almost deserted place: a soul of melancholy and ennui; a semi-resigned soul that still had febrile, ardent, slightly crazed moments; a captive soul, not yet entirely in despair; a soul of dolor and indolence.

"Do you remember our Sundays of old, Marie?" asked Michel.

Marie replied affirmatively, but so evasively that Michel could not tell whether the Sundays had left her a pleasant or a bitter memory.

"They were long days!" he added.

"They were good days," she replied. And when he fell silent in his turn she went on: "I remember that I liked them for their monotony and their slowness—and you couldn't bear them, for the same reason. How different we are from one another! Personally, I liked that kind of ennui that gripped us in the morning and lasted until evening, but it exasperated you. I would have liked the time to drag more, but you were in great haste...haste for what, Michel? I often wonder. Did you foresee that you would be a famous scientist? Was that what you were waiting for with such impatience?"

"I don't know," Michel replied. And he interrogated himself about that haste, which had never abandoned him. Today, again, what did he want? Nothing—and yet he was suffering, as before, from the duration.

His old Sundays occupied his mind. He detested them too. Was it not them, with their insistent languor, the excess of their leisure, their enervating softness, that had made his soul avid and nostalgic?—his unhappy soul, his vaguely dreamy soul, like a pond incessantly overflowing its flat banks. Was it not them that had alarmed him once and for all, and which, with their frenetic ennui, had given him the perpetual desire that he could not define?

A little later, he said to Marie: "One summer evening, Papa took us for a walk out there, in the country, beyond the toll-house. It was a Sunday. We had our hoops, we were running, chasing one another, climbing banks. When we came back, a little weary, I took my father's hand and let myself be drawn along. I was sleepy. In the outskirts of town, a veritable sadness overcame me, at the sight of the little dark and shoddy houses of the workers. There were flowerpots on the window-sills, and bindweed climbing in strings. It was dismal, those poor houses under the mauve evening sky: those poor houses imprisoning lamentable existences, which were entirely accomplished there. I shivered with sorrow. Do you remember that walk?

"No," replied Marie, astonished.

"I wouldn't want to repeat that walk; I don't want, this evening, to go through that poignant part of town. I'd be afraid of recapturing that old sadness, which is doubtless still there, like a miasma...."

When Michel and Marie reached the house, Madame Bedée was waiting for them with an impatience that she did not try to hide. Tenderly, she asked: "Are you going out again soon?"

"If Marie wants to," Michel replied.

Marie resigned herself immediately, albeit bitterly. "No," she said, "I don't want to."

"Then we'll spend the day together, all three of us?" concluded Madame Bedée. "How nice that will be!"

She was radiant with anxious joy.

\* \* \* \* \* \* \*

After lunch, Madame Bedée, because it was Sunday, did not

do her knitting, nor Marie her embroidery. Michel, between the two women, on whom their idleness weighed, sensed the conversation languishing. He was fearful of the interminable afternoon.

Madame Bedée perceived that. She put on her spectacles, picked up a prayer-book, and read. Michel got up and went to look on his father's bookshelves for the first volume of *Mémoires d'outre-tombe.*[4] When he came back, Marie had discreetly started reading a life of Saint Chantal. Sitting on a chair, she was holding the book in one hand and a bookmark in the other, maintaining a rigid, austere attitude, as if obliged to do so by some rule or ritual.

Michel pushed a large Voltaire armchair upholstered in red with a white floral pattern over to the window, sat down in it and put his book on his knees. His reading was not very active, but it served as a pretext for the inevitable silence; it concealed a slow and perpetual reverie.

It was raining.

"You did well not to go out," remarked Madame Bedée.

They all looked through the widow. The rainstorm crashed down and rebounded from the hard ground of the avenue; streams swelled and joined up.

Michel experienced a kind of wellbeing; he savored the tranquility of the house he was in, and said to himself: *Isn't it here, the haven of desirable peace? Why did I leave the everyday happiness of good children who never stray far from their other's skirts? But it's too late now. The good child was foolish enough to run away; he's gone elsewhere, to labor and sow foreign fields, bad fields, stony and sterile. Don't ask him to stay any longer; he needs to go and watch the paltry crop that he has sown grow....*

---

4. Chateaubriand's autobiography, begun in 1809 and finished in 1841, published in 12 volumes in 1849-50. Beaunier became something of an expert on Chateaubriand's life, works and circle of acquaintances, and edited several volumes of the memoirs and thoughts left for posthumous publication by his friend Joseph Joubert.

Soon, Michel was no longer reading at all. His gaze fixed itself on the wallpaper, yellow with green foliage; on the copper clock in the style of Louis XVI; he was attentive to his swift and staccato heartbeat. All that seemed to him to be pretty, charming, lachrymosely sad. He looked at his mother and his sister, dear loved ones, both growing older—the aging of his sister, still young, being sadder: it would put an end to her grace and beauty, which would have passed without making any noise.

He leaned over his book. He experienced a great desire to make the two women he loved happy, but he sensed the impossibility of changing anything in the life into which they had settled in definitive renunciation. Then, such was his pity and despair, that it seemed to him that the surrounding universe of reality and dream was devastated—but he did not budge.

Several times, he remembered Geneviève; he started thinking about her—but he set her aside, without roughness, a one pushes away a child that might trouble a meditation with a gentle hand. He even asked her pardon for moving her away. But in the intimacy of the afternoon, the souls of Michel, his mother and his sister had come so close together that the ideas of each were touching the others, and, instinctively, Michel feared that his mother, thus alerted, might suddenly interrogate him. Then, he would have too many things to say: dolorous things, impossible to say and difficulty even to think. He pushed away the memory of Geneviève, and shivered.

And the day passed like that, only varied by episodes of tea, a visit that was received, vespers and the benediction ringing, and intermittent chat.

In the evening, Marie played the piano. After the storm, the evening was soft and pure. The sky was a greenish blue when the stars began to come out. In the garden, the clumps of trees darkened; the chestnuts captured and imprisoned more light than the others. The odor of plane-trees spread. Flocks of house-martins screeched in the firmament. Michel went to lean on the window-sill....

Then, suddenly, the memory of Geneviève presented itself,

so clear and so ardent, that Michel could not escape it. He imagined her so young, so pretty and, in her bright summer dress, so enticing! But she drew away....

Marie sang a ballad. Her high-pitched voice vibrated in the evening air, and dared not expand. The ballad was seductive, almost voluptuous; it invited a chimerical lover to a voyage; it involved stars and the lake. Michel sensed the surrounding sadness more painfully, by virtue of contrast, and when Marie closed the piano, he knew that she had no wish to continue that tormenting music any longer. An overly strong odor was rising from the damp grass and flowers, an overly acute emotion emanating from that enraptured ballad. The distress that was beating down on Michel's thoughts left him miserable.

Melanie brought the lamp and put it on the sideboard. Marie blew out the candles on the piano, went to her mother's armchair, and sat down in such a way that Michel understood that he too had to come into the lamplight.

He wanted to read, or put on a semblance of it, but he saw that neither Madame Bedée nor Marie had picked up a book; unoccupied, they were expecting conversation. Michel offered to read aloud; it was the last alibi to which his dolor might have recourse. The offer was welcomed with excessive delight.

For the tenth time, he read his mother and sister the childhood of Chateaubriand in the wild Château de Combourg, in the midst of the rosy heather of the heath. He read, and he felt, fixed upon him, the dear, soft, sad eyes. Then his thoughts abandoned Combourg, Brittany and the heath. Melancholy ideas arrived, touched his soul, and awoke resonances therein, as the light evening wind was causing the leaves of the trees to rustle.

Then he divined that his mother and sister were content, and he thought that a fragile flower of happiness was blossoming, slowly, like a pellitory growing between the cracked mossy stones of an old house...a pale, slightly dewy flower, very tiny... flowering unperceived, timidly...so fragile that in looking at it one inevitably thinks of the inevitable end of all things....

Abruptly, Michel remembered his mother's old age. Inwardly,

he made the pathetic calculation of possible years to come; the numbers played in his mind, haunting him; he compared them to the duration of the life already lived. He became frightened. He continued reading, but while he read, cascades of words passed through his head, saying: "Yes, everything is there... nothing moves...this is happiness, like those little villages that are half asleep in the warm autumn sun...everything is calm, tranquil, at rest...."

Michel was increasingly inattentive to his reading. He stopped in mid-sentence. A few seconds went by, infinitely gentle for him, deliciously slow, casting a benevolent spell....

"What's the matter, Michel?"

Madame Bedée and Marie were looking at him, astonished; their anguish was manifest.

"What are you thinking about?"

Making no reply, Michel lowered his eyes and resumed reading. His cheeks were burning, his eyelids swollen. He read quickly, in a curt voice, uncomprehendingly. Suddenly, one sentence from the book, detached from all the rest, entered his ears and sounded a knell within his head: "Oh, let it not be too dear, the hand that will give us fresh water, in the fever of the throes of death...."

Michel closed the book on that, decisively. It seemed to him that a flash of lightning had lit up the darkness in which he had been groping for days on end. It seemed to him that, at the extreme limit of alarmed sensibility, he had found the indispensable remedy.

He rose to his feet and declared, firmly: "It's late; I need to go to bed."

Tender goodnights, thanks and cajoleries did not move him; nor, the following morning, could desolate goodbyes and tears persuade him to prolong his stay. He had made his resolution. Science, to which he was returning, appeared to him to be the rigorous convent in which he had to immure himself, where he had to flee forever the intoxicating martyrdom of sensibility, where he had to annihilate his unfortunate individuality.

A rigorous convent and refuge of despair: who enters here renounces everything; who enters here dies within himself. But Michel, at the limit of individual suffering, no longer desired anything but to die within himself, voluntarily.

* * * * * * *

When Michel left his mother's house to go to the station, at nine o'clock in the morning, he saw the Alchemist, pulling his door shut behind him rudely, going out for a walk, his hands behind his back and his cane beating his heels. Before turning left, as was his habit, the old man had glanced at Madame Bedée's house; he had seen Michel and swiftly turned away.

Michel wanted to run after him, but he thought about his mother behind the widow, lifting the curtain, accompanying him with her gaze and watching over him. Then, pretending that he was not in any hurry, he drew away. Once, he waved goodbye toward his mother's window, and was filled with sorrow. Then he continued on his way The old man did not slow down, and Michel dared not hurry; they each mastered themselves, both having to struggle to resist their equal desire to come together and chat.

As soon as they were out of range of the sentinel window, Michel ran.

"Bonjour, Master."

"Bonjour," the old man growled, and he put on a semblance of hating that encounter—but he stopped, noticed the valise that Michel was carrying, and asked, in a surly tone: "Where are you going?"

"Paris," Michel replied.

"To do what?"

"To work."

The Alchemist's face lit up with joy—and, extending a shaky hand toward Michel, he hid his emotion behind a laugh. "It's none too soon!"

He took his pupil's arm, and accompanied him toward the

station; he walked quickly, buoyantly, and said: "So you've changed your mind? So much the better—oh, so much the better, my little Michel. Thank you!

Michel was silent.

The old man began rambling.

"Has it been hard? You've suffered, I understand that. Yes, one suffers; I know that. No matter! Thank you for science. And thank you for me, Michel, even though I'm not important. All the same, you've put me in a bad way since yesterday. I said to myself: 'Well, if the best, the only ones, are cowards, deserting, science is done for. It's not me, or fellows like me, who are sufficient for that task!' And, as you see, I no longer had any momentum or zeal. I got up this morning like any other day; I lit my fire—but I wasn't able to work. Impossible! If the generals go over to the enemy, the soldiers can only throw their guns into the nettles. That's why I came out for a walk. Oh, Michel, you did well to change your mind. Thank you my boy, that's good!"

The old man rambled on:

"It disgusted me, you see, to think that you might desert— you, Michel. It disgusted me too much. I said to myself: 'The whole history of humankind is there. If humans, since they've been provided with intelligence, had worked hard, science would be complete. But no! Sentimentality has always doomed them! Sentimentality, egotism, the senses!' No matter. It's good, it's famously good, if you've broken those carnal ties—because, you know, one can only be an ascetic or...a pig. There's no middle way."

The old man added: "You're going to tell your wife?"

Michel was on the rack; he replied through clenched teeth: "Yes."

The old man burst out laughing, so forceful as his joy. He took Michel to the train—and when he left him, as the train moved off, he cried: "Adieu, Michel! I'm going to work!"

"Me too," Michel replied, making a great effort to prevent his face shuddering.

\* \* \* \* \* \* \*

When Michel got home, after hours on the train—after hours of methodical and stubborn reflection—he had everything organized, in theory, in the neatest possible fashion. He had fixed the program of his intentions rigorously; he had the arguments and the conclusion: the entire theorem of his renunciation.

And he thought: *I shall say....*

But the image of Geneviève immediately appeared; and the words that he had to say vanished, unraveled, lost. He recaptured them, put them back in logical order, in the order of battle. He fought against himself, and defeated himself.

His theorem was designed to convince Geneviève and himself—especially himself! With her, he thought the task would be easy; and as for himself, less comfortably, he told himself that, in truth, this life could not go on much longer, this life of anxiety, multiplied suffering, jealousy—was it jealousy?—in sum, sterile and vague mental susceptibility. No, it was necessary to end it. He would never be able to be happy, nor make anyone else happy. "Work, work!" he said to himself, again. "There's no more appropriate suicide, for a wretch of your sort!"

And he cursed himself.

To give himself courage, he also tried to abuse Geneviève as well as himself, but, although he could not find many reasons for rancor, he detested them more than the rest. Ingeniously, he assumed all the responsibilities—they were, to his tenderness and vanity, less harsh than Geneviève's responsibilities.

*I'll tell her....*

He had even prepared the words.

He saw Geneviève again. She was waiting for him. He saw her again, exactly as he had imagined her, with the dress that he had supposed, at the place in the antechamber where she would come to meet him; but he was astonished by her strange expression, her vivacity, her feverish manner.

She came toward him to kiss him, but she did not kiss him.

She offered her cheek for a kiss, after having offered her lips momentarily.

She was charming, with a color more animated than usual, her hair a trifle untidy; a blonde curl striped her forehead delicately. And when he kissed her cheeks, he felt the little bosom that he pressed against his own, with a voluptuous gesture. Then he feared that all his resolutions would weaken.

He was stilted; he was gauche. He hurried more than was reasonable, because he was afraid of weakening.

Soon, he said to Geneviève: "Listen. I need to talk to you. What I have to say is serious, almost terrible—but it's inevitable. You need to help me, in all sincerity. Otherwise, it seems to me that I'll forget all the promises I've made myself."

"Geneviève looked at him with her beautiful periwinkle-blue eyes. She trembled and murmured: "What's the matter?"

Michel took her hand, sat her down, remained standing in front of her and began, in spite of the anguish that was suffocating him: "Don't tremble. I don't mean to do you any harm; I'm only thinking of your own good. I love you very much. You have to answer me two questions, in all frankness. First of all, tell me: you're not happy, are you?"

"No," she replied, simply.

"I knew that."

He thought he might sob. He mastered himself and went on: "Secondly, yes, this is my second question....is Pierre Dauzanne in love with you?"

She went pale; her face contracted. She stood up an, her lips taut, replied: "You have no right to ask me that question."

Michel was bewildered. The entire series of decided sentences escaped him. He reacted, and, with a reflective stubbornness, went on: "That's true. Except that I have to. I demand that you answer me...or, rather, I beg you to answer me."

She remained silent and motionless for a few seconds. Then she said, very calmly and forcefully: "If I answer you, Michel, if you demand it, that's all right. But know that from that moment on, when I shall have submitted you to that humiliating torture,

I'll be detached from you forever; I'll be a stranger to you. That, I sense with certainty. Do you want that, Michel?"

"Yes."

"Well, then, Pierre Dauzanne is in love with me." And she went as white as a corpse.

With a stern passion, Michel went on: "He's told you that—that he's in love with you?"

"Ah! But whether he has or not, what does it matter? He had no need to tell me, if he has told me. A woman knows when someone is in love with her."

"Are you in love with him?"

The interrogation was, by dint of its rapidity, brutal. Geneviève rebelled. "Well, what if I were in love with him?"

"If you were in love with him, I would say this, which I'm ready to say to you: 'I renounce you, Geneviève. I've loved you a great deal; and if I love you still, my sacrifice, more cruel, is nonetheless absolute, sincere and complete. I have not known how, I have not been able, to make you happy. That's not my fault. I work hard. I have to work hard. It's impossible for me not to work hard. I don't belong to myself, any more than I belong to you. I'm a man who is bound to a task. It takes you, takes possession of you; one is no longer oneself; a monk, submissive to the rule of his order, is better than a man, and the kind of man that I'm not. So, here: I give you back your liberty. We'll divorce. You can go to Pierre Dauzanne, who loves you and whom you love...' I would say to you: 'Adieu, Geneviève; forget me and be happy.'"

"I refuse!" cried Geneviève.

Michel persisted: "But if...."

"I refuse!"

An immense joy suddenly exalted Michel. He groaned rather than pronounced: "So you don't love him?" He was begging.

Geneviève merely repeated: "I refuse."

They were both dumbfounded.

Timidly, Michel asked: "Why?"

"I don't know," she replied.

A little later, Michel kissed Geneviève's hands, wept, and asked for forgiveness. He said: "If you want, we can go away. We can go far away. You'll make me forget science and all that. Soon, I won't think about it any more. It's an old alchemist who has intoxicated me with his mania, as it's said that monks indoctrinate their pupils and make them enter the convent. But you'll save me. Do you want us to go?"

"No," she declared. "We'll stay."

"You don't want to?"

"No, I don't want to."

"I'll be recaptured, then!"

"You'll work."

"You'll be unhappy?"

"Yes."

"Let's go, then—I beg you!"

"No!"

And Michel savored the delights of love, the restful pleasure of being a coward, of abandoning himself to life, of feeling that it was stronger than he was, and letting it do what it would."

Then, he said to Geneviève: "I pity you."

Geneviève replied: "Michel, I pity both of us."

# CHAPTER TWO

It was a beautiful midsummer morning. The light spread out with perfect equality, and the heat was not yet punishing. The garden was radiant with the evident felicity of the trees.

Michel Bedée got up early, as soon as he could without worrying or astonishing Geneviève. He had slept fitfully all night, painful awakening following brief and difficult somnolence; there was a sharp pain in his fingertips. He knew what it was; they day before, unsuspectingly, he had been handling his sirium chloride, and the bizarre compound had burned him profoundly. At first he had not perceived it; now he was suffering, as if a thousand needles were incessantly traversing his flesh all the way to the bone.

He went downstairs, taking care not to wake Geneviève. He ran away, on tiptoe, and was only tranquil once he had shut himself in his laboratory, a large wooden shed, which one reached by means of pathways of pretty sand between flower-beds; abundant vegetation masked the building.

The house in which the Bedées were resident was charming, one of those old dwellings in Auteuil that have retained the appearance of olden times, and which made one think of Boileau, Racine and La Fontaine, of a simple life still regulated by hallowed custom.

Michel took refuge in his laboratory. He examined his wounds with a magnifying glass. He had difficulty moving his fingers; at the extremity of the phalanges he experienced a kind of exasperation of the sense of touch. If he applied the slightest pressure, the multiple needles went in deeper; the flesh became icy one moment, and hot the next as if it were about to cook and burst through the skin.

He could not see anything much, though, even on the thumb, where a recent cut had left an open wound. The impalpable emanations of sirium had penetrated, had hidden and were continuing an obscure and terrible work in the deep tissues. Michel resolved to observe and monitor the evolution of the phenomenon. As the trouble had developed in a matter of hours, he expected rapid episodes.

He sat down at a table and looked at his fingers, He was suffering and he was amused; on the one hand, he was in pain and, on the other, embarked on a scientific adventure. The two series of manifestations did not mix, and Michel soon noticed that his sense of self had divided. As he studied the two portions scrupulously, each of them constituted by a state of rich individuality, a third person overlooked the other two, contemplating them curiously. It had supremacy.

Michel wanted to write it all down. He picked up a pencil but could not hold it comfortably, either between the thumb and index finger or the index finger and middle finger. He feared, by increasing the pain, that he might modify the true data of the problem.

Then he remained motionless, watching out for the appearance on his skin of a patch or some other symptom. He thought he could distinguish a little redness, a brief tremor of the epidermis, but he was not sure. When the pinching of the nerves extended to the palm of the hand, however, he repeated an aphorism of Newton's in a whisper: "O physics, save me from metaphysics!"

He was enduring a torture cruel enough, but also interesting enough, for him to be occupied by it to the extent that his mind was entirely confined by it; that were courses therein that habitually led to hazardous voyages in ideology. Michel wondered whether metaphysics might not be a malady of spiritual leisure. For the sake of the peace of his soul he preferred his own malady, which had a positive quality.

Geneviève came in.

When she came in, Michel's eyes were fixed on the calendar, seeking dates in order to record the modification of the wound day by date. The twenty-fifth of July! That day shocked him: it was the second anniversary of his marriage. He remembered voluptuous weeks; he was remembering them with ardor and with fright when Geneviève, perfumed and fresh, was suddenly beside him, and planted a kiss on his forehead.

"What are you doing?" she asked.

As if he had been caught doing something wrong, his voice was abashed as he related the story of the sirium and his fingers. She was alarmed; she felt pity for Michel—but she said: "I can't see anything."

Then she touched Michel's fingers; and Michel did nothing but look at that hand, so gentle, white and plump. Suddenly, however, the pain was so intense that he went pale, and his injured fingers pulled away, contracting.

"We need to call a doctor," said Geneviève. "I'll telephone Pierre Dauzanne...."

At that name, Michel's suffering increased, and worse. He suffered jealousy, more dolorous than his wound. After a few seconds of hesitation, he said: "I beg you not to call a doctor."

"Why?"

That question, which was not difficult to understand, made him desperate; the impossibility of finding a good answer had the effect of a wall into which he had bumped violently.

"Why, Michel?"

He succeeded in mastering his emotion and said: "Because I want to study my wound without anyone disturbing it."

He would have preferred to find something else; he knew full well that that would make Geneviève indignant—and it did. She talked about absurd suicide, and detested the science to which Michel made too many sacrifices. She added: "For love of me, permit someone to look after you."

For love of her, what would he not have given? He would have given anything, and his life, more contentedly than to science. He would have given anything, except to let Pierre Dauzanne, who was in love with her and did not hide it, near to her again. As for asking for another doctor, no—it would be tantamount to admitting that he was jealous of Dauzanne, which he did not want to do.

Geneviève wept, and said: "You don't love me very much!"

He had no reply at all to make—absolutely none. Having searched rapidly, Michel knew that. But he looked at her, and he loved her. He sensed her, in her morning peignoir, nude and charming, soft to the touch—and at that imagination his hands hurt, tormented by invisible needles. That suffering called him back from far away, and he mastered himself, as his head, with his tempted senses, was setting out on campaign.

"Would you do me a favor, Geneviève? Will you write my notes to my dictation?"

"Yes." Except that she made a gesture of such disappointment that he regretted even having asked.

He continued, all the same: "I can't write at present. So, here goes...."

And he dictated what he had observed, hour by hour. First, though, there was the date. And when he said: "Twenty-fifth of July," his voice nearly failed. He was afraid that Geneviève might point out the anniversary—and afraid, too, that she might not have noticed it. And he watched.

Meekly, Geneviève repeated: "Twenty-fifth of July."

She was obviously on the point of saying something. He dictated. He thought that Geneviève was congratulating herself for not having carried on. Then his heart gave him no less pain than his fingers.

He dictated, and Geneviève wrote. She seemed not to be thinking about the petty torture that he was describing with such industrious scrupulousness; he had a desire to exaggerate, gradually, in order to see exactly when she would sympathize, but he was ashamed of that artifice and was exact. Geneviève repeated the sentences mechanically, thus inviting him to continue. Suddenly, she became conscious and rebelled:

"Michel, Michel! This is crazy! Look!"

He noticed, in fact, that the skin of his fingers was swelling, and that singular blotches were appearing.

"It doesn't look like a burn," he said.

"Does it hurt?"

"I don't think so," he said—and he was sincere, with extreme attention. "No, no, it's not painful...I can hardly feel any pain any more. The sensitivity is still there, however. If I move my hands I can feel the coolness of the air."

He waved his hands like fans, He had sweat on his brow. Then he thought that he did not know whether his flesh might have been affected in its most profound cells, whether the illness might progress, gradually, and whether, in the end, he was going to die. That possibility only troubled him in one respect; he divined that, widowed by him, Geneviève would marry Dr. Dauzanne. Then, the ideas in his head capsized.

He questioned himself; he wanted to know whether Geneviève had formulated that hypothesis, and welcomed it pleasantly; he wanted her, in spite of himself, to summon the healer.

He asked her various questions, with artful hypocrisy, but she scarcely replied, as if, in fact, the absurdity of the occurrence caught her unawares. He tried to interest her in his scientific curiosity; as ever, he felt that that in that regard there was a separation between them, like a wall. He did not say anything to her that she did not gladly admit, but the words and the ideas did not reach her. Michel saw them—the words and the ideas—fall before reaching her, like well-fired arrows that lost their momentum in flight by virtue of some force, as when the gods protected a warrior in a mythological battle.

She had a fine mind, so intelligent that he admired it in her, and was so nimbly imaginative, so rapid to seize the most delicate nuances of thought, that he had called her "little enchantress" in the days of their first love, when he amused himself by telling her what he knew about paintings and sites, everywhere they traveled. When he praised sirium and its marvelous properties, however, she was no longer listening.

"That doesn't interest you?"

She was honest and pitiless. "No," she said. "What do you want? No...I can't do anything about it; it's stronger than me. I've done all I can, but no. I know that you're a man of genius... but so what? Your sirium, which one can't see, is of no practical use, and has done you harm. If only it could cure!"

If only it could cure! Michel understood that Geneviève, perhaps without knowing it, was thinking about Pierre Dauzanne, a scientist himself, who could cure, a scholar of the benevolent science. He understood that Geneviève, in accordance with the old instinct of dolorous and ardent humankind, hated the uselessness of a science that did not augment the sum of pleasures, which did not diminish the sum of suffering, a science of curiosity. Geneviève thus pleased him more. He loved her for conserving within herself, so imperious and so strong, the desires of ancient ages. It seemed to him that their dialogue continued a centuries-old and poignant misunderstanding—the same one that, in the epochs of rude energy, had burned philosophers and their books.

His mother, too, did not admit that search for vain truths—except that his mother condemned it in the name of dogmas, wile Geneviève refused it in the name of life, in the name of beauty, sweet and amusing life, which was well worth living for its own sake.

Michel mused secretly on all of that, while Geneviève polished her nails with a corner of her handkerchief, meditating with a sad expression.

"Are you still in pain?" she asked.

"No, hardly any."

"So you don't need me any more?" she asked, then.

"No, no," he said.

And she went away. On seeing her go, however, Michel did not have a more bitter chagrin than feeling her so close and yet so distant, a stranger to him. When she reached the door and was about to go out, however, he could not control himself.

Yielding to his impulse, he called: "Geneviève!"

She seemed surprised. She looked at Michel. "What is it, my love?"

Michel was obliged to say something. He said what he had wanted not to say. "It's the twenty-fifth of July today—our wedding anniversary. Did you remember?"

"I remembered. Did you?"

As she was visibly more sad than annoyed, he softened. He begged forgiveness, without quite knowing what sin he had committed—but he accused himself at hazard, in order to pick a quarrel. He loved the infinite sweetness of repentance and pardon; he experienced, in taking all wrongs upon himself and meriting all indulgence, the disturbance that had once rendered the shade of the confessional delightful for him.

"You're kind, Michel."

And she talked to him like a child. He was touched. Furthermore, Geneviève's beauty tempted him, for she was more ravishing than ever in her morning robe, pink with ribbons. He remembered the time when be had loved her to the point of no longer inventing the words that he spoke to her, and he borrowed the words of others: "How I love you in that dress, that undresses you so well!"

And he wanted to stroke her, since she was cheerful and smiling; he wanted to hug her in his arms, and drew her toward him—but suddenly, his imprudently excited fingers hurt him, and he uttered a cry of pain. He felt weak, and he sensed that Geneviève was stiff and icy in his arms, which were no longer able to hold her.

He and Geneviève looked at one another without saying anything. He opened his arms in order that she could go. She went, having found one or two petty remarks of pity, of amicable politeness—one or two gracious and terrible petty remarks.

She went away, though.

Left alone, Michel thought: *It's over...I'm consecrated...I have the stigmata of science.*

He looked at his fingers, definitely marked by the redness of burning, with a curious distress.

* * * * * * *

In the afternoon of that same day, Michel was languishing miserably beside the silent Geneviève, when Dr. Dauzanne was announced.

Geneviève's physiognomy suddenly became animated. Michel, who was looking at her, saw her, at that name, light up like a landscape in a furtive sunbeam.

"Did you ask him to come?" he asked.

"Yes," she replied.

That was not true—but the assiduity of Pierre Dauzanne was unwelcome to Michel, and Geneviève took advantage of a facile lie to give the imprudent lover's visit a plausible reason.

Michel did not hide his bad temper. "I didn't want him to come!"

She seemed to hesitate, and make a quick decision. "I was anxious."

"You telephoned him?"

"Yes."

She made as if to go into the drawing room. Michel retained her, a trifle impulsively.

"No, you're not going to receive him like that. Get dressed. That little robe is too intimate."

She became impatient, and Michel spoke tenderly: "No, those little robes, which don't hide very much, are only for me—you know that."

She gave in, and left. And Michel, without waiting, went to greet Pierre Dauzanne.

He was a handsome fellow, strongly built, with an opulent blond beard and a perpetual smile.

"There was no need to come," said Michel. "It's nothing."

"What's nothing?"

"No, I won't take your hand. You shake too forcefully; today, your forthright grip would make me cry out."

Paul Dauzanne evidently did not understand what he was saying.

"Geneviève didn't say anything!" Michel asked.

"Nothing at all."

"But she telephoned?"

"Not at all."

"But you came?"

"I dropped in as I was passing...."

Geneviève soon arrived. Michel saw that Pierre welcomed her joyfully, and not only for the pleasure of her presence, but because it was necessary that she be there, in order for a mystery to be clarified, a bizarre secret dispelled. Geneviève said *bonjour* and held out her hand, which he kissed ceremoniously.

"I thought that you'd called Pierre," Michel observed, "about my fingers?"

"Well, yes....."

"Well, no!" he said. And with his eyes, he demanded Pierre's testimony.

"You telephoned me?" said the doctor.

"Yes! You were out; your servant answered. Did he forget to pass on the message? It's not important."

"It's not important?" Michel repeated.

"Yes, since Pierre's here: it's not important!" she articulated the words so clearly that Michel had no desire to continue his enquiry.

*It's not important!* he thought, with a strange docility. But Geneviève was already talking about the burn, how anxious she was, and Michel's stubbornness in not wanting anyone to attend to it."

"Show it to me," said the doctor.

Michel jibbed. "No—it's nothing to do with you."

"As you wish...."

"But, after all, yes, as I wish!" He sought a pretext to leave. For want of anything better, feeling awkward, he said: "Excuse me...I have things warming up out there. If I leave them alone, they'll boil over." And he withdrew.

Scarcely was he outside, though, than he regretted it. He accused himself of stupidity, leaving Geneviève and Pierre together like that, doubtless glad to see him go. In his laboratory, as soon as he had gone in, he wanted to return to the drawing-room, but he dared not. And he started mulling it over.

Assuredly, he was not suspicious of Geneviève; he knew that she was sincere and abrupt—in sum, capable of telling him that she no longer loved him, that she was abandoning him, incapable of betraying him. But why, in saying that she had called Pierre Dauzanne, had she lied? For he had no doubt that she had lied.

"It's not important!" Michel repeated, internally.

But he did not stop quibbling painfully over that, with too sharp a lucidity. He set out from authentic facts and he drew from them, with an appearance of rigorous logic, extravagant corollaries; he perceived the strangeness, but he trusted the accuracy of his reasoning and did not know what to think. His bad mood persuaded him to imagine nothing but catastrophe, even at moments when he sensed the pull of the great and magnificent liberty of hypothesis that is, for the scientist, an immense reserve of uncertainty, sometimes secretive and sometimes lucky.

Then he checked the time and counted the minutes that Pierre Dauzane's visit lasted. It lasted too many. Michel tried to guess what the two individuals, solicited by an evident affection, were talking about, and he wondered whether they were still talking about him, and if so, what they were saying about him. But no, that was over now, and they were talking about themselves. But where were they, in their confidences? Michel entered into the pathways of an entirely natural dialogue, which developed according to the habitual course of a law an innocent thought— and then he arrived at a crossroads of ideas and no longer knew which way to go. He was lost. He soon took the bad roads of jealousy, sadly inventive.

He kept watch on the hands of his watch, and detested their

slowness. He only counted a minute after the hand had passed the black mark and left white space behind it. In addition, he was careful not to lean his head to the left in such a way as to favor the illusory march of time.

And thus he sank into the bleakest reverie.

\* \* \* \* \* \* \*

"Why did you come?" Geneviève asked Pierre Dauzanne.

"To see you," he replied, bravely.

Such was the impetuosity of those words that Geneviève, initially arrogant, could not bear them. But Pierre Dauzanne, exalted by an insistent love, went further, and declared: "To see you, because I love you."

Then Geneviève retorted: "You don't love me very much, if...."

He seemed so unhappy that Geneviève softened her tone. "Pierre," she aid, "don't oblige me to give you pain, when I have nothing in my heart for you but friendship...but would you like us to talk more frankly?"

"I'd like nothing better," he said.

"Sit down. Try to stay calm and listen to me. And try to see things my way, because, all the same, a woman's energy has its limits...."

"I'm listening." He had the meek expression of a docile child who is going to allow someone to chide him when he had been naughty, and knows that he will be forgiven.

Geneviève sensed that, in sum, there was nothing more to do than talk; she also sensed that the horrible difficulty lay therein. For a second she sought among her ideas for the one that it was necessary to choose. She hesitated, became anxious, began to sob, without tears, wrung her interlaced fingers, and moaned: "I really am too unhappy!"

Pierre's compassion, at the ready, promptly launched, quickly recalled her pride. As he came closer she pushed him away with a gesture. "No, no, don't feel sorry for me; it's not a matter of feeling sorry for me. But it's necessary that I speak to you and that I tell you...oh, I've a lot to tell you, so much that I'll never finish...."

And she despaired, with regard to the future.

Pierre interrupted her. "But Geneviève, what's the matter? I don't want to displease you. All the same, I can't bear for you to be in such a state without being permitted...."

"Listen to me," Geneviève resumed. "Listen to me. The other day, when you came, when Michel had gone to see his mother in Brittany, we were insane...."

"Oh! No!"

"Yes, we were insane. I know that you haven't said a word that could offend my desire to be an honest woman. No—and I haven't said anything to you that I have to hold against myself, but after all, our conversation took on, without our thinking about it, a strange softness, by which I'm still alarmed. What we said, I no longer know. First, you talked about your profession, which is so fine, so moving—and then, it seems to me, we talked about anything at all, without even attaching any importance to what we were saying, solely for the pleasure of listening to our voices...."

"Geneviève!"

"Yes, yes...that's not all. Let me tell you...when you had gone, after two hours I thought you had only stayed for a few minutes, the hours having passed as if by enchantment, and I thought that you had stayed for a lifetime, so rapidly had habitude developed between us...it was like that, wasn't it? Did you experience the same thing?"

"Oh, yes!" he replied vehemently. "We love one another...."

"It's possible," she said.

They were both in ecstasy, not moving and feeling their mutual love. Pierre was happy, with a sort of anxiety; and Geneviève, multiplying the words of felicity, seemed to be contemplating a disaster. She reacted at first against the emotion that held her captive, and said, very simply, as if she were enunciating an evident truth that Pierre knew and accepted.

"Now we must part."

"Already! When shall I see you again?"

Then she remembered that she had to tell him her resolution. She was astonished that he did not know it, that he had not guessed it; she blushed at having so tenderly abandoned herself in her words without him understanding that she was saying goodbye. And she said, hotly: "Never!"

He protested, but she went on: "Never! After such moments, such confessions and such pleasure, there's nothing we can do but not see one another again."

He did not give in easily. He protested against the futile sacrifice, affirmed the sincerity of his love, battled as best he could against Geneviève's determination, and despaired when he sensed that Geneviève was imprisoned in that determination as in a citadel.

Henceforth, she fell obstinately silent. After the words of exquisite love that she had pronounced, or, rather, confessed, she said nothing more. She even seemed not to hear Pierre's ardent declarations. She looked at him, but perhaps did not see him. Pierre had the impression that he was talking into the wind, and that his words were dispersed on the edge of his lips. He wept. Then, when he ran out of arguments, he said: "Can't we continue to see one another? Michel doesn't suspect anything!"

"Michel knows everything," Geneviève replied.

And Pierre was dishonest, as one is with a subtle kind of honesty. "What does he know? What is there to know? We haven't done anything wrong. I've only begged you to love me. I haven't even begged you; but we've fallen in love without wanting to, without being aware of it, by virtue of the intimate ardor of our souls. It's not our fault—it's not a fault at all."

She perceived the danger of that sophistry, and, since the truth alone could triumph over too ingenious an error, she had recourse to blunt frankness.

"Let's not play the comedy of innocence," she said—and braved the words of which she was afraid. "If I had been your mistress, would we have deceived Michel any more than we have done...with our souls, as you put it?"

He avoided replying. He was already turning away from the conversation. She brought him back violently.

"Would we have had those hours the other day, if Michel had been there? Oh, it's necessary not to put the question otherwise; that's the way it is."

He said nothing.

"So," she went on, "goodbye."

And she stood up.

"But we love one another; I can't give you up!"

"You must."

"I don't want to abandon you to an existence in which you're unhappy."

"It's necessary."

"It's not necessary! One doesn't have the right—Michel doesn't have the right to annihilate someone, someone like you, who are so beautiful, so young, so dazzling, so beloved!"

It was as if he were fascinated. He was reciting litanies, which were insignificant but which delighted them both. He looked her in the eyes and their heads reeled. He came toward her and she did not recoil. There lips were like drops of water that are about to join up and mingle.

Suddenly, Geneviève, trembling, stiffened with a powerful effort of recovered energy. She opened the door and murmured: "Go away. Quickly, quickly! Goodbye!"

And Pierre went, driven by that dominant energy.

* * * * * * *

For some time, Geneviève listened to the doors that had to open and close for Pierre Dauzanne's departure opening and closing. She watched through the curtains over the window, standing far enough away to be unseen from the outside. He left; his step was a trifle unsteady; the gravel of the pathways moved under his feet and caused him to skid.

Michel's voice rang out. "Pierre!" he called.

Pierre turned round. He was pale. Michel soon caught up with him. They talked briefly.

Geneviève examined them with mortal anguish. The beating of her heart was so strong that she put her hand on her breasts and applied as much pressure to it as she could. She was on tenterhooks. She thought about walking toward the two men, in order to separate them if their mutual rancor threw them into conflict, but she was immobilized by fear. She had a desire to shout, but her mouth would not open. She had a desire to die, but she remained paralyzed in a state of suffering.

She watched the two faces—and suddenly, they smiled at one another. She was ashamed, and wanted to go and hide. That ridiculous bonhomie irritated her.

Michel showed Pierre his fingers and Pierre made a sign indicating ignorance. They chatted again. Then they separated, as comrades.

When Michel came into the drawing-room, Geneviève was slumped in an armchair. Her hands were on the arms of the chair and she was staring straight ahead, often blinking her eyes, as if it were necessary continually to drive away a dream that was afflicting her and resume possession of a reassuring reality.

Michel asked whether she was tired. She said no—but when he persisted, politely, she told him that the air was strangely heavy, and that there was a storm brewing. Michel agreed. He moved a curtain aside with the back of his injured hand to display the garden. The sky was covered; a crepuscular light, devoid of vivacity and unreflective, lay dormant, imprisoned beneath the network of branches and leaves. No breath of wind agitated the trees or the grass. The garden was waiting, tranquilly, for the rain. The silence was also that of calm expectation. Only the chirping of the birds, which had already taken refuge in their hiding places, did not seem to be waiting—because, in the obscurity, a tiny light does not radiate far.

"I showed Pierre my fingers," Michel said.

"What did he say?"

"Nothing. He doesn't know."

Geneviève did not say anything. He added: "I thought that I was wrong to study my wound without the aid of an expert...."

"Are you in pain?"

"No, not any longer, but odd things are happening; the skin is swollen. I told Pierre that I didn't want treatment, but I need him for diagnosis, I asked him to call in every day...."

"No!"

"Yes. Why not?"

"Is he coming?"

"He told me that he hoped to come, that he would try. Oh, these people aren't curious!"

"If you don't want him to treat you...."

"But there's nothing to treat, truly."

"Yes there is."

"No."

"Yes."

And on that, neither one would yield. The quarrel, apparently both pedantic and puerile, was fundamental to their perpetual misunderstanding.

The polemic lapsed, and the conversation with it.

After a pause, Michel said: "You chatted? What did you say?"

Geneviève was about to say something inconsequential, and then, impatiently, thought it better to put an end to it. "I asked him not to come back again."

"Why?"

"You know why."

She preferred being sincere than submitting him to the annoyance of a lie by omission; all the same, she wanted Michel to be content with a summary.

"What's that?" he asked.

"I asked him not to come back in order not to hear your questions, not to have stories to hear and susceptibilities to protect. What do I know? Spare me, Michel; I've had enough—too much. Leave me alone, please."

The final words were shaken by brief sobs. Geneviève, upset by so much emotion, was no longer, in Michel's presence, anything but a fearful little girl. Doubtless, he felt sorry for her, but a masculine resentment prompted him to riposte, and the least he could say was: "I've offered to leave you alone, to leave you absolutely. It's you who didn't want that."

"No," she said. "That's right." ·

They both felt certain that it was necessary now to take refuge in silence. They had a great deal to say, but they were so closed to one another that no thought was transmitted between them, even carried by the most vivid and adroit sentences. Geneviève closed her eyes, in order to mark her desire to be alone. Michel looked at her momentarily, and he drew away from her as if from a sealed tomb near to which one fears to linger.

* * * * * *

In the days that followed, Geneviève was gentler that usual. In appearance, she was calm—but she was quieter than ever, and not because she wanted to be silent in order that Michel might be annoyed thereby. He saw that she was a captive of her silence, incapable of emerging from it.

He was careful not to torment and pester her with questions, but he observed her with a scientist's tenderness. As he loved her, he could read her well, and he classified his observations methodically.

She tried to organize her life and sought desperately for an everyday activity, hazard having not provided one; she lacked the simple occupations, for lack of a child, for lack of a lover, for lack of wifely fervor. She could not hide the fact that Michel was a singular companion for her, who disconcerted her and was far from guiding her. Then again, she did not have a mania to serve; being serious in character, she would not devote herself to nonsense. Her existence seemed to be surrounded by a void.

Amid that universal distress in which she refused to languish, she came and went very punctiliously, more attentive to the housework, to her accounts, to her daily correspondence, to visitors, to all the routines of mornings, afternoons and evenings, but sad to the point of no longer even experiencing the desire to weep, or any desire at all. But she did not think of seeking a remedy. As Geneviève did not address herself to him, he did not offer anything; they were both aware of the insurmountable distance that separated them—a distance of dissimilar minds.

Michel's fingers peeled, causing bloody sores. He examined them curiously, but he no longer asked Geneviève to record the bizarre episodes of his illness. His scientific attitude revolted her, and he sensed a great desire in her to look after him. She would have been happy to put compresses on, to tie fabric dolls on his fingertips and watched out every day for signs of healing, just as he felt the attraction of the continual progress of the ravages.

One evening, when he was showing it to her, he saw that she was disconcerted by his refusal of medical attention, as Dauzanne had been when he had rejected it, and he understood that the souls of those two individuals were in profound accord. He suffered as a result, and pitied the grim solitude to which his jealousy had condemned Geneviève.

"It's absurd that Pierre doesn't come," he said.

"No it isn't," she replied, in a low voice.

"Yes, I assure you. It might even interest him, professionally. No such wound has been seen before. It's the first."

Geneviève said nothing, but Michel observed that the mere mention of Pierre Dauzanne provoked a long torpor. He persisted. "Write and ask him to come, please."

"No," she said.

Eventually, Michel's wounds healed, as if miraculously. The flesh, after the scrupulous work of corruption, came away, and a new skin formed, perfect, healthy and exactly similar to the one that the sirium had burned, except that it was slightly pinker. There was not even a visible scar, and the earlier cut on the thumb had disappeared.

"Look," said Michel to Geneviève. "It's a remedy I've found. Do you see? It's no longer a diabolical invention, but a remedy. Look, I'm cured. Touch it!"

She examined the miracle of sirium. For the first time in a long time, her eyes were cheerful. With a gentle timidity, he asked: "You're glad, aren't you?"

And it was necessary to tell her every detail of the physiological adventure. She loved him passionately. She asked Michel twenty questions, and he admired her enthusiasm.

"Do you understand?" he said. "If the wound had simply scarred over, I would have concluded that the sirium burn wasn't serious and no more—but that's not what has happened. No, the burn was deep; it corroded the tissues considerably, and then the flesh was rebuilt, intact. It's not a matter of scar tissue, but new tissue."

"So?"

"So I'm wondering what would happen if one burned, with the same sirium, a cancerous or ulcerated wound, for example—or even, I suppose, a lupus...."

And Geneviève concluded, ardent: "The diseased flesh would be eaten away, and replaced by another, healthy and brand new."

"Perhaps," Michel agreed.

At first, he was tenderly amused to see Geneviève so excited, to sense that transformation, for her, into a marvel of a science that was passing from virgin uselessness into fecund efficacy. Then he became thoughtful—and now it was Geneviève who was on watch, waiting for a word, a comment. She had emerged from her solitary tower and revived.

"It's absolutely necessary that I talk to Dauzanne."

"Yes," said Geneviève. "Go and see him."

"No, let him come here."

And Pierre Dauzanne came. Geneviève and he saw one another again, Pierre Dauzanne bewildered at first, and Geneviève tranquil, appeased as if by forgetfulness, appeased by a great hope that uplifted her, gave her sovereignty over the contingencies of her individual destiny.

Pierre Dauzanne had the bitterness of finding her thus; he had dreaded her disturbance, but was critical or her indifference. As for the story of the wound so well-healed, he greeted it with skepticism. Then the commentaries of Geneviève and Michel rendered him more attentive. He argued; he admitted the singularity of the fact.

"It's necessary to see," he said.

"Yes, yes—see!" Geneviève replied.

"I have an old Chinaman in my service whose face is devoured by lupus. Would you like me to try?"

Michel hesitated, but finally replied: "I daren't...."

Geneviève and Dauzanne fell silent. Michel continued: "It's not my business. No, no...let's leave it there. I daren't. If the unfortunate fellow were to die...no, no."

Dauzanne said: "If you're only anxious that the Chinaman...."

"Well?"

"He's my Chinaman, you know...." He attached no importance to the Chinaman.

"In that case, do as you wish," Michel concluded.

* * * * * * *

Afterwards, he was anxious. The Chinaman haunted him perpetually.

"Let's go see," hazarded Geneviève.

He refused to go, and in order to stop him telephoning Pierre Dauzanne to tell him to abandon the experiment, she had to keep watch on him. As he had shut himself up in his laboratory, she went out, went to see Pierre Dauzanne, and bravely asked him to bring the Chinaman. He obeyed. She had arrived in such a way, with so much simplicity and fine boldness, that he did not say a word to her about their love or their quarrel. Had she not forgotten all that? He wondered, in amazement, and did not interrogate her.

When he returned she said to Michel: "One can't even tell any more that he's a Chinaman. He had almost no face. And he cries! He's neither Chinese nor French—he's nothing but suffering."

She was upset by it..

"Is he going to die?" Michel asked.

"Yes, yes, certainly; he's going to die."

"Then I can't. Pierre has to treat him some other way, as best he can. It's madness. I don't know anything about it. Pierre shouldn't have said anything."

"Wait."

"No, no. I don't want my science to be murderous. It's done me enough harm already. To me, that's all right—but not to others. Science isn't a cure. People are always asking it for something other than it gives."

"What does it give?"

"The truth, that's all. It only gives the truth, with which there's nothing to be done—nothing at all. The truth isn't a drug. The truth, one looks at...and doesn't touch."

The more he argued thus, the more he excited, in Geneviève's mnd, the opposite idea. She was on the point of arguing, but she was afraid to do that and said: "I have confidence in the discovery."

On that, Michel got carried away. His discovery had no medical quality. No, he had found sirium; he was studying its properties, and that was all.

While he spoke, vehemently, Geneviève's statement came back into his mind, charged with a new significance that began, softly, to move and astonish him. He stopped thinking about what he was saying. He was no longer annoyed and he asked, as if to assure himself of a pleasure: "You have confidence in my discovery? Why?"

She replied that she had never doubted Michel's genius and that he was unjust if he thought that.

He was content, but he waited for some more affectionate effusion; the genius accorded to him he would have traded for Geneviève's arms to be put around his neck, as before.

He detested the moribund Chinaman, on whom depended, in too calamitous a fashion, Geneviève's confidence—the confidence that was all he retained of a voluptuous love. He was tormented by scruples because of that old man, come from who knew where in the marvelous Orient, one of millions come to him, come to this precise spot at this exact date, in order that ill luck should inflict upon him the first application of sirium to a human face. He imagined someone traveling through strange lands and over admirable seas, lingering or hurrying without wanting to, at the whim of a ingenious fatality, the organizer of coincidences. Then he arrives: here he is. His costume of embroidered silk has been taken away, he has been laid down in a hospital bed. His face is destroyed, his features disappeared—and that Chinaman is no longer anything but anonymous flesh, at the disposal of an adventurous science. He is going to die, after having received the baptism of a discovery.

In his meditations, Michel restored a personality to him, a kind of soul that protested obscurely against hazards, its malevolence and carelessness. And he was the target of the protests of that small, sharp and vindictive soul.

Two days later, Doctor Dauzanne arrived, when Michel and Geneviève, after lunch, were doing nothing but dreaming, variously, side by side, departing from the same idea along paths that would never meet.

Straight away, Dauzanne declared: "It's magnificent!"

"He's saved?" Michel exclaimed.

Dauzane smiled. "Oh—no, not him. He's dead."

Michel went pale; his fingers were trembling—his healed fingers, at the tips of which responsibility was quivering.

Geneviève was all ears; she waited for Pierre to speak, and watched Michel's face anxiously.

"He's dead," the doctor continued, "but he was on the way to being healed."

That honest summation wounded Michel like a sick joke. "In brief, he's dead," said Michel. "Did he suffer?"

"Oh! Yes."

"What I'm asking is whether he suffered more."

"No...I don't think so. There's a maximum of suffering that can't be surpassed."

Geneviève perceived that Michel was tortured. "But you say

that he was on the way to a cure?" she said.

"Yes. The wounds on his face had progressed rather like your fingers," Dauzanne said to Michel. "In places, the skin was reforming, and when I carried out the autopsy I found tissues that were already reconstituting...."

"Only, he's dead!" replied Michel, in a tone of dolorous irony.

"Oh, listen—you shouldn't put on mourning-dress for the Chinaman, even so. What do you want? It was too far advanced. For a first experiment, I didn't dare...I was wrong. It's a matter of starting again, that's all."

"I forbid it!" Michel exclaimed.

"Are you mad? The experiment has yielded astonishing results. If the method isn't perfected, we'll see what can be done; we'll investigate, and gradually, we'll get there...."

"And others will die?"

"Well, yes."

"Well, no. It's over. Bring back my sirium today."

"Never!"

"Today."

And they argued, the one who had pity on a few individuals and the other who glimpsed fine cures in the future. One ideology collided with another. But they also argued like two men solicited by rancor. Geneviève, beside them, sensed that, and because of it, did not take Dauzanne's side—but she was in compete sympathy with him. She knew what she would have said in response to Michel's scruples, and when Pierre Dauzanne passed over good reasons to choose brutal and paradoxical ones, her head was full of a persuasive eloquence, which excited her to the point of making her feel ill.

Pierre Dauzanne said to Michel: "It's a bizarre thing. There's no scientist bolder than you. You've formulated hypotheses and established doctrines that have thrown science into confusion. The bravest men would have been afraid to announce a quarter of your rude theories—but when it's necessary to pass on from theories to their practical consequences, you're all doubt and pusillanimity; in concrete reality, you seem to me to be like a little child."

Michel listened meekly to this diagnosis. He recognized its justice with alarm, and he had no reply to make.

"And why?" Dauzanne continued. "What difference do you see between your experiments and mine?"

"The difference," Michel said, "is the pain. When I work, there's no pain. And I can go forward—what does it matter? But concrete reality is full of pain; one doesn't do anything there without exciting pain; one can't touch it otherwise. Yes, the more I think about it, the more I see that that's what I'm afraid of." And he looked around fearfully, as if he felt all the reality of the world ready to shiver, ready to signal its infinite distress by cries or mute gestures.

"That's not brave!" Dauzanne riposted.

And Michel went away, to go and shut himself in his laboratory with his abstract and insensible meditations.

"You're going to carry on, aren't you?" said Geneviève to Pierre Dauzanne.

"Certainly." And after a brief silence, he added: "You're no longer the same. What's happened to you?"

She did not conceal the fact that she wanted to avoid that conversation. "Work," she said. "It will be fine, superb. And if you like, I shall be the friend of your benevolent task."

\* \* \* \* \* \* \*

Pierre Dauzanne multiplied his experiments. Michel knew that, and tolerated it, but on the condition of being completely uninvolved. He shut himself away in his laboratory, more tightly. And he was even more unhappy there, because it seemed to him that, outside the planks of his refuge, a crop of pain was growing that he had sown.

For a long time, the experiments did not succeed. Dauzanne came to tell Geneviève about them. He observed partial results, but he determined that he needed to hesitate further before determining the doses of sirium, the duration of the applications and the appropriate combinations. There were deaths—as many deaths as experiments. In addition, although the patients were condemned, several died more rapidly, howling under the torture. There were protests.

If Dauzanne took fright, Geneviève encouraged him. If he sometimes seemed gripped by uncertainty, she found the best ways to reassure him. Better than words, she had her veritable love, which said nothing, but was there; she experienced joy because of its efficacy. When Pierre went away more ardent than when he had arrived, she congratulated herself on her good influence. She also told herself that Michel wanted her to be the same for him—an intelligent companion in his labor. But what could she do? She had offered; he had not refused, but had simply desired it without taking it—and that nonchalance separated them.

Soon, Pierre Dauzanne triumphed over the difficulties. The sirium worked wonders, of which the press was aware, and which were advertised therein. On the day of the first victory, when it was observed that the drug arrested the hemorrhages of a cancer and reduced its extensive progress, Geneviève and Pierre, moved by the same delight, told Michel about it.

He was working, and only said: "That's good—but I had already verified that property of sirium on my fingers." He was studying the formula of the electrical emissions of sirium, and did not raise his head. "Excuse me," he said, "I'm working."

Such dryness chilled Geneviève. She cried: "You felt so much grief for the Chinaman!"

"So?"

"You might be a little glad for the poor woman who's just been saved. I think so—that would be human."

"Yes, yes," he replied. "I'm glad...but I'm working."

There were a few seconds when Geneviève detested him.

When she and Pierre went away, Michel did not even watch them go—but when the door closed behind them, he abandoned his task; he could no longer resist; he simply accepted suffering. And he said to himself: *I'm suffering, though, like a human being.* That was his reply, belated and secret, to Geneviève's reproach: "That would be human." And he understood, better than ever, the poignant particularity of his case, the exile to which his austere idea of science confined him.

He was, however, jealous—yes, like any other human being; he was suffering from the vulgar malady of jealousy. In spite of his distracted manner, he had perceived the delightful intimacy of mind and soul that united Geneviève and Pierre. He envied such happiness, which he had allowed to be stolen from him. And he regretted not defending himself; but whenever the impulse took him, a numbness overwhelmed him. If he separated Geneviève and Pierre, she would not come to him; she would languish alone, and he would not profit from it, for she would remain as distant from him as ever. He pitied her and was scornful of her. Except that, by virtue of suffering, he was capable of bad temper; that was why he had sent away the triumphant pair a trifle rudely. He wondered, moreover, whether the cancerous woman's cure delighted him. He concluded that it did not, and concluded that there was no longer anything human in him but suffering.

The cures, or their promise, continued their victorious progress. At the hospital and Dr. Dauzanne's consulting-room, invalids presented themselves in such numbers that it was necessary to turn most of them away.

Geneviève was desolate about that. One day, she had an idea: to make her house available, so that patients could be accommodated there. She would retain, for herself and Michel, two rooms on the second floor. The rest would be a hospital, where Pierre and his interns would make applications of sirium, and she would serve as a nurse.

Michel consented to it, because she showed, for that project of devotion, a keen enthusiasm that rendered her even rosier and more lovely—and for lack of that pleasure, what could he offer her? In brief, he only reserved in laboratory.

Then, with a joyful zeal, she soon informed him of a new resolution by which she was excited. She would sell her furniture, her jewels, her charming luxury, to buy, instead, beds, sheets, apparatus—all the equipment of a hospital. Michel resigned himself to it, because it was, after all, the natural extension of his abnegation—which was a fact, like the others, laden with consequences. And he saw depart, in several carriages, all his memory of happiness: the divans of their tender idleness, the mirrors of coquetry, the pictures by which their reveries had been amused. All that went away, carried off by people who had the indifferent brutality of lists, who passed through one after another, each taking his booty; and the clearance of the house was similar, in its pace, to that great perpetual thief, time. Michel watched the procession from a distance, and thought that death was working, that day, more quickly than ever in preparing him for oblivion.

In a matter of days, however, the beds were set up, the white curtains hung, the white sheets extended, and Geneviève was dressed in white and coiffed in white, like those nuns who, in order to care for human corruption, don the insignia of perfect purity.

Then a lady who was astonishingly rich, and who, no longer being young, had penances to make with a view to eternal life, donated the sum necessary to buy the building next door and transform it into a hospital. It was a former convent, once inhabited by some two dozen good sisters who had taught little girls to read, write and calculate, and had thus become a danger to the republic. Other good sisters were summoned, a dozen in number, who wore the uniform of lay nurses in order that the republic could tolerate them without anxiety. Beds were installed everywhere, even in the former chapel, its usage changed just as the nuns had been laicized, but no more; in spite of the new installation, the little nave retained the air of a sacred place, with its lanceolate windows, its stained glass, its pleasant isolation, and its flagstones, where the sound of footsteps would have had the same ring as in a church—although everything there invited silence, and people walked on tiptoe, speaking in whispers.

In that unexpected environment, Geneviève immediately

seemed at home—and while Michel was disorientated and lost there, she came and went with assurance and familiarity. One might have thought that she was recovering old habits instead of having taken up residence along recent things. One had only to look at her, so simply happy and natural, to see that she finally had the surroundings she needed, and Michel perceived that previously, in the midst of futile elegance, she had been like a stranger who could not settle in, nostalgic for the past. As a nurse, she remained pretty and charming, with her delicate and flexible figure, her firm step, her youthful bearing and her pink face; her features gained even more beauty, by virtue of the satisfied bounty that animated them. And when Michel remembered her dressed as an elegant young woman, she seemed then to have been in disguise.

She spoke to the interns without timidity and without confusion; she spoke to the patients amicably and without excessive sensitivity, with attentive correctness. She gave orders to the servants and did not multiply vain activity, but when she brought tisanes, hot and odorous, she had the look of a benevolent enchantress.

People of all sorts arrived: men and women of various ages, various conditions and, soon, various nationalities. The rich had separate rooms; they paid for their sojourn in order that the poor could be admitted gratuitously.

Workers arrived from the poor outlying districts; their ferocious expressions made modest and amiable because of illness, which did not permit them to be menacing. They tried to be polite and humble, but their behavior often became involuntarily brusque and demanding; they easily forgot that no one owed them anything and that they were simply receiving charity.

Peasants arrived from Normandy, in blue blouses ornamented at the collar by a little white braid; and from Brittany, with their short jackets, their metal-decorated belts and their beribboned hats; and Provençals who talked volubly about their ailments.

A negro arrived, whose jeremiads were sinister and puerile; his chatter resembled a tall story which had mistakenly chosen for its theme a terrible adventure of desperation and folly. A Zealander woman arrived, helmed in copper beneath a lace bonnet, her arms bare and her skirt so large that she was reminiscent of the Old Woman Who Lived in a Shoe; the frightful thinness of her face already lent it an appearance of death, and that death's-head was horrible, thus costumed, as if for an absurd and macabre carnival. Bearded and booted Russians arrived, a Siberian muffled in a goatskin greatcoat and an astrakhan tiara.

A little girl arrived who hardly knew her name or where she came from, and remained haggard and uncomplaining. The son of a Balkan prince arrived, with eyes as large and black as a moonless and starless night—a little prince, melancholy and impertinent, who hid beneath his fine clothes the blemishes of a corrupt heredity.

Specimens arrived of all the dolor scattered throughout the world. There was an intermittent procession of the grimaces that disease imprints on faces of every color. There were faces destroyed by lupus; stomachs, bosoms, tongues and wombs eaten away by cancers; skin ravaged by ulcers; living flesh reduced to filthy pulp by gangrene; there were all the tears that physical misery extracts from eyes that no longer gaze and are no more than organs for weeping; there were the lamentations and the cries, the groans and the whimpers, of all suffering, sharp or chronic; and there was the bleak bestiality of beings in whom the soul is overwhelmed by the torments of the body.

Michel felt pity for all of that, but fearfully, and that unhealthy horde excited a religious horror in him. He lived increasingly reclusively; he felt more abandoned, by virtue of the fact that Geneviève's parallel existence was marvelously organized without him. When she had been bewildered in the midst of quotidian hazards, he had caught scraps of her; now, the zeal of active charity had taken complete possession of her, and she left nothing behind that he could plunder.

Then he retreated further into himself, but he could not succeed in confining himself within his studies, because the thought of Pierre and Geneviève, brought together by the same fervor, summoned him out of himself.

He tried to join them. He took that resolution one morning, and went into the hospital, with the determined desire not to be a vain spectator. It was to the chapel that he went first. Six women were lying there in parallel beds—six poor women. Two were asleep, very calm, under the supervision of a nurse. They were breathing easily, with broad regularity, but their bodies were ridiculously twisted, as if the old habit of being badly accommodated was preventing them from taking advantage of a good bed. The others, awake, opened wide eyes in which no race of sentiment was perceptible: vague and silent eyes. Michel approached one of them and said to her: "Are you feeling better, Madame?"

Her only reply was an unintelligible moue. Michel would have liked to say something else. It is said that there are words that do invalids good, which encourage them, give them patience, distract their unhappy minds, dispense them from gripping their distress again. Michel thought about that; then, as he found absolutely nothing, he was already drawing away when the nurse came. She did not have to speak; she only had to be there, smiling somehow; the poor woman smiled too, in a knowing fashion. In a matter of seconds, there was a mute dialogue, an exchange of numerous ideas, confident and sympathetic, to which Michel was not invited.

He stayed in the chapel a little longer, and he remembered that chapel in the cathedral where, with his mother, his sister and the devotees of the little Breton town, he had once prayed to the Virgin of the Seven Dolors, immobile in the demonstrative glory conferred upon her by the crutches, the soldiers' epaulettes, the ribbons taken from children's dresses and ex-votos of every sort. He remembered the chapel, and he remembered having felt there, once, the desire for a more human, curative and miraculous science.

*Now,* he said to himself, *here is that science. It has lost the pride of its haughty indifference. It is dressed as a sister of charity; it is leaning over manifest and hidden wounds, laying its hands thereon and healing; it is bringing tisanes and warming poultices; it is hand in glove with the poor and with destiny; it pities destiny, and, in favor of the poor, incites it to commit injustices. It is playing the moving and beautiful role of the Virgin in the legends that Christian hearts have adopted, because the number seven is here a symbol of infinity: with the seven dolors, the Virgin is moved to universal sympathy. But it is the dolors of the soul that she assumed, and for the dolor of the body, here is the new Notre-Dame.*

In the chapel where the six women lay there was still a blue and white Virgin with extended hands, whose feet were placed on a crescent moon. Michel saw that, and named her mentally the Virgin of the Eighth Dolor.

Then he felt the inclinations of old reawakening in him, pious and ardent. He was no longer in a state of desiccation and incredulity when he went up the staircase that led to the cancer ward. He saw Pierre, Geneviève and two interns standing next to a man's bed. Pierre was making an application of sirium over the stomach. He was speaking, indicating his intentions, giving instructions—and Geneviève was listening, as obedient as a servant. She was holding a large white bowl into which Pierre was throwing soiled cloths, and did not turn away; neither the odor nor the ugliness made her recoil. She was like those young Flemish women that old painters put into depictions of the Works of Mercy.

When Michel arrived, she did not look at him. An intern had to leave; Pierre wanted water, and quickly. Awkwardly, Michel was in his way.

"Sorry," he said.

Pierre had an impatient expression.

A little later, Michel asked: "Can I help?"

And Pierre, with brutal cordiality, replied: "No, old chap—you only have genius." And he laughed.

Geneviève looked at Michel with a kindly smile; there was admiration in it, for Michel, but he was insensitive to it. What he understood was that Pierre and Geneviève were perfectly in accord in getting rid of him; they had no need of him, and he was in the way. He did not reply to Geneviève's smile. He shrank; he only stayed there long enough not to seem too docile or vexed. Then he went away, without anyone even noticing. He went downstairs. When he went past the chapel, the door was open. He dared not look at the Virgin of the Eighth Dolor; she too, like the other, the Virgin with the heart transpierced by seven blades in the cathedral of his childhood, had driven him away.

* * * * * * *

On the afternoon of that day, autumn passed like a beautiful golden cavalier through the gardens already marked by its colors. It arrived borne by a warm wind, and the leaves, falling, clicked like small, exceedingly thin, pieces of delicately-carved metal. A red sun multiplied its phantasmagorias in the treetops, painting the branches one after another; then they gradually faded, becoming violet, brown, gray and then entering into the shadows that slowly sent the sun away.

Finally, dusk set in; twilight reigned, awaiting the imperious arrival of night.

On a bench surrounded by a grove of old linden-trees and willows, Michel abandoned himself to the melancholy of the moment and the season. He watched the alternating play of light and shade; the double decline of the year and the day coincided with his sadness. He savored that sympathy of nature and liked its ingenious participation in his ennui. A kind of vague well-being appeased him; a kind of soft bounty took possession of him and cradled him. He started thinking, without bitterness, about the invalids he did not know and who would owe their cures, unknowingly, to him. He was conscious of being their hidden benefactor. For the first time, he felt a link connecting them to him. But between then and him that link was Geneviève and Pierre, the two of them—always the two of them—united by common determination, the effort emerging therefrom, and similar success.

Suddenly, dead leaves stirred and were crushed. The two of them, Geneviève and Pierre, emerged from the hospital and went into the garden. At first, Michel had a desire to go toward them, but he could not move; a strange torpor immobilized his body, while his mind was on tenterhooks, extending toward them like insectile antennae.

They were gazing at the garden, whose half-light pleased them. They were not saying anything, but they were experiencing a delightful joy in being alone in the tranquility of the evening, after having worked side by side and becoming weary. They followed the path that led toward the door of the house but they did not go in. Without anything being said, they both stopped at the same time, their strides being regulated by the same sentiment, their gestures coordinated, their dream identical. Both dressed in unbleached linen, Geneviève in a long apron, Pierre in a long smock, they seemed, in the darkness two phantoms of love. They lingered in the delight that was their common solitude. They did not move; they looked at one another; in the sky, the first stars were coming out. And their happiness was more radiant than the stars.

Michel was tempted to tell them that he was there, that he had seen them, but the words failed him. He wanted at least to reveal his presence in some way, by making a small sound; it would have been sufficient for him to shift his position, to cough, but he could not. He reproached himself for acting badly; he was embarrassed by his hypocrisy, by his espionage; but most of all, he was afraid of what he might hear and see if he persisted in his imprudent perfidy. He was afraid, and he wanted it to end soon; he blamed the slowness of the amorous couple, who had no pity for him and were prolonging his torture with an apparent malevolence. Only a few minutes went by, but so full and abundant, for Michel as for them, that their duration seemed excessive. Then Pierre Dauzanne's hand, which was very close to Geneviève's, took it, held it and retained it. Geneviève did not shiver, so naturally did the movement continue the mutual caress of their souls.

Michel shivered for them; and that hand of Geneviève's, which Pierre did not release, made him feel ill. He thought of shouting; he thought of launching himself forward and shaking that chain of amorous hands until it broke—but Geneviève and Pierre, mutely holding hands, turned away and went into the house.

Michel had no desire to follow them. An idea, sudden and conclusive, had overwhelmed him; destiny had become manifest, inevitably destiny, its determination brutally indicated. He thought that destiny had brought Geneviève and Pierre before him in order that he could be informed in a clear fashion and cease vain inhibition. It was destiny that had obliged them not to go in straight away, when they were about to do so. They did not know why they had lingered; destiny knew full well. And destiny had not been overly cynical; it had spared Michel by only presenting him with a decent image of the truth of which it was informing him: a decent but evident image; they had not had to say a word in taking one another by the hand, in order to savor a marvelous felicity together, so much in love were they.

Dusk was complete, and night now took possession of the garden. Michel abandoned himself to the bleak quietude of despair. He felt some relief in feeling that he had arrived at the worst of his distress. He no longer protested; he accepted the misfortune wholly; he refused none of it.

He said to himself: *I shall go away. I have to go. And it won't be very difficult, because I've already gone, I'm already far away. I don't know exactly where I am, but far away, in a plain of silence that is like the vestibule of death. I have to go, because life here is perfect in its complete activity; it has the space it requires and fills that space; it moves there easily; it has no other imperfection but my presence, like a dead leaf that had fallen into a pool of water and spoiled its limpid mirror. Oh, take away that dead leaf! I shall go away.*

He was docile and found, in being so, his peace.

Suddenly, a voice emerged from the door of the house—the

clear voice of Geneviève. "Michel!" she called.

And Michel shivered. She was calling very loudly, as if her voice had to carry to the interior of the laboratory in order to reach Michel. He received it at close range and was bowled over by it. Then he was ashamed to admit that he was here, hidden, as he had been a little while ago. He waited.

"Michel!"

"What is it?" He came closer.

Geneviève did not notice that he was only coming from the cradle of lindens and willows.

"A visitor...a visitor that will give you pleasure...."

Soon, in the lighted corridor, whose glare was dazzling, he recognized the Alchemist. That was, for him, a terrible blow, because of the conversations he anticipated.

"How nice, Master!"

"Yes...the old fellow has come to Paris, for you. Oh, it had to be for you! For twenty-five years...."

"Come."

"You're taking me away? Excuse me, Madame."

In order to come to Paris, the Alchemist had put on his ceremonial costume, all black, with a frock-coat, a little white cravat and a top hat whose nap was capricious and its style outdated.

"Let's go to the laboratory," Michel said.

"Bravo! And we'll talk."

"Will you stay for dinner?"

"Gladly."

Michel guided the Alchemist; and they advanced, feeling their way. They went into the dark laboratory. Michel flicked the electric switches and the large room was revealed in such a way that he scarcely recognized it. The Alchemist scanned it with a circular gaze; he seemed to hesitated., and then said: "That's odd; it doesn't give the impression that anyone's been working here today.

Michel made no reply. He offered his armchair to the Alchemist.

"Sit down."

The Alchemist sank into it, putting his hat on a table and taking off his gloves. "Well," he said, without further ado, "where are you up to?"

That question set Michel aback, as the crux of an interrogation disconcerts a guilty party. He wondered where he was up to, precisely. Then he said: "I'll show you the hospital."

"There's plenty of time for that."

"No, because the patients will be asleep...."

"All right."

Michel took his master from ward to ward. The asylum of malady was already getting ready for sleep. The light had no glare. It seemed drowsy, like the people. In a soft voice, Michel added dribs and drabs of commentary here and there, and then further details in the corridors.

"It's curious," said the Alchemist "it's curious." He obtained information about the treatment, about the results, and he approved of it all calmly. Then, when he knew how the sirium was working in the flesh of the cancerous, he was content, and asked no more.

There were still two wards to see. "It's all much the same," he said. "Let's go talk."

They returned to the laboratory. Then, imperious and suspicious, the Alchemist repeated his question. "Come on, where are you up to?"

"Well," Michel replied, "you've just seen."

"Yes, yes, I've seen. But I want to know where you're up to in terms of chemistry, in terms of science, damn it. All that's very nice, but it's only medicine, at the end of the day, and no more. I know that there's been a devil of a noise about all those machinations—but, between us, seriously...?"

Michel was nonplussed. The old man went on: "Come on, you're not going to tell me that you've set up as a physician too, Michel?"

"No."

"Not even a physician—a pharmacist. No? You've found a drug. That's good. It might be useful, like jujube and licorice.

But let's talk about something else, between ourselves."

Michel stammered, confusedly, and the Alchemist exclaimed: "Ah! You're not up to anything, are you, wretch! I suspected as much." He groaned, and then said: "I suspected as much. Really, that's why I've come. Tell me—what's wrong?"

He was so pressing, that Michel wanted to tell him—but Geneviève came in, simple and cheerful. " Dinner's ready," she said.

That was salvation for Michel. As he stood up, the Alchemist said: "We'll resume this conversation later."

It was necessary to go up to the second floor of the house, to which Geneviève had relegated the dining-room. Pierre was waiting. Michel introduced him to the old man, and Pierre said a few words, to which the old man paid little heed.

At table, Geneviève tried to chat, but the Alchemist did not say very much. He was grim; he uttered a few words ill-humoredly, and then obstinately shut up. Besides which, he was watching; he was studying Geneviève, Michel and Pierre. He was not loath to examine them with curious and severe eyes. He ate, but he renounced eating at times, as if he were reflecting privately, and harshly. Geneviève made fun of him timidly. In order to break a silence that went on too long she hazarded: "Are you proud of your pupil, Master?"

"No!" said Michel, annoyed.

The Alchemist grunted. "No. Not for the moment."

"You don't admire the amplitude that his discovery has acquired?" Geneviève persisted.

"The cures?"

"Yes."

"No, Madame, no. The cures aren't my concern, or Michel's. That's medicine. We don't concern ourselves with medicine, Michel and I. We're scientists, men of science."

"But when science results in cures...."

"No, Madame, science doesn't cure."

"If it diminishes human suffering...."

"No, Madame. That's not the business of science.[5] If it were only a matter of ending suffering, it would merely be necessary to pierce the planet deeply enough, plant a strong dose of dynamite and blow it all up in the blink of an eye. That would put an end to suffering."

Geneviève laughed. She riposted: "But one can try to cure without killing!"

"To what end?"

"To multiply life."

"That, Madame, is the business of love—but science, beautiful science, is not that at all."

"What is it, then?"

Geneviève put her elbow on the table, her chin on her palm, and listened to the Alchemist. As he preferred to remain silent, he assumed a knowing expression and rapidly swallowed grapes, nervously—but when Geneviève interrogated him, he replied.

"Science has only one goal: the truth, whether it cures or kills. That doesn't prevent physicians and pharmacists from going about their business. In any case, I approve of liberating people from their suffering, because pain preoccupies us and turns us away from the truth. But first of all, it's necessary to seek that truth, in order to have it to offer to people who are cured. Otherwise...."

Pierre made the observation that one could not, however, wait for the completion of science in order to fight against disease, or humankind would be at risk of dying before the supreme discovery.

---

5. Author's Note: "If anyone is astonished by the bluntness with which my Alchemist refuses to take much interest in the practical applications of science, it is only necessary to read the introduction to *La Valeur de science* by Henri Poincaré: 'The search for the truth must be the sole objective of our activity; it is the sole objective that is worthy of it. Undoubtedly we ought first to strive to relieve human suffering, but why? Not to suffer is a negative ideal, which would be more surely obtained by the annihilation of the world. If we wish to liberate human beings increasingly from material concerns, it is in order that they can employ the liberty thus gained in the study and contemplation of the truth.'"

"That's all the same to me," said the Alchemist. "I don't mind if humankind dies while seeking the truth, provides that it seeks it. All its dignity is there."

There was a silence. The Alchemist hesitated a few seconds over saying everything. The he burst out: "Anyway, if one wants science to progress, it's first necessary to let scientists work...."

That fell into the general silence—but he went on: "So, Michel.... He was a great scientist, Michel: the greatest scientist of the age...."

"No, Master!" said Michel, imploringly.

"Shut up. We were counting on him; we were waiting for him. He was leading us to a new idea of matter. He was at the threshold of the truth, I swear it, and he was about to open the door—and look at what you've made of him, of Michel, the two of you: a nurse!"

He got up from the table. He was quivering. He added: "I beg your pardon...but it's just too abominable, you see! I can't bear it, as a man who knows what's at stake. Michel, possessed by you, is science held back, perhaps by a century, or ten centuries.... I tell you that he was on the point of finding something that might never be found without him!"

The Alchemist was shouting.

Geneviève was no longer laughing. "But I'm not stopping him from working, you know!"

"Yes, Madame. Let's not argue about that: it's a fact. So I beg you, I implore you, give him back to me. I'll take him away. We need him. You, on the contrary, have no need of him. With Monsieur, you'll be occupied with your hospital—that's quite sufficient. I'll take Michel away."

"Excuse me," said Pierre Dauzanne. "I have to visit two patients before I leave...."

"I'll go with you," said Geneviève. To the Alchemist, she added: "Michel is perfectly free, and you're wrong to believe that we're keeping him prisoner. There he is: he's all yours."

\* \* \* \* \* \* \*

When the Alchemist and Michel were alone, the Alchemist stood directly in front of Michel, and with the brutality of a resolute man determined to go all the way, he said:

"Oh, my poor boy, so you're not seeing clearly?"

"What?"

"You can't see that your wife and that handsome doctor...."

Michel was appalled. "Master!"

"Oh, I'm not making any accusations—but they're in love; that, you know, is as clear as daylight."

"No!"

"Yes. Yes, I tell you. And you know it full well. And it isn't worthy of a man of science to hide the truth, even from himself. No, no—shut up! And if you want, we won't say any more about it—but don't tell me that I'm mistaken; you'd be lying. Let's not talk about it any more. Except, Michel, you can't stay here. It's disgusting, I assure you. You have to get away—I don't know where—to work. Oh, it's essential, damn it!"

"Perhaps I shall go away," said Michel.

"Yes! Because it's still necessary for us to know whether a body is able to produce any energy whatsoever without losing its substance; and then, it's necessary to know what matter is, whether it's only a molecule, and what everything is. Isn't it? Go work, my boy. Where will you go?"

"I don't know. I'll think about it."

"No, no—right away. You need to go right away!"

"Not this evening, though!"

"Not this evening, no—but something like tomorrow evening, for example. Is that agreed?"

"Perhaps."

"No, not perhaps! It's essential, Michel."

And the Alchemist protested against Michel's final hesitation. He was glad, however, to have persuaded him so easily. He understood that the service of science was not the only efficacious argument, in the event, and that, if he had convinced Michael to leave, he had found him already on his way out. *One only commands nature by being obedient to it*, he thought, in the terms of Bacon.

He continued: "You can't stay here. You're degrading your-self by staying here. There's still time—save yourself! You aren't even happy. If you were, I'd command you to go all the same, because it's not important to be happy, but look at you!—you're downcast, you're jealous, you're humiliated, you're debased. Save yourself, my boy, with science in your hands, as one carries away a treasure in saving oneself from a burning house."

"Where shall I go?" Michel asked.

"Oh, I'd like take you with me. I'd like to install you in my house, in my laboratory. What joy! And I'd be your assistant. But no—impossible! It's too close you your mother's house, too close to your childhood. You'd escape me. I know you, my poor boy! You have to go to a place where you have no amusement, no memories, nothing that can remind you of anything. Like Spinoza, when he left Amsterdam one day, where he'd been so much in love and so disappointed—he took refuge, all alone, in Rijnsburg, in a region of peasants and cabbages, and then he occupied himself solely with arranging his ideas in geometric form. That's the example."

Michel said nothing. He was thinking about Spinoza. He had no need to say anything, for the Alchemist was satisfied.

The Alchemist continued: "*Au revoir!* Until tomorrow. I'll come back tomorrow to fetch you, in the evening. I'll take you away. I'll take you to the station, like the other time, when Maman nearly got you back, and I'll say goodbye, so that you can be alone and free."

Michel thought about the words of the gospel in which Jesus says that he will separate the father and the son, the daughter and the mother. Thus science was separating him; it was sepa-rating him from everything he had loved. Aloud, continuing his train of thought, he said: "The doctrines are hard!"

"What?"

"Until tomorrow. I'm going away."

"Yes. I'll give you until tomorrow evening to put your affairs in order, to make your preparations. I'll come in the evening. If there's no train—that will depend on the place we choose—well, we'll spend the night in a hotel and you'll leave tomorrow morning. But tomorrow evening, you're leaving this house, eh?"

Michel acquiesced.

As he withdrew, the old man added: "Inform your wife—and don't be afraid of causing her chagrin. Tell me, do you both sleep in the same room?"

"Yes."

The old man looked Michel in the eyes and, while shaking his hand, said to him: "I'm counting on you, Michel. Don't be a coward, or a...."

He opened the door. Geneviève came in.

"Adieu, Madame. I'm taking my leave!"

Immediately afterwards, Geneviève said to Michel: "Is he a lunatic?"

"No, no; he's not a lunatic, he's a sage."

He waited for Geneviève to question him. She did not. He waited for her to ask him whether he was leaving; he divined that she was not thinking about anything else, and that the question was on her lips, but that she did not want to formulate it. He was ready to say, spontaneously: "Yes, yes, I'm leaving, tomorrow, forever"—but he kept quiet, because he could not admit that Geneviève had nothing to say.

Soon, he thought he divined that Pierre had begged Geneviève not to say anything, not to oppose, even with an imprudent politeness, a departure that would liberate her, would give her to him and organize their splendid happiness. The attitude that she was adopting was not natural to her, and Michel detested sensing that she was doing someone else's bidding, experiencing hated and disgust. *How he holds her!* he thought. *How he possesses her!*

An hour went by. It was a strange, funereal death-watch, over the corpse of their love. They were there, facing one another in two similar armchairs by the fireside, not saying anything or doing anything. A maidservant came in to clear the table. That took five minutes, and they were less unhappy during those minutes than they would have been alone with the corpse. Then the maidservant withdrew, closing the door, and in the mortuary chamber, the silence was enclosed with them.

Michel was tempted to pronounce the decisive words: "I'm leaving tomorrow," but he feared false protestations, and remained silent. Geneviève waited, and her mute silence did not conceal the fact that she was waiting. Then, after an hour, she got up, came to Michel, put her hand on his shoulder, kissed his head and said: "Goodnight."

"Goodnight," he replied.

* * * * * * *

Until the following day he lived in a dream, submissive to fatalities that he sensed were in great haste to take him away. He imagined them analogous to the divinities of fable, forming a group of diligent spinners midway between him and Heaven. It was easy for him to obey them.

That idea haunted him. Meanwhile, he continued coming and going. He ate lunch with Geneviève and Pierre. He did not talk; he could not talk; but he was thinking very clearly. He carefully avoided opportunities to be moved or irritated. As he began, at the commencement of lunch, to observe Pierre, to deduce his thoughts from his mannerisms, to hate him, he succeeded in diverting himself from that cruel discipline. In the afternoon, when Geneviève and Pierre were both in the hospital, he made the preparations for his departure, gave instructions, wrote the list of what he would take with him. A trunk and a valise, with underwear, clothes, books, a few implements of chemistry, small in number. He did his accounts and quickly resolved questions of money.

At six o'clock, which was the time Geneviève habitually left the hospital, he waited for her, and hoped that she would come; he had to talk to her. Pierre was with her, but he made his excuses to him.

"Five minutes," he said. "I need to talk to Geneviève for five minutes. After that...."

He was so awkward that all three of them were disagreeably embarrassed. Michel took Geneviève to the laboratory.

"What is it?" she asked. And she looked at him with anguish, and also with pride, with an offended expression, of not deserving it. She was pale and stood up straight, rigidly.

"I wanted to tell you, Geneviève," Michel replied, "that I'm leaving."

"Oh!" she said. "Where are you going?"

"I don't know," he replied, "but what does it matter where I go? What's important, and what you need to understand and admit, is that I'm going."

"Yes, I understood that yesterday evening. And I admit it, because, in sum, I've never stood in the way of any of your plans—not one."

And she stopped, as if she expected a reply. She was provocative, reflective, determined. She added: "Have I?"

"Not one," Michel admitted.

"Will you be gone long?"

Michel had to assemble all that he had of scattered energy and bewildered strength to reply: "Forever."

"Good!" she said. "Good!"

Seconds passed, during which a crazed vertigo spun them in its turbulence. Their surroundings danced, whirled and crumbled.

Geneviève recovered first. "Before you go, Michel, tell me—I need to know whether you have any reproach to address to me."

"No."

"All the same, one doesn't leave one's wife and one's home like this, for the sole reason that an old man, a lunatic, has come to say...."

"I'd decided to go before he came."

"When?"

"Well, as it happens, yesterday...."

"Yesterday?"

It was necessary to finish. And Michel, with his courage failing, declared: "Yesterday, yes. At a similar time, when dusk was falling, as it is now, I was there, not deliberately—there, on the bench in the lindens and the willows. You and Pierre came out of the hospital...oh, I didn't want to tell you, but you're demanding that I speak. Too bad! I saw you...."

His voice caught in his throat.

"Well?"

"Well, I saw you. And I understood...never has anyone understood anything so clearly...I understood, in such a way as no longer to be able to set the idea aside, that there was one man too many here, and that that man was me. Oh, don't take the trouble to console me or tell me that I'm mistaken. I saw you, like fiancés that nothing in the world could separate. He took your hand...."

"No!"

"Not so? You didn't notice it....I was sure that you didn't notice that, at that moment, he had to take your hand. He had to. It isn't your fault, and perhaps it isn't his. Your hands, your little hand and his, came together, like this, very gently, just as your souls have come together; and your hands did, unknown to you, what your souls were doing."

There was a more profound truth in that than Geneviève had yet discerned in her adventure—so much truth that she was frightened to see it all of a sudden. She began trembling; and she was not only surprised to have been caught, but she was afraid, for herself and, independently, for Michel. She was no longer haughty now, and Michel's ardent jealousy was softened by compassion.

He added: "So, adieu, Geneviève."

She shivered. She sensed the irreparable happening, and stammered: "You're pitiless."

"No, no," he said. "It's not me who is pitiless. If it were only a matter of forgiveness...but I have nothing for which to forgive you; it's not your fault. Nor am I punishing you—I'm simply leaving. And I'm saying goodbye. I offered to go once before.

You refused. You shouldn't have refused. This time, I'm going."

"Adieu," she said.

They went at the point of breaking into sobs when someone knocked forcefully on the laboratory door with the head of a cane.

"Come in!" shouted Michel.

The Alchemist came in. He did not seem to be comfortable. Geneviève looked at him fearfully.

"Madame...."

Geneviève turned away from him.

"Well, Michel, are you ready? Your bags are packed, I see. That's good. So...."

"So," Michel said, "we're going."

"Do you have everything you need to work?—your observations, your notes, your equipment? Where have you put your sirium? That stuff can't be easy to lug around."

Suddenly, Geneviève became wary. She made an abrupt movement when she saw that Michel was hesitating.

The Alchemist noticed it and added: "Where have you put it?"

Geneviève did not wait for Michel's reply, and shouted: "You're not taking it!"

"No, no, I'm not taking it."

The Alchemist was annoyed. "You're not taking your sirium? Come on—that's crazy!"

Michel tried to calm things down. "No," he said, "I can easily do without it. I've done a great many experiments now...."

"Don't tell me stories, my boy. I may be only an old imbecile, but I know what the work of a chemist involves. It's not a matter of metaphysics, damn it! Where is it, your sirium?"

"I beg you...."

"Where is it? I asked you where it is."

Geneviève intervened. "But the sirium's in the hospital, where it serves to cure the diseases of poor folk who would otherwise die in abominable suffering."

"Aha! Tell me Michel—you don't have any more?"

"No. I had seven decigrams in all. I lent them to the hospital. I don't have any more."

"And how long has that been going on? Four months. It doesn't surprise me that you're not doing anything. Couldn't you get more of it?"

"It took me three years to obtain seven decigrams of sirium from four quintals of pitchblende. No, I can't start again, no."

"And even then, we'd have to wait three years." The Alchemist turned to Geneviève. "Madame, I ask you to be so kind as to return Michel's sirium. He needs it in order to work."

"Never!" cried Geneviève.

She was ready for battle. The Alchemist recoiled momentarily.

"Michel, will you please ask your wife to return your sirium?"

Michel said nothing, and the Alchemist resumed: "Look, Madame; I'll explain. Michel is going away to work. His work is important to the entire future of science. He was not in good conditions here to accomplish that great and august work. It demands tranquility and solitude, so he's going...."

"Yes, yes, I know. You've put ideas in his head that are making him leave. He's going, taken by you, as it were. That's not important. But...."

"But he needs his sirium, for the sake of science."

"We need it," Geneviève replied, "for our patients."

The Alchemist could not contain himself. He forgot all courtesy. "I don't give a damn about your patients!"

"I do!" Geneviève riposted.

"If these dozens of moribunds complete their dying, what difference, I ask you, will it make to the world? When a general leads his troops into battle, he sacrifices men: what are a few men? Well, science is more than a war; it's more important; it's everything. So, if science sacrifices people, too bad: I don't hesitate."

Geneviève was gripped by the same fury of ideas. "But I tell you that, if Michel's discovery can diminish the suffering that there is on earth, that's beautiful, and splendid—and that if Michel took it away from the poor folk that it might heal at close range, he would be a criminal...the worst and most savage of criminals."

The Alchemist, having run out of arguments, said: "At any rate, the sirium is Michel's; are you going to steal it from him."

"I have stolen it from him!"

"No—give it back!"

"Never!"

"You must."

"Never, never, never!"

She went out. And Michel could not help thinking that Geneviève had not fought like that, like a furious lioness, to keep him, Michel. He was not uplifted by the scientific fanaticism of his old master, nor persuaded by Geneviève's warrior fanaticism; he was simply thinking about people, who are not ideas, nor are they humankind.

The Alchemist was silent for a time. He put a finger to his lips, meditatively. Suddenly, he said: "Stay here, my boy. I'll go see whether the carriage has arrived. I've ordered a motorized taxi. Wait for me."

Michel waited. He did not know what would come of this bizarre dispute; he no longer knew anything. He remembered having once seen a church clock that had broken down, the hands of which were spinning madly. The worst absurdity is when time goes mad. Michel remembered having gazed with amazement at the frenzy of delirious hours—and he experienced the same malaise now, feeling that a demented fatality was carrying him away. He wondered whether he would see Geneviève again, or whether he would leave abruptly, thrown out of his home by the prodigious velocity of events. If a leaf blown by a tempest were able to think, or to feel, it would have experienced the same abandoned panic to which Michel was yielding.

The Alchemist returned. He was hiding something inside his frock-coat, and he was laughing. He was laughing wholeheartedly. And he said to Michel: "I have it! Here it is!" He displayed the little iron box that contained the sirium. "I've stolen it, or very nearly. I went to the hospital. I bluffed the old woman—you know, the old nurse you introduced me to, in the pharmacy, who looks like an owl. I told her a story—you needed your sirium right away, to do an experiment with me in your laboratory. You couldn't come yourself so you sent me. I spoke with authority; she believed me. She gave me the sirium—and here it is! Open your trunk, quickly—quickly. Hurry up, let's go! Now their patients can die—their filthy patients won't get in the way of science any more. Come on, open it!"

Michel opened the trunk. The old man put the little iron box inside, with religious precaution, and said: "It's sacred; it's science. If I hadn't lost the habit of kneeling, I'd say a little prayer in front of that little tabernacle of iron where god—the true, good god—is." He added: "Let's hurry. I'll go tell someone to fetch your bags. Where's your overcoat? I'll send it to you—and I'll wait for you in the car."

"Give me four minutes, Master?" Michel implored.

"Four minutes—not one more." He went out.

Michel, who was at the utmost limit of despair, found a sort of supreme calm there, and an astonishing facility of sacrifice. His thoughts were lucid, his determination clear. He opened the trunk again and took out the box of sirium. He put it to one side. When someone came to collect his bags, he handed them over. He had his overcoat, his hat and his cane—and the box, under his arm. He waited for the bags to be taken away. He looked at his laboratory, switched off the electric lights, and emerged.

His footsteps, in the garden, made a sound that displeased him. He looked at his house. The shutters were closed; light was passing through the interstices in the wooden slats, high up. Geneviève must he in her room—their room. He gazed at the thin rays the light that was illuminating Geneviève, and groaned, very softly: "Adieu, my darling Geneviève!"

He walked on tiptoe, but, instead of going straight ahead, as if to rejoin the Alchemist, he turned left, toward the hospital. He went up the stairs. He put the sirium back in its place, exactly.

He thought: *There—and no one will every know anything about it. Now, I have nothing more that I can renounce—absolutely nothing more.*

And he thought, in the form of a prayer, because at moments when the soul reaches the high points of its ups and downs, it recovers the language of childhood: "Lord, I have nothing more to return to you. I'm as naked as when you gave me birth. All that I had, all that I loved, Lord, I no longer have."

The old nurse with the face like an owl appeared, and he simply said to her: "Goodnight, Madame Rose."

He went downstairs. He went through a patch of darkness and took the path that Pierre and Geneviève had traveled amorously. He opened the door of the house and went into the corridor. When he reached the foot of the stairs he stopped; he thought that he could not, physically, continue on his way without having said another goodbye to Geneviève. As he hesitated, though, he door facing him opened, quietly, by a crack.

"Michel!"

The Alchemist's head, with its big nose, passed through the gap, harsh and impatient.

"Michel!"

And Michel left.

# CHAPTER THREE

Michel Bedée arrived in Holland at daybreak. The Alchemist was with him.

When the Alchemist had asked him, at the moment of departure, exactly where he was going, he had felt bewildered, as if he were at a crossroads where all the roads in the world intersected, and he had no preference for any of them. But the Alchemist had said to him: "What if you were to go to Spinoza's homeland? The man who was able to vanquish life and be alone could teach you about solitude."

So Michel had decided to go to Holland. He thought: *Why should I be in one place rather than another from now on? God, who renounced choice, is everywhere—and we, in uncertainty, ought to be nowhere. So, in the meantime, what does it matter?*

The name of Spinoza, which the Alchemist had dropped into his train of thought, caused a considerable stir of ideas there.

*In Rijnsburg, when he had been chased out of Amsterdam by the rancor of people and the deceptive love of a woman, in a bleak landscape, Spinoza was nowhere. And nowhere is where I'm going....*

Michel was in a sort of quietude, a condition of resistance against the sharp temptation of tears that were rising to his eyes; at the same time, his ears were buzzing, his head was filled with a bizarre seething—but he mastered it, and the attentive effort of his will kept him busy.

Facing him, lying on a banquette, the Alchemist was asleep—sleeping well, like an honest man whose hour has come.

Dawn came stealthily.

Through the windows of the carriage, Michel watched it. First there were a few tufts of cloud that became paler; then, in the intervals between them, silver light appeared. Then, there was a profound liberation of the heavens, which brightened; the clouds became darker. They passed a file of trees, still black. The light was freed when the meadows manifested their verdure, under the shadows and the mist, but it was sad and confused. There was no explosion, but a slow transformation, devoid of episodes. The progress was imperceptible. Michel's eyes grew tired trying to discern the nuances and their metamorphoses. Besides which, his back was so weary and his legs so heavy that he scarcely dared change position in order to get a better view.

In The Hague, they went to see Spinoza's tomb.

It is in the New Church, vast, square and ugly. They were guided by a good woman who only spoke Dutch. She said a great deal, but from all her chatter, Michel only retained the smiling familiarity with which the old woman supported the proximity of a poignant tomb. She led them between chairs and pews; she took them to the pulpit into which the pastor climbed, every Sunday, in order to affirm the superiority of Calvinism to his flock. Facing it, she pointed out a platform to which the young queen came, willingly, to learn more about Calvinism and its superiority.

When they asked for the tomb of Spinoza, the good woman cheerfully tapped her foot on a stone slab; her movement agitated the bunch of keys hanging from her belt and made them rattle. The Alchemist took her by the wrist and moved her aside.

There were two stones side by side, worn, with no inscription except for a number on one of them: 21. The good woman had enough sign language to inform them that the 21 covered Spinoza's body.

"No name," said the Alchemist to Michel. "That's good. The man merited having no name to dispense all his genius and reduce his individuality in order that ideas could be at home in his head. I believe that he achieved it, and he merited that tribute.

He was called Spinoza simply for the sake of convenience; no one knew him! In truth, ideas met up with one another there, that's all."

Under the next stone was one of the de Witt brothers—and on the two slabs stood the pillar supporting the pulpit.[6]

Michel gazed obstinately at the stone covering the body of Spinoza; he looked at the pillar, massive and charged with the entire weight of the pulpit. On examining that architecture, he had an almost suffocating sentiment of oppression. It also seemed to him that on Sunday, when the pastor was there, a bearer of abundant eloquence, that Calvinism must oppress the light body, which strove energetically and artfully to be free, even more heavily. The pillar seemed to him to be a powerful leg, whose heel was pinning a slain enemy to the ground.

"No matter!" said the Alchemist. "No matter! He was free in spirit—and given that, what the parish priest preaches can do nothing."

In spite of those arguments, however, Michel, whose flesh was more squeamish, shared in his imagination the perpetual choking of the cadaver.

The Alchemist went on: "Don't you think it's beautiful, that anonymous stone? It would be even more beautiful if one didn't even know that Spinoza is here, and if one no longer knew who he was, that he had existed. What was in him that was only him would have disappeared, and nothing would remain but the book, the encounter of ideas. Can you imagine that stone, if no one knew what was underneath it? You might say that then...but no; the things are sufficient, which are the truth."

Outside, he said: "He was a man of short stature. Since we know that, let's take advantage of it. He was a little man with pronounced features, a discolored complexion, a big nose, eyes

---

6. The tombstone in the grounds of the church nowadays identified as Spinoza's burial-place was not erected until 1956; his body presumably still lies where this account places it. Johan de Witt was a seventeenth-century statesman notoriously murdered on the orders of King William III after a military defeat by the French for which he was held responsible.

florid in his head, very dark eyes, as shiny as jet. He didn't dress flashily. In every aspect of his life, he sought decency, in order not to attract attention, so that he would be left tranquil."

Michel allowed himself to be guided from street to street, in the same way that, as a child, he had been guided by his father. He allowed himself to be guided by the old man's words, and whenever the thought of Geneviève came to alarm him, he chased it away, and he listened assiduously to the old man.

The latter said: "He died on the twenty-first of February 1677, the Saturday before the carnival. He was living close to here, in the house of the Van der Spycks. That day, he did not seem more ill than at any other, but his constitution was weak and he was on a strict diet. Van der Spyck and his wife went to church. A few minutes earlier they had been chatting to Spinoza, who urged them to follow their custom while he smoked a pipe at the table. When they returned to the house, Spinoza was dead in his little hard bed. He had received a visit from a physician; the fellow ran away on the night boat, having stolen some money and a knife with a silver handle—those people! Spinoza, when he died, left his clothes, a few books, prints, pieces of polished glass, instruments used in polishing glass. At auction, the lot fetched four hundred florins thirteen sous. That paid for the barber, the funeral prayer, the church, the artisans, the notary. All that was settled—and nothing remained of Benedict de Spinoza on earth. He had passed through delicately; after his death, all trace of him was effaced; he had done no harm to anyone and he had not been useful to anyone. He had simply lent his head to ideas; and he wrote those ideas down, so that after his death, his ideas would not be without shelter; they were in the book."

They arrived at the Hofvijver. The air was mild, the architecture and the water composed a pleasant study in gray. There was a fortunate harmony there, an exact equilibrium of objects, an agreement of hues, a neat amplitude of lines, which invited the soul to repose and leisure. The Alchemist and Michel sat down on a bench. Michel put up no resistance to the delicate charm of the place and the moment—but the Alchemist, obstinately, talked about Spinoza, citing dates, relating authentic facts in such a way that every one became an emblem and an example. He yielded to the evocative force of memories and preached to his uncomfortable disciple, organizing a religion for his solitude.

Michel thought: *They have their saints, like the others; they have their little chapels and their devotions; they have their legends, their lives of the saints, their gospels, their litanies....*

He observed that, but he did not refuse the piety that was being offered to him.

Suddenly, the Alchemist, concluding aloud thoughts that had only stirred him, said: "He had been thoroughly subdued! But, he was only a philosopher; we could do without him. But you, Michel, a scientist, will be sublime!"

Michel could not help smiling, as if, carried away by his zeal, the Alchemist were confessing his edifying intentions.

\* \* \* \* \* \* \*

They left for Amsterdam.

They arrived at dusk, when the city was red, black and gilded. They walked alongside canals in which the water was hardly flowing, devoid of reflections, color and clarity. Leaves were falling into them, which floated there, little squadrons of the dead with which the water nonchalantly played.

Early the next morning they went out. It was raining, or, rather drizzling, to begin with. The water of the canals rose up in a mist that mingled with the low sky. The great city was outlined like a Biblical phantom. There were big ships going like gliding shadow who knows where—perhaps to India and its sunny ports, splendid distances, over magnificent seas. In the harbor, there was a strange odor of spices, of shoddy Oriental goods.

The Alchemist took Michel through back streets and over hump-backed bridges to the Waterloo-Platz, which was once called the Burgwal, where Baruch Spinoza had been born, among Jews, contented businessmen.

"The house was here, my boy. It's no longer the same one; it's another, built in the same place. At any rate, little Baruch was born here, at this exact spot in the universe. That was a freak of chance, of course. His family came from the Orient; then they had prospered in Portugal; then they had ended up, after those peregrinations, here—so that he was not a man from here more than anywhere else. And he wrote in Latin—a dead and universalized language suited to a man with no homeland. All the same, he had to get out of the ghetto. He walked here, where we are, with his satchel and his Bible under his arm. He might have met a boy who lived not far from here, Rembrandt. Obviously, they did meet. I think they must have. They would have had so much to say to one another, those two! All the more so because Spinoza loved prints. They can't have known that they had met; destiny is a fool, which squanders everything."

They went to the Portuguese synagogue. A beadle they questioned appeared not to have heard of the Spinoza he was being asked about. From his sign-language and confused babbling, it was obvious that he only wanted to be officious, but this "Spinoza," whose name he pronounced with a strong accent, no, he had nothing to say about him, no, no....

He seemed sorry, but also sly, and the Alchemist insulted him in French, a language incomprehensible to him: "Dirty liar, you know very well who he is; you're denying him, and avenging your old rabbis...."

Michel thought that the quarrel between philosophy and the synagogue was beginning again.

In front of the synagogue there was a large courtyard framed by walls, like the parvis of a citadel. When the Alchemist and Michel came out, they were assailed by a horde of beggars, humble and insolent, chattering, sniggering and grumbling. Where had the band come from? It had not been there a little while before, but now it came out of the corners of the courtyard, like a swarm of woodlice, hurrying, limping and hopping;

it displayed wretched miseries, stumps, wounds, withered arms thinner than twigs of dead wood, at the ends of which hung swollen hands; it undulated, living putrefaction beneath sordid rags; it bowed and saluted; hideous mouths approached, trying to kiss the fabric of sleeves, touch the hands of benefactors.

Michel was afraid of that contact; he threw a few small coins, and the vile, battling horde fell upon the windfall. The Alchemist, for his part, threatened them with his cane and growled. He cursed the filthy brats that had picked him out and were tugging at his frock-coat with a piteous manner. To rid himself of those horrible beasts it was necessary to plunge forward, shoving the boldest aside, tearing away the grasping fingers and shoving back the compact pressure. At the entrance to the courtyard, however, the horde stopped, continuing its active indigent prattle, but staying where it was, hereditarily docile to the habit of the ghetto.

While the Alchemist snorted and made sure that no one had stolen his purse or his watch, an adolescent from a good Jewish family went by. He was dressed in black, carrying books under his arm, and holding a little cane awkwardly in his right hand. He was taking long strides. He had the face of his race, thin with a long nose and pronounced lips, the lower lip overlapping the other. From his hat, pulled down too low, long wisps of black hair emerged. He resembled an young man and an old rabbi. When he saw the Christians having difficulty disengaging themselves from the horde he was ashamed, lowered his eyes and increased his pace.

"Look at him," said the Alchemist. "Poor boy, perhaps proud! I can imagine our Baruch walking like that, at eighteen, vey wise, disgusted with the synagogue, tormented by feeling something fraternal within him that he scorned. He had not yet launched himself beyond the Scriptures then. He was arguing with the Bible, colliding with verses and sometimes emitting long commentaries. Poor boy! Do you think he should have used his elbows and been quick, clever and determined, to escape from all that, as we escaped that ill-clad and loquacious horde.

Anyway, he got himself out of it. And it was here, or hereabouts, that a Jew accosted him one day, a fanatic, and struck him with a dagger. His clothes were ripped, but not the flesh—but Baruch sensed then that his race hated him and that he was being cast out of the old Jewish communion. He had been saved, but at first, he only felt that he had been cast out. Others wouldn't welcome him. I think he suffered, bitterly. Solitude, which is a great marvel, didn't please him in principle, and I think that he had no idea what to do, expelled by the centuries of his race, already all alone, all alone!"

"I feel sorry for him," Michel replied.

The melancholy tone of these words and the distress they signaled moved the Alchemist. Besides which, he was watching Michel, and if he had led him to that allusion by means of his words, it was not unintentional. He wanted Michel to be conscious of the lesson, to take it to heart—and he also wanted to know what Michel, who was not saying much, was thinking.

Rudely, he replied: "You'll see. It's only a matter of time. You'll see."

"All of life is only a matter of time, to wear away," Michel replied. And he thought about the stone covering the dusty bones of Spinoza in the Calvinist church.

"To wear away nobly!" riposted the old man. "To wear away for the sake of science, day after day, relentlessly.

As the afternoon came to an end the Alchemist and Michel were still strolling through the streets of Amsterdam, on the banks of the canals. Michel gazed at the reflections in the dismal water, and the houses and ships composing inverted and immobile landscapes in which, for a while, sedentary life and errant life, patience and folly, came together: pretty landscapes, scarcely animated by the slow rippling of the water. As he saw the clear image of objects on the surface of the canals, he told himself that the world in the mirror of thought is as authentic as in reality; on that, he built an idealism that soon enabled him to renounce any fortuitous encounter with another symbolism, for he was not directing his reverie but wearily submitting to it.

It seemed to him that the ships were tugging hard on their moorings. The rings on the quays were grating. The masts, the pulleys and the rigging sometimes seemed to be moaning; little cries could be heard, similar to those of birds that want to fly away, but are held back by hands, Michel sensed the captivity of the ships, their exaggerated desire to travel, the tormenting madness that prevented them from ever savoring repose—and he told himself that the ships, old vagabonds, had succeeded in being nowhere; they had found that remedy for their infinite nostalgia.

As night fell, the water in the canals sickened. There were glimmers in the windows reflected in the black water, the heavy and oily water, the water whose ripples had the color of lead, then tin, then silver, and into which fell treasures of magnificent pearls and multicolored wisps of straw.

Afterwards, silence passed over the dormant waters of the canals like a night-bird beating short wings precipitately. Then the silence was there, on the canals, like a perfume in the vicinity of a flower.

In the vicinity of the phenomena of light and shadow, Michel was subject to an unfortunate susceptibility. The Alchemist allowed him to tint the landscape—which, in any case, lent itself to it, complacently—with his melancholy. He had resolved not to cure him immediately, and thus respected an emotion that was not intelligible to him in all its detail.

In the Jewish quarter, to which they returned, there was a vibrant animation. It was market day on the Burgwal: an astonishing market of old iron, old clothes and old things of every sort, broken and damaged chairs, tarnished lampshades, battered hats, artificial flowers, pegs, staved-in stoves, deformed roasting-spits corroded by rust, theatrical helmets, dented armor, all heaped up pell-mell, rags, pieces of velvet and satin, faded curtains, a collection of discarded gods, a bric-à-brac of the wreckage of life, a great cemetery of everything abandoned by elegance, poverty and quotidian vulgarity. All those debased things, from which attentive or idle souls had been withdrawn, were lying in

injurious disorder. They composed, with their sordid variega-
tion, a rich bronze color, with heightened outbursts of red and
gold.

In the midst of all that, a rapid, brisk and loquacious popu-
lation was wandering. There was haggling over rags picked
up, negotiated, released with reluctance, taken back, disputed.
There were cunning ploys, feints, victories. And what agitation!
The movements of stiff marionettes, which, forced to hurry,
were making all their movements out of step. And what persistent urgency, to dispute such derisory interests!

The Jews were of various provenance. From ancient Judea
their families had emigrated anywhere, subject to the tribulations of peoples that accommodated them as best they would,
enriching themselves at the hazards of love or climate, taking on
unforeseen characteristics, beauties or blemishes, singularities
of every sort, but retaining, in site of hybridizations, the perma-
nent signs of their race, and then, ultimately, launching those
specimens summarizing a multiple and centuries-old adventure
into a square in old Amsterdam. Pale, suntanned or olive-tinted
complexions; hair plastered to heads as if stuck there by an
ointment, or which hung down in supple spirals, or flowed in
pale cream-blond curls over narrow foreheads, old patriarchal
beards, glabrous chins; intensely dark eyes, others that seemed
colorless and others that were almost violet, between curt red
eyelids; men who made Biblical robes out of large overcoats;
others wearing tight-fitting jackets like disguises; fat, heavy
women, often beautiful among the thin, emaciated men: that
assembled humankind had various analogies to the stock of the
market of everything disused; it was no less scattered, numerous,
absurd; it was no less united in an ardent and complex tonality.

And the prattle of the Tower of Babel was resolved into a
mocking, quarrelsome, violent shrieking, which had its highs
and lows, its ebbs and flows, its surges and exhaustions.

Suddenly, there were singular movements in the businesslike
crowd. People were running back and forth, passing news from
group to group. Transactions stopped dead. There was a gallop

toward the quay; then, the laggards having caught up with those quicker off the mark, the square was empty.

The Alchemist and Michel did not understand that sudden exodus. They saw the buyers and the sellers rushing to the parapet of the canal; some climbed on to it; others, in the crenellations thus formed, leaned forward as best they could, trying to see, jostling elbows and stretching out curious heads.

The Alchemist and Michel came closer, and realized that a Jew had fallen into the canal—a Jew that the crowd knew, and whose name was passing from mouth to mouth. Everyone was gazing, keeping watch on the gray water, the perfidious water over terrible depths of mud, the water on which illuminating gas-lamps traced long yellow streaks, the water of the evening, bleak and opaque.

Boats arrived; they moved over the water, with their oars like legs, reminiscent of scurrying spiders. The rescuers reached into the body of the water with long poles; they threw harpoons in here and there, dropped ropes at the end of which stones were suspended, which splashed when they hit the water and then disappeared. The water, scratched, clawed, and rent, scarred over rapidly; the shroud of the water, which they were trying to part, closed again obstinately over the dead man.

That sinister angling went on for some time. The watchers only drifted away from the parapet one by one, slowly—and behind the ranks of people who had not moved, who were silent, following the search for the cadaver, there were hunched women, swaying their heavy bodies from one foot to the other, uttering indefinite jeremiads.

"Look at them," said the Alchemist to Michel. He pointed to the Burgwal house "It's from there that our Spinoza set out, traversing their frightened crowds, to go take up residence in pure ideas. What a road!"

Michel shivered. What he had seen left him with an impression of despair. With all the images of desolation that filed before him, like enigmatic but nevertheless persuasive symbols, the poignant memory of Spinoza was mingled, as the Alchemist desired. Michel saw him amid the crowds, going away from them; but they accompanied him, and he did not free himself from them without difficulty. He got away from them, but he retained their odor in the folds of his clothing—and he could not get rid of the resemblance to them contained in his features, even when he had forcibly extracted himself from their proximity, even when they had chased him away.

As they returned to the hotel in the sly shadows of dusk, the Alchemist said: "He escaped them completely—but to begin with, they held him hard. You've felt how hard they held him, back there at the synagogue, with the tight bonds of Scripture, the age-old image of rituals, family habits, the infantile memory of offices, the prestige of rabbis, the fear of ready-made rancor, and finally jealousy: pride humiliated, but pride nevertheless, that of a chance collectivity, which is persecuted but resists stubbornly. He went away, solely by virtue of the strength of his genius—but he was still attached. The fanatic's dagger that ripped his clothing also cut that tie. Good for the fanatic!"

The Alchemist laughed—and Michel, turned inwards, compared the Alchemist to that fanatic, in his own adventure; the Alchemist had detached him, too, from his Church.

The Alchemist continued: "But that's not all. There was still, to enchain him, that little she-devil Van den Enden. Not stupid—she knew Latin and music. She captured young Baruch's brain with the Latin—the Latin that had attracted him to free paganism—and I think that she was able to soften his emotions with the music. He was in love with her. Fortunately, though, she preferred Kerckring, a native of Hamburg, who had given her a necklace of three hundred pistoles. I can imagine her, that girl, quite pretty, mischievous, both clever and womanly. Yes, yes, conversation and corsage, a white skin. She's wearing a low-cut dress, and has Kerckring's pearls around her neck; she's proud of them, and Baruch is jealous. She excites his jealousy, without much malevolence, but in the way that women play. He's even more jealous than amorous; it gives him no pleasure but the desire and the pain are intensified in being excited."

Michel thought about the Van den Enden girl, desperately. He imagined her similar to Rembrandt's Jewish Bride, plump, fervent and content with a few jewels. He saw her young, already a trifle heavy, ingenuous and yet calculating, alarmed by love and possessed of the mischief of her race, graceless and yet, in trying to be genteel, attractive of compassion.

"Girls like that," said the Alchemist, "have what it takes to catch you and keep you, by means of the double concupiscence of body and mind. In the bric-à-brace of that Jewry, the girl was charming, and wore her three-hundred-pistole necklace well. Then again, he was lost, our Baruch, already a trifle consumptive, excitable, his continence causing his ears to buzz. But once again, there was a knife-thrust of deliverance. Full in the heart! The knife thrust was the Van den Enden girl's marriage, to the generous Kerckring. One can't stay, for things like that; he went away...he was free."

And Michel united, in thought, the life that came from leaving and the life that Baruch Spinoza had left, in fleeing Amsterdam. His own life appeared to him, noisy, ferocious and ridiculous—and he cursed it; but he also sensed how difficult and damaging the separation was, how vast and empty of liberty. He languished, and wanted to cry.

* * * * * * *

They went to Rijnsburg. It was there that the Alchemist had decided to install Michel and to leave him, all alone, with his work to do, following Spinoza's example.

They went into a broad landscape of air and wind. The sky was magnificent, with the abundant curls of its clouds, rolling and floating, reminiscent of squadrons in old marine paintings, plumed with sails. The clouds bobbed under the pressure of the stormy wind; their prows emerged, large and round, ornamented by three-dimensional emblems. Flotillas of small clouds, moving more rapidly, passed from one edge to the other. Then the naval combat of aerial fleets was lost in a confusion like that of smoke belching from cannons, soon filling the atmosphere; One might easily have thought that frigates and caravels had reached horizons of mist and nothingness.

The fresh vivacity of the air felt good on Michel's face and hands, which were warmed by a kind of fever. The Alchemist liked it too, and took off his hat in order to receive it on his brow. After the noise and bustle of Amsterdam, they appreciated the peace of Rijnsburg, a little village wrapped in silence.

The Alchemist said: "Listen! One can hear the silence." He added: "How tranquil it is! I don't believe there's a calmer village on Earth."

Michel agreed with that, and had the impression of finally entering into rest. His head was disengaged, his limbs relaxed. For a few minutes, he felt a slight appeasement. He thought that he would soon be able to sit down, to be alone before a blank sheet of paper, with a pen, ready to trace numbers or words or vague geometrical designs, such as one draws when thinking about something else. He would classify the elements of his chagrin, put them in order and make arrangements to live with them, almost meekly.

But the Alchemist, who was indefatigable, said to him: "First we'll go to Spinoza's house. Then we'll find lodgings for you. And then, my dear boy, I'll go, because it's time for me to go home now. That's enough vagabondage, for an old man!"

They had left Michel's luggage and the Alchemist's valise at the railway station. They asked for directions, but it was not easy to find Spinoza's house. They went astray, went further than they should, retraced their steps. The roads were slippery because of the mud and cabbage leaves with which they were strewn. An insipid odor rose from the cabbages and mingled with a miry odor that came from stagnant pools of motionless canals.

Furthermore, during their long detours, they met hardly anyone. They wondered where the peasants were, who were not to be seen either outside or in the little single-story houses whose wide-open doors displayed pretty and tidy interiors, with shiny painted faience, copper and tinplate pitchers, soft shade and discreet light. Thus, the silence was perfect—and it reigned over the entire landscape, beside its sister immobility.

There was only movement in the sky, where the clouds never finished unrolling their slow voyages, their marvelous phantasmagorias, and their extravagant and incessantly-renewed resemblances.

Looking at all that, the Alchemist said to Michel: "This is where he came, after the two knife-thrusts." He added: "The memory of Madame Kerckring, née Van den Enden, dissipated in such a place like those clouds you can see."

He seemed to find that quite facile and quite natural. Michel thought about Geneviève, whose memory would be persistent.

Spinoza's house moved them—that house in which he had lived, occupying two rooms, one for working and thinking, the other for mechanical work. The latter, with its steeply-sloping roof, formed a kind of ground-floor grain-loft, but there was bare earth underfoot.

That was the bench at which he had sat down to grind his lenses. It was a long piece of wooden furniture: the bench, the elbow-support, the wheel, the vice, the pedal. And he had sat there, short and thin; he had leaned over it, in order to work well, precisely, while his subconscious mulled over metaphysics. His foot, on the pedal, was diligent. The plank was worn away by the shoe; the support by his elbows, and the wheel no longer rotated since he had been put under a stone slab in the New Church of The Hague.

It was easy to imagine him, and to see him, so assiduously inclined over his work, sometimes straightening up to verify the transparency and the exact thickness of the crystal, the concavity or convexity of the surfaces. But the pedal supplied rhythm to a thought that could not be divined, which wandered too far away, too vigorously impelled to be overtaken, a thought whose wings beat too swiftly, as if it knew how to sustain itself in the ways of the dialectic. The pulse of that pedal rhythm was contiguous with the wing-beats of the thought.

Spinoza's bench seemed, to the Alchemist and Michel, to be a relic as august, venerable and holy, for the faithful, as that other bench at which, in his days in Nazareth, the fleshly son of the carpenter Joseph had served his apprenticeship.

Then, when he had turned his wheel long enough, when his thought had fluttered its wings long enough, Spinoza had returned to the room where, along with his bed, his books, his table and his writing equipment were. Then he had noted down the various episodes of his dialectic, the ups and downs of the logical series that descended from axioms through successive theorems to their scholia and corollaries. The axiom was more beautiful in its nudity; the final corollaries had a more numerous and pretty agreeability. And he rejoiced in seeing the various branches of the idea flourish, becoming gradually similar to the apparent reality of things, at which it is sufficient to look to find it abundant and marvelous. Then he retraced the steps of the series, in order to escape the scattered seductions of corollaries and take refuge in the austere silence of the axiom.

Sometimes, he went to the window, through the panes of which he looked at the countryside.

"He was twenty-eight when he arrived," said the Alchemist. "Twenty-eight years old! He came because he was in love with that girl, who was so white, knowledgeable and plump...and shut himself up here."

Yes, sometimes he went to his window, and through the closed panes—the window was very small and the panes neither very regular nor very transparent—he saw that landscape, that plain of cabbages, so monotonous that the violet cabbage among the quantity of green cabbages is the only amusement for the gaze. In the distance, there is the village of Katwijk on the Oude Rijn, house in the trees; further away, Katwijk aan Zee, before the open space of the sea and the wind. Beyond the cabbages, they could not see anything but a line of poplars, behind which the sail of a boat occasionally passed. They could only see the top of the sail, because the edges of the canal have high embankments.

That was all he could see, if one adds in delicate changes and shades that the play of light and shadow multiplies, with richness and taste on the surface of the most modest landscapes.

"So," said the Alchemist, adding a conclusion to the mute thoughts that occupied him and Michel, "he worked, for want of anything better—for want of anything better for his concupiscence, that is; for the liberty of the soul, there is nothing better."

They went out. They paused momentarily on the threshold, and the Alchemist said: "Sometimes he came here to take the air and smoke a small pipe of tobacco. I don't know what tobacco it was; strong tobacco, I imagine, brought by large boats from Amsterdam, with cargoes of spices, which must have reeked of the Orient, strange countries where the mind dares not adventure. Or else he hunted for spiders; he put them together and watched them fight. He was not wicked, but spider-fights gave him an opportunity to laugh, because he did not think that one could change anything in the order of nature, and he had acquired the philosophical habit of considering that which is real as necessary; so he amused himself, glad to be in a good humor, and knowing, once and for all, that nature is ferocious. Or he chatted in a familiar manner with the other people in the house, about anything that provides subject matter for a polite conversation, about trivia. One day, his landlady asked him if, in his opinion, she was doing well in following the religion in which she had been brought up. As he had no desire to correct the good woman, he told her that she was doing well and that all would be as well as could be if, in practicing piety, she led a peaceful and tranquil life. Oh, my dear Michel, everything is there. Now, let's find lodgings for you. Time's passing. Let's hurry."

They found two honest and decent rooms in a house in the village, which overlooked the same landscape as Spinoza's window. With his fists, the Alchemist made sure that the bed was sound. He asked for a better table—larger and steadier on its four legs. The housewife would prepare Michel's meals and bring them to him. The price of his accommodation was agreed.

Then the Alchemist said: "You won't do at all badly here! You don't need much room or much apparatus for your work. That's the beauty of your discoveries; they're exempt from artifice and perfectly simple, like the truth. There. Now, my boy...."

When the time came to leave he was emotional. He did not hide it very well. He even used the back of his hand to wipe away large tears that were sparkling in the corner of his eyes. Michel looked at him sorrowfully.

The Alchemist said: "It's stupid! Oh, I'm growing old. Come on, Michel, my little Michel; embrace me."

They embraced—and Michel had the sentiment of witnessing, with a veritable anguish, a scene that he did not entirely understand. Since his departure from Paris he had been living in a quasi-automatic fashion, without rebellion against or voluntary adhesion to the fatalities that were leading him but not persuading him. He had not been numbed by pain; his thoughts were as lucid and clear as ever, and as active, but they were working of their own accord, independently of him, without him perceiving any link between his thoughts and himself. While his alert thoughts labored, he had been in a kind of paralysis and torpor. The Alchemist's sudden emotion woke him up, as if with a start. His eyes were wide with astonishment, dazzled, as if he had opened a window to sunlight in a room where he had just finished sleeping.

The Alchemist experienced something of the same sort, in spite of the energetic rigor with which, during the last three days, he had carried out his plan, realizing his decisions point by point, exactly accomplishing his meticulous intentions. Suddenly, he had lost momentum—the momentum he needed to accept the final consequence of his action and to conclude it. He had a moment of weakness, not knowing whether he was right to do what he had done, asking himself whether the results of the poignant exile to which he had relegated Michel would be worth the voluntary sacrifice, the responsibility he had taken and all the effort of such boldness.

Then, if he had seen Michel hesitate, tremble before the solitude in which he was heaving him, he might have taken him by the arm and led him away, saying: "I beg your pardon, I've made a mistake. Come, I'll take you home; will you forgive me?" But Michel, whom he was observing with amicable compassion, gave no sign of despair. Michel had no precise consciousness of himself; he became formal rather than surrender to confused transports.

"Give me your hand," said the Alchemist. "You're magnificent!"

Michel was not magnificent—but he neglected to say that he was anything but.

"Work, then, my boy," said the Alchemist. He would have liked to bless him as he left, as an old patriarch of science who had just consecrated an admirable neophyte. A monk who trims the hair of a postulant is not touched by a graver mystery, or a holier horror, but he has the Latin words of the liturgy with which to conceal his disturbance, and in which to invest his fervor; they are impersonal, and have the noble modesty of symbolism.

In place of that, Michel and the Alchemist only had the vain, timid and poor clichés of separation—mediocre and useless words that one says in order not to be silent, and which are also symbolic, but quivering and awkward, mingled with allusions and lamentable: the offer to accompany the person who is leaving; the refusal; the aphorisms of a somewhat rudimentary moral hygiene; the flurry of farewells and an entire hypocrisy of courage that gives the lie to the meanest gestures, stammerings and mournful expressions.

"Adieu, Michel. Be well, my boy!"

"Adieu, Master."

And the old man left. He changed his mind and said, again: "I'll tell them to bring your bags."

"Thank you."

"Or would it be better for someone here to fetch them?"

"Perhaps."

"No—I'll find someone there to bring them. Don't move."

These vulgar cares occupied, as best they could, the final seconds of their parting.

\* \* \* \* \* \* \*

Left alone, Michel collapsed in a large armchair upholstered in chintz. He was facing his window, with the dull landscape of cabbages and the moving sky. He did not feel anything but fatigue. He let his head sag, and soon allowed his neck to rest on the back of the armchair. The glare of the sky blinded him; his eyes closed. He opened them again to look at his room.

A white, shiny paper was hung from the ceiling to the plinths, whose painting imitated black marble veined with green. There was a large dresser of sculpted wood; there was a bed, with ample curtains of starched lace; there were three white, green and red wicker chairs. On the walls, behind glass, there were two colored vignettes, one religious and the other gallant.

None of these objects was extremely ugly, and that very simplicity, in sum, was better, for contenting the gaze, than the gross composite luxury of Paris. Michel was saddened, however. Tears came to his eyes, and he weakened.

The mere fact of weeping did him good; that release of his body and idea rested him. In the same way that in a garden, after a rainstorm, the beaten-down plants revive, Michel felt his heart reborn within him. But then he began to feel sorry for himself, in his abandonment and isolation. He did not know what he was doing in that remote spot. The image of Geneviève passed before his eyes and his lips trembled. His throat tightened. He could not sit still. He got up, opened the window, leaned on the sill and, before the desolate landscape that would be the contemplation of his days, he sobbed uncontrollably, in despair, not because of one thing or another—he did not separate the various and numerous elements of his dolor—but because of his entire life.

Voices in the corridor and a discreet knocking on the door brought him round.

"Come in," he said—and tried to put on a brave face.

His luggage had been brought. There was an opportunity for words, reflections, ceremonies; the landlady offered to help him to arrange his drawers and his cupboards. He sent her away benevolently, and set to work.

First, he applied himself to straightening the pile of shirts, the pile of handkerchiefs—but what was the point? He transported the untidy heaps of his clothes from the compartments of his trunk to the dresser.

At the bottom of the trunk he found the few items of chemical apparatus he had placed there. Haphazard and incomplete, they seemed derisory. Why had he brought all that? Alas, in leaving Paris, had he not been playing a lamentable comedy of going elsewhere to work? Those burners were for gas, and there was no gas in Rijnsburg. The test-tubes, crucibles and flasks were so many knick-knacks. He deposited the vain apparatus of the abandoned science in a cupboard in the next room. Then there were his books, and the wads of paper that he had once covered with his fervent observations: all of it the flotsam of a shipwrecked science.

And no sirium! He remembered having left behind the iron box in which the precious substance was contained. He perceived the mad generosity with which he had ruined himself, on the evening of the great renunciation, when he had given the sirium to Geneviève and Pierre for their patients as he made his escape, and the joy of that forgetfulness. He did not regret it; his pride would not permit him to take back his prodigality, even in his imagination. He raised himself up in the certainty of his destructive will, and went so far as to forbid himself mere regret for his gifts.

But the poor old Alchemist who had just left him, Michel remembered—so humorously that he smiled. The poor old Alchemist who had thought he was locking up Michel and the sirium in a prison of science, Michel laborious and the sirium obliging...poor old Alchemist! Michel mocked him bitterly, for his credulity and naivety. He mocked him with the malevolence that he had against himself—for he was furious with himself; it was himself that he had sacrificed, with a kind of rage, and it was himself that he was killing, slowly.

When he had finished arranging all that remained of his life, he put his empty trunk and valise up in a grain-loft, went back to his room, and found authentic solitude there.

\* \* \* \* \* \* \*

The following morning, Michel, who had slept heavily, needed some air. He opened his window. The plain of cabbages was sunlit for a moment, then clouds came over; then the sun came out again—and the alternation continued, rapidly, for hours. Michel's eyes grew tired watching those changes, so complete that the landscape was not the same from one moment to the next. The shadows moved; the brightness and the shade moved, replacing one another everywhere, succeeding one another capriciously.

His mind, quick to philosophize, found emblems of doctrines there, distinguished from the ungraspable reality of the trickery of appearance, and sought, beneath the mobile multiplicity of accidents, for eternal substance.

He went out, as if he were going in quest, in the countryside, for the substance that the accidents concealed. Thus one parts undergrowth in order to discover roots; and thus one tears a veil in order to examine the mystery it covers. But the veil of appearance adheres to the reality—or, rather, there are numerous veils over the reality, in such a fashion that tearing one displays the next; one cannot tear all of them, and the last one tears is no closer to reality than the others, since infinity cannot be diminished. And then again, between the most profoundly-hidden roots and the extreme florets that the undergrowth bears at its tips, there are roads of sap, of which one can map the design; but between the substance and the accident, one can never know where the attachments are, or the passages....

Michel walked along the paths, accompanied by his ideology,

consecrating the landscape and its metamorphoses to the service of a stubborn metaphysics. He arrived on the bank of a canal and saw three large, heavy, slow barges devoid of sails laden with oranges. Agile men, putting their shoulders to poles that plunged into the water and were wedged on the canal bed, were marching head down, at a rhythmic pace, along the banks. The three barges advanced with in indolent continuous movement, guiding that magnificent, odorous sacred cargo—a cargo of sunlight—along the line of the canal.

He passed a pinnace full of chrysanthemums; one might have thought that the canal was in flower.

The fine weather was radiant. The clouds had dissipated. Light, even and warm, settled in and reigned in tranquil sovereignty. It was as if the veil of appearances were no longer shifting, permanently hiding the substance that was becoming, by virtue of its immobility, substantial.

The calm sunlight consecrated the appearance and divinized it.

Michel was the amused victim of these spells. He liked fine weather and savored its diverting mildness. He perceived that he was taking pleasure in it. He was afraid for his pleasure, being Catholic by nature and long habituated to mistrusting bodily delights, and also being sensual by nature, fearing the fleeting quality of those miraculous coincidences, good minutes—but he yielded to a charm stronger than the dread and the scruple. He was even satisfied to think that nothing was calling him elsewhere—not work, nor Geneviève, nor sirium—and that he was admirably free. At the end of his abnegations, in recompense for his renunciations and, in brief, at the conclusion of his despair, he received the gift of a glad frivolity.

He smiled at feeling Bohemian. It seemed to him that there was badinage around him, and he believed vaguely that nature was collaborating in his game. Amid the appearances he strolled cautiously, attentive to a fragile and graceful mystery.

He met a peasant and spoke to him. The peasant did not understand and replied in Dutch. Michel did not understand and replied in French. Politenesses were exchanged several times in the two languages—and Michel burst out laughing.

He met a pretty girl; she was carrying pitchers of milk. He smiled at her and she greeted him. When she had passed by her blew her kisses, jokingly.

All morning he frittered the time away. Then, gradually, his cheerfulness evaporated. A kind of sorrow fell upon him, as a little sly and fine rain sometimes begins to fall without one noticing it, and soon dampens all the surroundings. There was not, however, a single reason in Michel's surroundings for his change of mood. The sun continued to animate the region; the hours continued their admirable round, in a beautiful autumnal atmosphere—but he no longer had a welcome for the petty distractions of the route. He became bored, and even began to detest being so far away that he would now have to walk for a long time to get back home. He wanted to be at home, to shut himself up in his room; he was subject to the instinct that makes sick animals want to hide.

When he got back he had lunch. Then he did not know what to do. He sat down at his work-table with a book: Spinoza's *Ethics*, which the Alchemist had bought for him in The Hague and had given him as a breviary of solitude.

He read. He could ask for nothing better than to allow himself to be led from definitions and axioms to theorems and corollaries. He was docile to the rigors of that logic; having accorded everything to substance, he refused nothing to God or his modes. He experienced a perpetual difficulty, however, in fixing his interest on the dry and insidious formulae, which revealed nothing at first but their plenitude, and from which ideas emerged as if from ambush. That dialectic, clear and abstract, contrasted with the abundant melancholy he felt in himself. The malaise he endured ended up occupying him more than the scholia from which God obtains a little fabric.

He closed the book.

He was unhappy, to the point of perceiving a heavy discouragement of his hands. He had no desire to move, and languished in bewilderment by remaining in place.

With a mechanical gesture, he opened the book, and he read: *A man who understands his passions and himself clearly and distinctly loves God.* Then: *That love of God must occupy the highest point in the soul.* And then: *God is exempt from passions and is touched neither by joy nor sadness.*

In order to find peace, Michel wanted to love that intelligent and impassive God. In order to love him, he tried to know himself, and his passions—but he glimpsed nothing within himself but disturbance and vehement confusion.

*There is no passion of which we cannot form a clear and distinct concept.*

"Yes, by virtue of everything that has gone before," Michel thought, "But I have not accepted everything that has gone before, in order to seal that bargain."

And he applied himself once again to disentangling the elements of his tumultuous dolor.

*It is necessary for us to devote all our care to knowing each of our passions as clearly and distinctly as possible; thus the soul will reach the passion that affects it with the thought of objects that it perceives clearly and distinctly, and in which it finds a perfect repose.*

"A perfect repose!"

*And thus, the passion being separated from the idea of an external cause and connected to true thoughts, love and hatred will be annihilated.*

That promise comforted Michel, and he started searching within himself for the verity of his chagrin. It seemed to him that his body was suffering with his soul and that his nerves, his muscles and his brain were combining their tremulous excitation with a mental anguish to compose the total of his misery. He analyzed the torment, separating its fragments, and as he became confused in the subtle multiplicity of it all, a sharp synthesis was suddenly formed in his mind, and he groaned: "Geneviève...Geneviève...."

Then he knew everything and had no need to seek any

further—but he did not find repose in the idea of Geneviève, and the idea of Geneviève was combined, in the most offensive manner, with the idea of Pierre Dauzanne. Michel's jealousy began to torture him, no longer obscurely but with manifest cruelty.

He was no longer striving to know his dolor; he was striving to divine Pierre and Geneviève, back there. He pursued them, caught them, entered their hiding places, penetrated the hearts of the mistress and the lover. The lover and the mistress had no refuges in which to escape him; they had no hypocrisies that could deceive him; they had no secrets between themselves that Michel did not discover with the keen scent of a hunting dog.

Michel saw them, after his departure, the next day or the same evening—yes, that evening!—coming together, animated by a similar desire. And Geneviève letting herself swoon, Pierre catching her, Pierre taking her in his arms, Geneviève with her lead titled back on Pierre's shoulder; and Pierre, with his thick lips trembling, kissing her mouth ardently. She feels Pierre's beard and moustache...she shows the whites of her eyes...she surrenders to the seductive energy of the lover....

Michel passed his fingers over his eyelids and, with his palms, made a gesture of driving away the image.

The image came back, cynical and stubborn. Sometimes it relented mercifully, but then redoubled its ferocity. Pierre and Geneviève going for a walk, the two of them, like virtuous lovers for whom the happiness of being together is sufficient. Their paces were equal, their strides similar—and Pierre was speaking in whispers; Geneviève smiling, already wrapped in furs; she was wearing her Astrakhan bonnet, her muff swinging in her left hand.

"Geneviève! Geneviève!" murmured Michel.

Because of the people one meets in the streets they were keeping up appearances and Pierre had not taken Geneviève's arm. Because of people, not because of him! For they had evidently forgotten him, immediately. Oh, how Michel would have liked the people always to be there—the people because of whom Pierre was keeping slightly distant from Geneviève! And Geneviève was looking straight ahead, modestly, like a very distinguished little woman.

But scarcely had he desired that the thoroughly reasonable walk through the streets and then the pathways of the Bois be prolonged—it was evening, and there were a great many people outdoors, taking advantage of such a fine moment—than the lovers were transported, as if by a detestable feat of magic, to the end of their journey. Yes, yes, to Pierre's house, to Pierre's bedroom!

And Pierre, suddenly, locks the door. They are alone. Michel can see them....

Ah! Suddenly, Michel stands up. He strides back and forth in his little room. It is too small; he arrives at the walls too rapidly; he would bump into them if the increased acuity of the subconscious did not warn him to turn round and draw away with the supple promptitude of ferocious beasts pacing back and forth in their cages. By maneuvering, he avoids the walls; and by means of agitation, he also prevents the images from adhering to his retina. He runs away, and thus sees nothing but fragments of images through abrupt openings of thought.

He sees the genteel Geneviève climbing on to a bed, arms forward—bare arms. She is in her underclothes. Her legs are bare, her beautiful petite legs.

Michel is like a madman pursued by hallucinations, and can only escape them by flight. Sometimes, he stops and gazes insistently at no matter what: the modest sculpture of the dresser, the lace of the curtains. He applies himself to discerning, among the fibers of the wood, a bright or dark vein that hides and reappears, making numerous meanders, and fades away, lost in the thickness of the planks—or, in the lace, he counts the threads and disengages them from their knots; when one trail escapes him he attaches himself to another, which will soon go astray. He tries to occupy his eyes with an indifferent and manifest reality, in order that, full of the design that the veins of the wood or the threads of the lace form, possessed by the difficult research, he will no longer have any room for false and anxious visions.

He has scant success; the wooden surface realizes obscene figures and the threads of lace are lustful entwinings.

All day long, Michel struggled against the ignoble haunting. When he went to bed, early, he was so tired that he slept—except that he woke up, tormented by inept nightmares. He dared not go back to sleep again, lit a candle, ascertained that it was not yet midnight, and kept his eyes open.

He felt almost calm now that his room was illuminated. Mentally, he listed the strange properties of sirium; and since he had no sirium with which to embark on further experiments, he resolved to classify the results he had, in order to deduce their logical consequences; in that fashion, he could use up the length of his days.

Then, without any transition, but with such simplicity that the passage from one idea to another did not astonish him, he thought that that night of harsh insomnia might perhaps be Pierre and Geneviève's first night. In favor of that being the case there were arguments so persuasive that scarcely had he perceived them than he yielded to them. Michel had not enunciated them, but he felt their convincing force. In any case, he raised no protest. He did not quibble with the evidence, and he thought about all that almost without suffering, in the same fashion that he had formulated so neatly the singularities of sirium. He continued, in the same tone of lax reverie, a meditation that gradually went to sleep, just at the moment when Geneviève, in Pierre's arms, appeared to him with the whiteness of her skin and her ecstatic face....

Then he detested Pierre's hairy hands, his blond hands, because of patches of redness, whose hairs were gilded by sunlight. Then he cried.

He got up, no longer able to stay in bed. In a dressing-gown, at his work-table, illuminated by his candle, he searched furiously for the page in the *Ethics* in which Spinoza describes the phenomena of jealousy. His fingers were trembling, riffling through the pages of the book. And, his eyes burned by the words as if by letters of fire, he read:

*It is what most often happens in the love that one has for a woman; for the man who imagines the woman he loves in the process of prostituting herself with another man, not only because his appetite finds an obstacle....*

He skipped; those words were not the ones his folly demanded—and then he fell upon these frightful words:

*But because he is forced to combine with the image the beloved object, she....*

The frightful words tolled a grim knell in his ears; the words that Spinoza seemed to have wanted to be cynical, disgusting, filthy; the abject words....

And then the anger terminated in despair and unhappy affection.

*In addition to that, the jealous person is not greeted by the beloved object with the same face as usual, a new source of sadness for the person who loves.*

Was there, then, more sadness in the anger? And was there, even in unleashed fury, still affection? Michel sensed that.

Michel wanted to recount the torture that he was enduring; he wanted someone to feel a little polite compassion for him. He could not get used to being alone without weakness—and he started inveighing against Spinoza. He said to him:

"After you had written those lines, did you feel better? Did it do you good, to get to the bottom of your rancor? You resented Kerckring, but it was yourself that you martyrized in throwing your fiancée into the arms of a man bolder than yourself: your naked fiancée. And you wrote how you saw them, the little Van den Enden with Kerckring. You wrote that voluntarily, to avenge yourself. Did your quill tremble, in writing that?"

He riffled through the book, and he said again, silently:

"After the two knife-thrusts, when you arrived here all alone, no one knows what there was in your sick heart, your discontented flesh. You were a mild and polite man. You were an astonishing maniac, a manic arranger, a collector. You dug into the little pigeon-holes of your thought and your dolor. After that, you were better...were you better?"

And he began to sneer at Spinoza. Afterwards, he went to sleep as best he could, in his bed, where he could not find a comfortable position.

* * * * * * *

In the following days, he fell into a kind of languor. That new state was less painful than so much excitement.

He was indulgent toward himself and, weakly, no longer tormented himself. He rarely went out. Time, with its slowness, ceased to be his mortal enemy.

In any case, he busied himself with organizing the hours of his days. He regretted not having some futile task to perfect. No matter! Perfect futility—which is, after any discouragement, the supreme desire—he realized marvelously in the planning of his life.

He resolved to work in ideas, to build the physics and metaphysics of sirium, carefully, line by line.

He reread his old notes with a reasonable assiduity, and he asked himself: "What's the point?"—but he was satisfied in not finding any response to such a question, which saddens imprudent youth but reassures a sage.

Crises of jealousy returned from time to time. Michel succeeded, not in avoiding them, but in softening them. The vile images were less frequent, and more often, Geneviève appeared on her own, in morning costume, coming and going in the house, making no noise, simple being the Geneviève of old, becoming, before long, a lady, and learning to govern her home.

Michel gazes at her; he dares not speak to her—no, she would only become the other Geneviève, or one other, which she became a little later, when she became impatient so easily! Michel gazes at her and he weeps; his tears are not bitter. He weeps softly; and then he works.

He decided to conclude a molecular theory that would

account for all the bizarre phenomena of sirium. He started to construct an unforeseen physics, which did not have for its principle the equal transformation of energy, since sirium produced an energy that did not appear to come from anywhere else. It was, in sum, a complete revision. The old hypothesis fitted the totality of previously recorded phenomena, not the phenomena of sirium. A new hypothesis was necessary, which accommodated the phenomena of sirium and the others, in order to reconstitute unity. On that subject, Michel commented at length.

"Unity," he thought, "is beautiful and comfortable—except that I don't know, personally, that unity is anything but a desire of the human mind—a taxonomic procedure, let's say. No matter. Science only requires multiplicity to be combined in unity. It seemed that multiplicity is the appearance and unity the substance. If it's mistaken, that would be rather droll; scientists would be doing the work of a Bouvard and Pécuchet,[7] arranging and classifying. Oh, it's not important; we're working for science, and since science doesn't require any more, well, let's search for unity. Then everyone will be content...."

Uncertainty led him to a kind of nihilism. He did not suffer in consequence.

His work detached him from the thought of Geneviève. As before, she was not associated with his work as a scientist; he did not rediscover her in the course of his task—but it often happened that, the minute he was no longer working, he saw her again, and imagined that she was mocking him a little. He would smile, as a sign that he was not taking all that very seriously.

Sometimes, when he went for walks, she accompanied him. Along the paths, he talked to her, but she scarcely made any reply. And when he sat down again at his table, before his papers, his figures and his black scribbles, he left her behind. He had to leave her behind, attentive to the timetable that he had fixed to discipline himself. Then he hesitated, and experienced

---

7. The eponymous characters of Gustave Flaubert's last, unfinished novel.

impulses to leave, to return to Paris, to see Geneviève, in reality. He wanted her...but no. *The jealous person is not greeted by the beloved object with the same face as usual.* So, no! And he had some slight difficulty in picking up the thread of his argument. He was restive, like a horse that has not rested for long enough. And then he trotted, meekly, in harness, his blinkers hiding the temptations of the roadside.

He thought about Geneviève less and less, his mind being otherwise occupied. He glimpsed her from time to time, but he did not stop to look at her. When that gave rise to rancor, the memory did not last long. Jealousy had succeeded love, gradually, jealousy disappeared; the love was no longer there.

A day came when Michel thought about Geneviève for the last time. As he did not know that it was the last time, he paid no heed to it, and it is thus that one allows cherished individuals to die within one, without consecrating to their final moments a fervor that will henceforth have no further opportunity, not knowing that they are about to die, numbly squandering the supreme grace of their presence. But they die, and one is informed by that of the sin one has committed; one repents of it. Michel was not informed; it was, for him, a day like any other, and others followed.

The memory of his mother and sister had also faded away without making any noise. That was how Michel only became alone a long time after believing that he was. Once he was, he did not have a clear consciousness of it.

He scarcely spoke to anyone. With his landlady, a good and precise woman, he only exchanged words of quotidian courtesy. He had no instructions to give, because the order of his days was precisely regulated.

He worked. He built phenomena into laws, and he assembled particular laws into more general laws. The mechanics of sirium elevated him to a pure and simple notion of life. He was in the realm of metaphysics.

In the same way that once, during mass in the cathedral, while the organ was singing the glory of the Son, he had conceived the hypostases and the efficacious virtue that flows from the Father to the Spirit via the Son, now, once again, he speculated about the trinity of the conscious, the subconscious and the unconscious—three states of being—and the inexhaustible fecundity of sirium was the symbol of the fertile unconscious. Except that henceforth, his dialectic was stripped of the splendid vestment of myth. It was naked, or almost naked, scarcely clad in words that adhered better to the idea. Between the unconscious activity of matter and thinking individuality, he found no other difference than memory. It sufficed for him, and he took it as an absolute. He built a metaphysics of memory, but in order to unite it with a physics of spontaneous fecundity, he worked. He spent laborious hours in the service of unity.

The period in which he constituted that metaphysics of memory was the one in which he became, with regard to himself, the most forgetful. His individuality was then subject to singular ups and downs. As he only thought attentively about ideas unconnected to him, and as his days were deprived of incidents, he acquired the habit of not reporting to himself anything that occupied his mind. He became disaccustomed to being happy or unhappy. He was, in accordance with the Alchemist's desire, a location where ideas constructed their own logic.

Outwardly, he continued to act like any other man. He took the same care in his appearance, his nourishment and his sleep. He looked at the clock and did not fail to set it right. He responded amicably to the *bonjours* that were said to him, and he walked unhurriedly along the roads, faithful to his itinerary, not seeking any amusement there.

Weeks passed, and then months.

Winter arrived. Michel asked for a fire.

But what was done for him was not done entirely by himself. There was a part of his intelligence that was, as it were, detached from him, which watched over him in the manner of a servant. He did not perceive it.

Through the panes of his window, he could have seen the plain covered with snow; he could have seen delicate arborescences of frost congeal on the panes, landscapes of little trees with heavy branches, and supposed that the distant line of poplars was reflected there, had left its image there, fixed in thin ice; he could have seen, some distance away, people going about, doubled up, slipping on the difficult ground, some laden with dead wood, others with sacks, forming processions of black shadows in the white countryside. He looked at all that, but he did not see it. Except that, when he went out, he put on his overcoat, raised the collar and put his hands in his pockets; the secret servant had forewarned him.

He knew what time it was, but not what day. The change in the season did not lead him to tell himself that he had been there for a long time. He was patient; that was because he was living in eternity.

* * * * * *

By the end of winter, he had built the system of his ideology. He had realized its unity.

Nothing remained then but to contemplate it.

He was pleased with it, after a time. The series of theorems formed narrow and sure pathways in which his thoughts loved to roam, in both directions, alternately, whether he was tempted to go and see how concrete realities were divided, at the extremities of the routes, or whether anxiety soon gripped him and he wanted, like a prudent shepherd, to bring those follies back into the fold of unity.

He grew bored, though. The active effort that his hard metaphysical labor had compelled him had left him in a laborious state, and he no longer had anything to do. He told himself that, in order to extend his doctrine further, he required new realities, but he did not have any more. In any case, he did not want others, for he feared putting his doctrine to that proof.

His doctrine was beside him, like a tower. He had been its architect; he was no longer anything but its warden. He grew bored, like those old soldiers retired from service, who sit in their wicker chairs from morn till night, at the foot of the monument that has been confided to their vigilance. Their canes trace arcs in the sand, and they wait for bedtime to arrive. If they have previously traveled the world with conquering armies they remember the countries to which they went and suffer from nostalgia in spite of their lassitude; and if the monument commemorates an action in which they played a part, they love it—but they do not look at it incessantly, and they languish alongside it. Thus Michel languished.

The pursuit of ideas is a hunt in which the mind seeks amusement; their contemplation rapidly becomes fastidious.

Michel realized that the mind is not made for contemplation; it needs movement and is fearful of rest.

In the presence of his fine and solid tower, Michel was analogous to those provincial adolescents who find the days long and go to Paris. One says to them: "You have such a beautiful cathedral in your little town!"—and, indeed, the cathedral is beautiful, as if the entire region had been devastated in order to build it. It is broad and tall, sculpted with delicacy even in its nooks and crannies, illuminated by its stained glass, rich in its treasure—but there is almost nothing around it any longer; all life, all fervor, opulence and ingenuity are enclosed within the space of its walls; since they have built their cathedral, people have not had anything else to do, and the human generations have, in the course of the centuries, become torpid. The little town is dismal, and the adolescents reply, hotly, that they cannot go to the cathedral incessantly. There is nothing alive there but the devotees who take sanctuary there out of constant habit.

Michel was not a devotee of his tower. That fine but cold architecture satisfied him, but did not enchant him. It was not a sanctuary, and no god dwelt within it. Michel climbed its staircases from time to time, but when he reached the top, the view was nothing but an immense desert. Only the bold and powerful architecture could interest him—but that was all.

Should he build another tower? He did not have the materials. All that he possessed of facts and ideas he had put into it:

the solid facts for its foundations, then the ideas in stages that gradually diminished and became at the summit, the point of a steeple, unity. But the steeple had no bells to summon any worshiper.

So, Michel could not build another tower. To build another, he would first have had to demolish that one, but the other would be similar or less perfect. That one, in which he had been able to place in consummate order every stone and all the cement, was better, and it was necessary to be content with it. It was, in structural terms, a masterpiece; but it was not very pleasing, because of its perfection.

When spring began, Michel had bad days.

A terrible malaise was visited upon him by the timetable that he had fixed for the employment of his time. The hours of labor were empty. Sometimes, he looked at the tower, and if, by change, he perceived a slight flaw, he repaired it rapidly, cutting, smoothing and carving the stone, refining a joint. Then he fell back into his nonchalance.

He resolved to reread the *Ethics*. It seemed dry and arid. It also seemed, as theorems were placed on theorems, than another tower was being built in his mind alongside his own, and he feared seeing them side by side, hostile and peevish. In any case, they had no quarrel; each of them as unassailable in its ill-tempered solitude, and there was no projectile by means of which either could destroy the other.

And Michel realized that human thought had, throughout the ages of history, built many towers on the indefinite plain of dream, many towers of various heights, all terminating in points. He saw them, in all their variety, forming an extravagant landscape. Several had crumbled of their own accord; rubble attested that there had once been architecture there; fragments of stone still bore the traces of the saw or chisel. Others were incomplete; the ridges of their profiles indicated the desired intentions, and the eye continued the proudly rising lines, extrapolating curves whose amplitude was only indicated by their departure; but they sometimes ended in such an entanglement of capricious curves that one could understand why the builder had become discouraged. The other towers—the ones that had their steeples—Michel saw at close range, numerous, making up a crowd, and prodigiously sealed. Each of them had only a single inhabitant. People had come, had looked, a few had even gone in and then had gone away and build their own some distance away.

The solitary inhabitants of those towers were dead. Yet others were built, in which other solitary inhabitants enclosed themselves, and where they died, captives of their constructive ingenuity.

Among those towers, Michel saw his own, the most recent of those that were finished; he preferred it. He perceived the faults, poverties and fragilities of others, some of which were threatened by ruin, and some of which only owed their duration to stays or replastering. He preferred his own—but he did not like it much. It was so thin! Tall, yes, but narrow.

He remembered cathedrals, which were not so tall, but which sheltered multitudes. He did not like cathedrals, or multitudes. He sensed that he was a man of the solitary towers: a man of one tower, his own, to which he had given birth and in which, like the other builders of towers in theirs, he would die.

At the point he had reached, there was nothing left to do but die. When one has built one's tower, one resides in it, one is enclosed by it. Except that the towers are uninhabitable by the living; they are not dwellings but tombs. And Michel wanted to die—or, rather, he felt that his death would be the most timely incident. But while he died inside more completely every day, something in him endured: the mechanism of life.

Thus, it was necessary to occupy that mechanism and not leave it to operate in the void, like a windmill whose sails have kept their canvas to the wind, although there is no more grain between the millstones.

*But on the other hand, why?* Michel wondered. Why not let the sails of the windmill turn crazily, since that is their function, as the wind pleases? But no—he was a windmill conscious of his turning, not wanting to turn in the void.

Why? He did not know, to tell the truth, why that demanding windmill refused to be, in the spring sunlight, sails moving under the caress of the light breeze—but he was suffering and he did not wear suffering well.

There was nothing more to do but die, or to contemplate.

As he leafed distractedly through the *Ethics* he fell upon these strange lines:

*It is therefore useful, above all, in life, to perfect understanding or reason as much as one can.*

"Good!" he said. That I've done, and I have no more reason!"

*It is in that alone that the best felicity, bliss, resides.*

He repeated, mentally:

"The best felicity, bliss...."

And the words seemed to him to be a slightly absurd paradox, and he smiled, bitterly.

*Bliss, in fact, is nothing other than the tranquility of the soul that gives birth to the intuitive knowledge of God; and the perfection of understanding consists of understanding God.*

He thought: "Now, I know God; God is unity. I have placed him at the summit of my tower; he is its point. I am, therefore, undoubtedly in a state of bliss...."

It was necessary to occupy that bliss. "For," he thought then, "God himself made himself human, in order to occupy his bliss, even more perfect than mine!"

God had come into the world. Around Michel, however, the world was desolate; he had employed in the building of his tower, if not the world, at least that portion of the world that surrounded him.

And leaving God out! But he remembered Spinoza, who, to occupy his bliss, had ground spectacle lenses. And Spinoza would not have made the pedal of his machine beat regularly, if he had not had the lens of spectacles—real lenses for real spectacles—to grind.

Michel was deprived of that work. But the man who lodged him had an orchard next to his house and a vegetable garden.

He worked there constantly, alone, unaided. Michel asked him to employ him—oh, only for amusement and in order to get a little exercise. Besides, Michel affirmed that he was not entirely ignorant of the art of gardening, being a countryman—he ought to have said "provincial," but he exaggerated.

He had a spade, a hoe, secateurs—the various implements of gardening, and the time that he had once devoted to bringing theorems into the world, he devoted wholeheartedly to favoring the growth of fruits and vegetables.

He preferred that new work, finding it less harsh than the other and more pleasantly varied. He had to prune the trees and train their branches; he had to shift the earth, to sow the cabbages, to plant out others; he had to get rid of weeds. In the early days, there were unwelcome contortions; he had a girdle of pain around his midriff. He remembered Blaise Pascal, his own enemy, who wore a girdle studded with nails on which he tapped with his elbows, driving the nails into his flesh, in order to learn not to be lustful. Michel smiled in a melancholy fashion at the idea that he had no need of that discipline; reclusion was sufficient, with work and modest nourishment, to deaden his flesh—and he mocked himself mildly, and humorlessly.

When the first buds appeared, he rejoiced. He examined them; he observed their daily growth, their red and pink tint, their inflation; he watched their velvety and sticky tegument extending, bursting, under the outflow of sap. And one morning, under the lovely sunlight, the flowers showed themselves, small and delicate, pale pink and charming. The day before, they had scarcely been detectable; a warm dawn had opened them; they were the delicate miracle of the prelude of spring.

There were no leaves on the trees; the trees were like those in Japanese paintings, their short branches brown and pink, neatly outlined, seemingly fragile—and because of that, more precious. The slightest breath of wind caused one to fear for them, but they resisted flexibly, and stood proud again when the wind had passed. The contrast between the old bark and the fresh buds was, in the orchard, like a poignant and gracious emblem of ancient and new nature, the earth that is mortuary and fecund. Michel admired the patience of the seasons, and the beautiful succession of obstinate springs.

At any rate, these phenomena diverted him. As he did not try to arrange them into a dialectic, he experienced, in considering them, the pleasure of free play, and as he had no interest of any sort in the success of flowers, he loved them for their simple beauty; all that was an agreeable pastime. And when his train of thought inclined to the austere unity of delightful flowers, he told himself that ideologists were mistaken in always climbing toward tedious unity, when the ravishing profusion of flowers invited them in the other direction. He repented, but soon dreaded the sophism that had seduced him: the flowers were the allegory of all the peril he had escaped for months while he was taking refuge in the direction of unity.

He dug the soil with his spade and dared not lift his eyes often to the miracle of spring. If the ideas of dissipation that emanated from the renewal brushed him, he turned away and, like the divine gardener of the orchard of Jerusalem, he murmured: *"Noli me tangere!"*

He sensed danger. He evaded it, and gardened as monks garden, to tire their muscles.

One day, however, there was a letter for him. A great marvel! It was the first that had reached him since his departure. Only the Alchemist knew his address, and he never wrote to him.

Michel examined the envelope; the handwriting was unfamiliar. He detested the Paris stamp.

He had his foot on the iron of his spade, with the shaft applied to his belly. He tore the envelope open and read the contents.

"Ah! Good!" he said,

It was an advocate that had written to him, on Geneviève's behalf. Yes, on behalf of Geneviève who wanted a divorce.

*That's perfectly just*, he thought.

And he was astonished not to have thought before about that detail. On departure, he had had the illusion of liberating Geneviève absolutely—but no; it was necessary that it be ratified by legal tribunal; it was necessary that he, Michel, be legally suppressed. The advocate indicated the best means— the quickest and least scandalous. Quite simply, would Michel allow himself to be found in default, would he be kind enough to let himself be condemned for not being there? Yes, gladly. Michel admired the ingeniousness of that procedure, how little it disturbed him. It was sufficient for him to write to the advocate, and not to budge.

Right away! He plunged his spade into the earth, and went away to write that short letter.

When he came back, he resumed digging.

He struggled hard against it with good arguments, but he felt more abandoned. Certainly, before that announcement of divorce had arrived, he had given no thought to returning to Paris, or getting Geneviève back, or even of seeing her again. She had even disappeared from his memory. Now the image of the genteel woman presented itself to him with such insistence that he did not know how to drive it away.

He dug, with a rhythmic action, tracing long furrows in the fresh earth; he beat down clods, flattening their ridges; he pulled out the ends of dead roots and shook them. Then he stood up and breathed momentarily. If the image of Geneviève came a little too close, then, he murmured: *"Noli me tangere!"*

He shivered—and resumed work.

He did not know how long the formalities of the divorce would take; nor did he know exactly what the procedure involved. He reflected on that, as if it were something important, even though he did not care about it. Deep down, however, in the secret intimacy of his heart, chagrin settled in, like a great sheet of mist over a landscape: the bleak chagrin of conclusive abandonment.

Toward evening, he became even sadder. It was the hour when once, in the time of his happiness, he had been afflicted by a kind of anxiety, but when Geneviève said to him: "I'm here!" And she laughed, and so did he. To cheer him up, she called him "the bad Michel of the dusk." The lamps were lit; and all was well.

\* \* \* \* \* \* \*

The following morning, while Michel was working in the vegetable garden, another letter arrived. Michel received it impatiently. This time, he recognized the Alchemist's handwriting.

"Oh," he exclaimed, "why can't I be left in peace? I ask no more, but they won't leave me alone!"

Rather than opening it, he stuffed the letter in his pocket; then he worked. He was angry; what did the Alchemist want? Doubtless something to do with sirium, and the transformation of energy.

"Do you want my tower, Master? I'll give it to you!"

He added: "I'll give it to you, for what it's worth. And it's worth as much as any other, and not a sou more, damn it!"

He laughed. Then he became sufficiently curious about the letter to require an effort not to open it. It seemed heavy in his pocket, and unwelcome. He did not want to give into himself, however, and continued to sow small seeds in the furrows that he had prepared, with the result that he eventually forgot the letter and the Alchemist, and the rest of the world too, to be nothing but a good gardener busy ensuring that he would soon have fine vegetables.

That day passed like the others. Michel, with the letter in his pocket, was the usual Michel. He did not think about Geneviève much, and he did not think about anything much. Sometimes he looked at his watch, and when it was time for a walk he went out. He walked, as he did every afternoon, along the canal, following paths that never led anywhere.

He went as far as the point at which the sea air blowing from Rijswijk brought a saline odor; he breathed that odor in, and went home along the main road. He dined and he read, as he did every evening. But when he emptied his pockets before getting undressed to go to bed, he found the letter. It displeased him. He accused the letter of being stubborn and following him. He tore it up into four pieces, which he threw away.

Then, without thinking any longer, and as if he could not do otherwise, he bent down; with a submissive gesture he picked up the four pieces. He pulled a piece of paper out of a corner of the envelope. Words leapt to his eyes like strange beasts, to claw him:

*My dear...your poor...died....*

He thought that his mind was invaded by madness. He tried to put the fragment of the letter together again, but he became confused; his fingers were trembling, dropping one fragment and presenting another upside-down. His eyes were veiled, or dazzled. He had to take it all in his hand, with his lamp in the other hand, to his table, in order to perceive words that drove him to despair, divining them before he read them, and finally reading:

*My dear Michel,*
*Your poor Maman has just died....*

Then he did not read any more. He got up, marched, tottered, stopped, breathed in as much air as his lungs could contain— and he fell on his bed, his body folded in two, his forehead on his sleeve.

He called: "Maman! Maman!"

He was nothing but an unhappy child. He suffered like anyone else, and with his entire being, ordinarily divided but the elements of which suddenly fused to compose a terrible unity of grief.

When he had reacted against the first shock, he suspected that he might have been the victim of a nightmare. That had happened to him before—dreaming that his mother was dead; he woke up with a start; and then, by touching the wood of his bed, by listening, by lighting his candle, he had verified that it was not so, that he had been duped by a frightful lie. Moreover, he had never heard of anyone's death without thinking, for a second, that it might be a mistake, and retaining a little hope.

But he read, again:

*My dear Michel,*
*Your poor Maman has just died....*

It was that abominable certainty, against which his discouraged imagination could no longer contend; he battled momentarily, and was vanquished.

He wanted to leave, to go back there, to be there soon enough for the farewell given to that inanimate body. But how! In the middle of the night? No, there were no more trains...

He had, no matter what, to wait until morning, to wait like this, in distress....

But the letter, he had had since the morning; the Alchemist had written to him the day before, or the day before that; why a letter and not a telegram? It would take him more than a day, no, to go from Rijnsburg to Brittany. One day, two, three...oh, to late, too late! He would not be there; it was finished, finished forever; oblivion had triumphed; oblivion had come surreptitiously!

Finally, Michel read the whole letter.

*My dear Michel,*

*Your poor Maman has just died....*

But that was so absolutely complete that Michel could not get past that word, and he had to resume several times before being able to continue:

*I only found out just now; you know how secluded my life is— but she passed away the day before yesterday, in the morning. More exactly, your sister found her, the day before yesterday, in the morning, no longer breathing. She seemed to be asleep, but she was no longer alive.*

*I learned that just now. As the cathedral was tolling the knell, I asked who it was. Usually, I don't ask, no longer having any friends in the town. I did well to ask. Old Marie-Claude told me that it was Madame Bedée and that they were ringing for her funeral ceremony. She told me what I am writing.*

*It's too late for you to come. You can't have been told, because I didn't know and I haven't given your address to anyone. I regret that; but also, I couldn't betray the voluntary retreat in which you're working. I only gave it, under the seal of the greatest secrecy, to an advocate who wanted to write to you about the divorce.*

*My dear Michel, I feel very sorry for you and the grief you will endure. I've known that, and you're much more sensitive than I am. I implore you to be strong. Work; there's nothing else to do. Thus, one becomes less tender every day, less tearful and prouder, more capable of refusing suffering. Life is horrible; that's why men like us don't accept it and take refuge in science.*

*Don't come. There's no longer any reason for you to come. It's said that your sister is going into a convent. I approve of that. For want of science, which is not at her disposal, the convent is always better than life. But don't come. The emotion that you would have to bear here would lose the profit of your long solitude. It's necessary to stiffen yourself; that's all I can see.*

*I hope you're working, and soon, I'll ask for an account of what you've done. If you want me to come to see you, say so; I'll come. But it's doubtless better for you to compose yourself on your own. You only have to write, though.*

*Michel, I shake your hand.*

Michel had to reread all of it to take it in. The words went past too quickly; he could not retain them, and some lingered when others had already fled.

He only retained the gist: the dates and the fact. For four days his mother had been dead, for two, buried.

He made the sign of the cross. He knelt down and recited the *Pater*.

He had not decided to do that; it was spontaneous, almost mechanical.

In Padua, in the Church of the Arena, there is a painting of the *Death of the Virgin* by Giotto. The Virgin dies down here, on earth, surrounded by the cares of pious individuals, but in the heavens, Jesus suddenly becomes a child again and rests, a little orphan, in the arms of the Father.

In spirit, Michel similarly became a child again, and, scarcely aware of what he was doing, bore his orphan soul to the bosom of the Father. And he wept.

When he got up from his prayer, he did not know what to do. With regard to death, he lacked the occupation given to those who are there: the arrangements, the preparations; the funereal care, and, finally, the desolate protocol whose details at least prevent one of falling into an oblivion similar to that of the very recent death. Michel had the sensation of drowning in a whirlpool of despairing ideas.

The sentences that had announced his mother's dead were in his mind, in his ears and in his eyes; he could hear them and see them.

He wondered whether his mother had been obliged to suffer. He told himself that she had not, and that she had gone to sleep peacefully. Yes. However, at the last moment, at the very instant of dying—for oblivion is not, after all, a simple continuation of sleep—at that instant, had she realized that she was dying, and had she thought about him, to desire to see him and to criticize him for his absence? Michel feared so.

And he thought that he saw his dead mother, lying on her back, her hands joined amid the beads of a rosary: her white hands, which he loved and remembered, with their blue veins and delicate softness. He could still recall the contact of the fingers, on his own fingers and face, for she had once caressed his cheeks while cuddling him.

He devoted the entire night to remembering his mother. He made that pious vigil, troubled with tears, at a distance, at a great distance. He remembered his mother as he had loved her, of old and recently. He saw her again, young and old: the little mother who took her children out for a walk, showing her paces, who had a blue umbrella; now here she was, a widow too son, dressed in black forever; and here she was grown old, too quickly grown old and impotent.

How rapid that transformation had been! The years that had elapsed between the youth or her motherhood and old age, he had forgotten; it seemed to him that they had not gone by. He understood that those years were those of his own adolescence, and that, like all boys, he had not thought about anything but the amusement of being a young man. He had squandered all that time, that lovely time, not taking advantage of the presence of his mother, living as one lives, without absurdity, as if life might last forever. Afterwards, she was old, his poor Maman, old and captive in an armchair.

And now she was dead.

The periods of life went by so swiftly, in his mind, that he thought he was old himself, almost at the age at which one dies. Was he not already half-dead? Except that he perceived himself more clearly than ever. Tens of years went by, in his imagination, so rapidly that the days and nights were momentary—except for that night.

Michel lost any accurate notion of time; he measured a tormenting meditation at whim. All that he knew was that he other seemed to be present very few days, and that that night of regret went on indefinitely.

Weariness made him drowsy.

When he woke up, he wept, because of his mother's dress, because of her black dress, which he would never see again, which he would never touch again, and of which his fingers retained the memory.

Once, he had said to Madame Bedée: "You ought to have a new dress."

"She had replied: Oh, since I don't go out any more...."

And in that distant epoch, he had wished that she might be a little more elegant, for the sake of the gaiety that elegance supposes; but he was also pleased to find, after all of his journeys, the same black dress, so perfectly proper, which he recognized. He had also wished that his mother had worn a less rigorous mourning. One day, to be obliging, she had put on her black silk bonnet with a mauve ribbon. It had disconcerted him; she had perceived it, and was in black for ever more. Michel could not console himself for that life all in black.

* * * * * * *

In the morning, when he went out to go, as usual, to the garden, the new spring realized its masterpiece. The air was so pure that sight could distinguish the slightest detail of the plain in the distance. The trees on the horizon, though smaller, were no less clear than the objects in the foreground. Slack sails were passing on the canals, taking advantage of an imperceptible breeze. The light was limpid. At the ends of the branches, florid and motionless twiglets, extended toward the beauty of the landscape, seemed to be casting a spell, like the wands of invisible fairies.

And Michel, as on other mornings, set to work. He remembered the death of his father. One such a morning, once, during his childhood, his father had just died. Michel and his sister had gone down into the garden of the house of their birth to pick roses and place them beside the mortuary bed. Since then, he had forgotten so many things that he retained, in sum, almost nothing of those years—but the odor of those roses remained in his memory, importunately. The flowers of the orchard in Rijnsburg reminded him of it so precisely that he dared not look at them He scented an odor of death around him, and the marvelous spring thus appeared to him as a slightly ornate cemetery.

He thought he could see, in that earthly cemetery, a grave.

It was the grave in which his father had been sleeping for thirty years; the grave that he had once visited frequently, with an emotion that the years had rendered less poignant; the grave that had suddenly become again, by virtue of the presence of his mother, more moving, and was covered with the fresh flowers of the interment.

As he straightened up after having driven in his spade, he perceived over the hedge, some distance away, a young woman dressed in black. He recognized her and shivered, murmuring: "*Noli me tangere!*"

He had recognized his sister.

Yes, it was really her, evidently looking for him, asking people for directions and taking a wrong turning. He should have run after her; he should, at least, have called out to her. Michel tried to do that, but a strange paralysis of the body and soul gripped him. He could not move, he could not even shout. And he stood there, gazing at Marie as if he were devoid of all strength.

A voice within him begged: "*Noli, noli me tangere!*"

He was afraid of that young woman in black, who appeared to him thus as a courier of death, and who was his sister.

He feared that she might see him and he leaned over the soil, hoping that she would not see him, that she would give up trying to find him and go away. He was afraid of a tenderness that was coming to him, still alarmed, which would speak to him, and cause him to die of grief.

He raised his eyes; he looked over the hedge and no longer saw anyone. He waited his heart was beating forcefully. He was in anguish. After a while, he thought that Marie would not come; he felt sorry for her, but he was more afraid that she might come. And while he worked, he was all ears, a poor creature subject to a threat, which could not resist or struggle against it, and was trying to ignore it.

"Michel!"

And Marie arrived. They embraced.

And then they were in front of one another, no longer knowing what to say. They looked at one another with eyes full of tears. Their arms dangled.

Michel said to Marie: "Come to my room." He took her by the hand and led her there.

That vast space around them, that ample and cheerful light, and the dazzling sky, numbed them.

When they went into the little room, they experienced a slight appeasement. The shutters were closed with the window open. There was too much shade, and also too much air. Michel opened the shutters and closed the widow. There was light and silence in the room: desirable tranquilities.

"Sit down," said Michel—and he brought two chairs together.

The brother and sister sat down next to one another. They did not say anything, because they were not animated by the same concern, Michel only thinking about talking about his mother and Marie astonished by the strange state in which she found him.

"What are you doing here?" Marie asked him, finally.

He was ashamed of himself. How could he explain as rapidly as possible the absurd and detailed adventure that had brought him a young scientist from a good family from Brittany to Rijnsburg, to become a gardener?

Michel replied: "What are you doing here?"

She replied: "I'm going to enter a convent."

She explained hat she had already had a vocation for some time, and that she had only postponed her vows in order to care for her mother.

"At present...."

She affected that lightness of spirit with which all the desperate who have nobility in their heart dress up their renunciation when they have reached the point of even refusing compassion.

Michel interrupted her. "Well, as you see, I too have entered a convent!"

She seemed not to understand at first; then she said: "But this isn't a good convent. No...it's not a convent at all." In a low voice, she added: "It's a convent without God."

Then there was an abyss between them: an abyss that their tenderness could not fill in, an abyss so profound and wide that their words would have fallen into it, instead of going from one to the other, like arrows launched from too far away.

They fell silent again.

Then Michel asked: "How did it happen?"

"Maman was confessed, on the evening of the day before. She had talked to the abbé for a long time. After that, I saw her more serene than I had seen her for a long time. Her face was as it was when you arrived. Yes, a joy of that sort, but without the apprehension of a departure...as if you had come, and were not going to leave again. A great, placid contentment. The next morning, I found her the same, except that she was no longer moving, she was no longer breathing. She possessed eternal joy."

Michel wanted to know whether, in her final days, his mother had asked from him, whether she had suffered from his absence. He did not say a word—and Marie seemed to be relying to Michel's mute thoughts when she said: "God alone can give that joy, because he never goes away; he's the perpetual presence."

Michel asked her about earthly things, and Marie only spoke about heavenly matters. Thus, their dialogue did not satisfy them. They seemed to be chatting but their speech passed one another by, each clinging to a separate rosary of ideas.

They ate lunch together, Michel and Marie, in the little room. They hardly spoke, although they had much to say—but what touched their hearts, they did not say, and they restricted themselves to vain words, whose vanity even offended them. Silence was better, painful and embarrassing as it was.

They went for a walk, but Marie soon confessed that she was tired; her large crepe veil pulled her head forward. Only then did Michel notice that he was not dressed in mourning himself.

"When are you leaving?" he asked.

"I don't know." And Marie dissolved in tears. "I would like, most of all, to take you away."

"No," he replied, harshly. "You have your convent; I have mine."

"If you knew how much I feel that you're wrong!" she said. "But I'll never be able to persuade you. No, no, I can't. I'll pray for you, Michel."

"He answered softly: "Yes, Marinette, pray for me. That I'd like, very much. But are you right to go into the convent? You're young...."

"I'm not young and I'm not old. All I want is eternity."

*That's the most likeable name for oblivion*, Michel thought.

He took Marie to the station. Oblivion and eternity said goodbye to one another.

\* \* \* \* \* \*

After that, Michel understood, in a more decisive fashion, that his mother was dead. Before then, he had only felt the dolor of the separation; now he was aware of the absence.

He was also aware that he was, henceforth, a being separated from everything, with no human attachment in this society, where hazard had abandoned him. After half a year, did he not know it? No. From a distance, from afar, his mother had governed him, his mother, his sister the little town, the cathedral. Even after he had enclosed himself in his grim meditation he had been obedient to a mysterious influence, a moral rule, denuded of its god but nevertheless conserved and observed with rigor. A monastic rule; he had been a monk in his narrow cell.

*In his narrow, empty cell,* he thought, *without a crucifix, without any painted image to recall the sacrifice that Unity made for human beings!*

He continued:

*For the Unity is scattered throughout the world. Except that it has not told the Multiplicity that it is necessary to live in one fashion rather than another. The Unity has not made its wishes known. It has no wishes. It has no other wish than to spread out with a magnificent profusion, while remaining the Unity. Afterwards, it is indifference itself. And there is nothing vile in the house of Unity.*

Michel remember a passage from the *Ethics*. Back in his room, he searched for it, and found it:

*It is certainly not wise for a man to use the things of life and take delight in them to excess, because then there are no more delights; it is wise for a man to refresh and repair himself by moderate and agreeable eating and drinking, profit from the perfumes and beauty of verdant plants, ornament his attire, enjoy music, games, performances and all the diversions he can provide for himself without harming others.*

He did not want to reread the preceding axioms and theorems and he omitted all the cogent argument that had led to that sentence and in the tight network of which the sentence was insinuated. It seemed to him to be singularly flourishing amid the aridity of its environment. It had a strange charm for him. He savored its engaging mildness—and he abused it, mentally; he took it further than it went of its own accord. In the following days, when his grief gave him a certain release, he had such an impression of liberty that he was bewildered by it. He felt freer than one is with security. Geneviève was divorcing him, and now his sister was going into a convent, and, above all, his mother was dead; in sum, all the links were broken—all the links that had ever attached him, in the distant or recent past, to any affection or habitude.

He was as free as a minute in the course of duration of which no one in the world is conscious, and which no memory binds to the continuity of time. He no longer had anything to retain him but science, the prison of ideas to which he had retired as if to a monastery.

He decided not to stay there any longer.

One cold, gray morning—one of those dry wintry mornings that interrupt the jolly preludes of spring—he was suffering from his free solitude and was griped by the spite that one sometimes has against oneself; he decided to be even freer; he wrapped up his physics and his metaphysics in a parcel bound with string. Without any letter or commentary he send those papers—his tower—to the Alchemist; and when he came back from the post office, he swung his arms, which no longer contained anything, broadly, offered his forehead, which was no longer thinking about anything, to the freshness of the air, and surrendered his soul, which no longer loved anything, to the wind.

He repeated internally: *There is nothing vile in the house of the Unity—nor outside it!*

And the passage in Spinoza invited him to use the things of life, to enjoy the perfume of flowers, to seek diversion. The words in the text which moderated all of that he neglected, hearing nothing but adventurous advice.

In any case, he did not obtain any gaiety from it. The bizarre invitation took hold of him at the peak of his distress. It did not promise him pleasure, or consolation, or even forgetfulness. It proposed veritable hazard to a vagabond expelled from everywhere and who no longer wants repose, a shelter for his body among human beings or a shelter for him mind among ideas.

One day, he went away.

# CHAPTER FOUR

Michel arrived, one spring morning, in a small town in a mountainous region. He had not decided to come to it, but he was passing through and the landscape pleased him. Then, as he had no more reason to be anywhere else than there, he stopped.

The little village, Swiss in appearance and French in language, was asleep in the depths of a bay formed by a lake. Was it Swiss or French? It did not matter to Michel. An eternal silence was resident there; an immemorial past continued there.

A river that flowed into the lake passed through a confused accumulation of old houses with projecting roofs and divided the small town into two villages. One of the villages was darker than the other because of the high mountains looming over it, which deprived it of sunlight, but the other, built on marshy ground from which reeds emerged at intervals, had an odor of mud and fever. A convent rang the hours there.

To cross from one bank to the next there was a large flat boat, which was not easy to steer. It was, however, manned by a girl: a strange girl, pretty in spite of her suntan, dressed entirely in black, with a black hood like a nun's. If she had no one to take from one bank to the other she remained seated, head bowed, on the bench of the boat, between the two limp oars and recited her rosary, but she only had to be hailed and she would arrive with her boat. She hurried; her small hands worked hard; she pulled her oars with all the strength of her slim body, thrown backwards. To the man, woman or child who wanted to pass over the water she showed a profound reverence, and, placing her arms in a cross over her rounded bosom, she said: "I beg your pardon, very humbly."

No one paid any attention to what she said. On disembarking, no one thanked her or gave her a sou. She recommended the reverence of humility, and then begged pardon again. And the man, woman or child drew away. Then, at a rapid pace, she went to a wooden pile supporting the first section of a bridge that had disappeared—nothing any longer existed at either bank but the stump. She knelt down in front of the pile, made the sign of the cross, kissed the damp wood, made the sign of the cross again and went back to her boat, to row or to pray, according to whether she was required or not.

Michel watched her for some time, with surprise and compassion. He asked about her and was told: "That's Brigitte."

Eventually, he learned Brigitte's story.

A little girl was thus named. Her father was an old widower, religious and morose. At play, she had more enthusiasm, gaiety and zeal in running and jumping, always wanting to be first, and was more amusingly inventive than her companions—but her ardor sometimes disappeared rapidly, and then she went away, with obstinate quietness.

She could be seen roaming the streets, a well-behaved child, her school apron tightened by a belt, her face inclined forwards. She had a handsome and mobile face, which smiles illuminated and melancholy rendered angelic. Her hair was blonde and as shiny as brass, pulled back, hanging in a plait terminated by a black ribbon. Her eyes were brown; and their gaze settled at length, but sometimes only opened on invisible thoughts.

At that time, the two banks had been linked by a bridge, which was known as the Bridge of Death. The rails were solid wood, at the height of the shoulders of passers-by. The girders, distant from one another, provided a view of double landscape of the lake and the valley, soon as narrow as a ravine. Those girders supported a tiled roof, so that the bridge was like a corridor. The ancient architects who had constructed it had not attempted to take it straight from one bank to the other; it affected the sinuous form of a caterpillar moving between pebbles. Under the roof, in the triangular spaces between one upright and the next, there were panels of painted wood on which some artist of old had represented the numerous episodes of a Dance of Death.

In the course of her tenth year, Brigitte had looked at those paintings one day. As she had always seen them, it required a freak of chance to bring them to her particular attention.

It was a subject of painful astonishment for her.

In the first picture, she saw skeletons still clad in a few muscles, who were dancing; one of them, for that purpose, was playing the fiddle, another the pipes and a third a triangle. Brigitte thought that she could hear that music, with lively notes and a brisk beat.

In the second picture, she saw a pope officiating. He was saying mass in his miter, elevating the host. Behind him, however, in the guise of a choirboy wearing a surplice, was a skeleton. In his left hand, the fellow was holding the hem of the pontifical chasuble; in his right, he was shaking a hand-bell frenziedly—and he was laughing.

In the third picture, she saw the Emperor visiting his beautiful domains, ornamented by golden fabrics and furs, wearing a crown and carrying a scepter. A courtier accompanying him, pointing out the opulence of the palaces and gardens, bowing respectfully, was a skeleton brazenly mocking, bantering and jesting.

Brigitte looked at those bizarre images. She did not understand all of their significance, but she was subject to a powerful attraction. She stopped for a long time in front of each of them, allowing the uncertain and tremulous ideas to penetrate her soul along with the colored forms.

She saw the Empress and the ladies-in-waiting; she saw the King and the Queen, and the Bishop, the Duc, the Abbé, the Comte of the Holy Empire, the Comtesse and the Knight, forming, from one picture to the next, a long procession, with which skeletons mingled, fearful nonentities in plumed hats, velvet doublets and buckled shoes—and the hideous, elegantly costumed individuals were joking and sniggering.

Brigitte was astonished to observe that the Emperor, the Empress, the King, the Queen and the other powerful lords or clerics did not perceive the mortuary company in which they were, and did not notice the jokes that were being made about them, and did not know that they were advancing in a funereal procession.

In another picture, a monk was dying, lying on an iron bed. A skeleton had climbed on to the mattress; with both hands it was shaking the shoulders of the dying man, whose mouth was open, panting.

Then there were the Judge, the Flag-Bearer, the Advocate, the Merchant and the Philosopher. Trade and philosophy provoked the same irony in the skeletons.

An architect was building; workmen, on the scaffolding, were hoisting stones, and he was tracing the plain of the edifice with his compasses—but a skeleton crowned with gold was confusing his calculations; another was causing workmen to stumble; a third was unfurling a banner on which one read: *Sic transit gloria mundi.* Brigitte could not understand Latin, but she divined that the edifice would collapse, because of the malice of the skeletons.

A painter was striving to represent the important members of a guild naturally, but while one skeleton smeared the colors in various directions another insinuated its horrible face between the radiant faces of the drapers or goldsmiths who were posing, and having itself portrayed in their stead.

A captain brandished a standard in order to excite the courage of his troops, engaged with the enemy. A skeleton had seized the edge of the cloth and was pulling upwards, with the result that the shaft was slipping through the captain's fingers.

Lovers, in whom Brigitte could only see a handsome young man and a beautiful young woman, were walking along the pathways of a flowery park. They were holding hands, walking in step, their eyes ecstatic. Skeletons dressed as pages at festivals surrounded them, officious, ceremonious and mocking.

Among the various peasants, gardeners, artisans, the teasing of skeletons was always subtly introduced.

One panel showed a clockmaker's shop. The man was meticulously contriving the delicate combinations of wheels, cords and counterweights in a machine that would beat the measure of time and according to which credulous people would calculate the future—but he did not see, behind him, the cradle in which his baby was sleeping, which already had the form of a coffin and on which a skeleton was balancing on one desiccated knee.

When she saw that, Brigitte was afraid. She ran to her father's house. The religious old man questioned her about her disturbance,

"I've seen death," said Brigitte.

He took her to the bridge and immediately led her to the final panel. That was the final judgment, God the Father in his glory, surrounded by cherubim, dominations and angels with bells and trumpets. Lower down, bodies were resuscitating. Some, emerging from the terrestrial mire, had recovered their form and freedom of movement; others, still half-embedded, were making a great effort to hoist themselves up with their arms; others were lifting the lids of coffins.

The religious old man commented on that scene in the spiritualistic mode. He wanted Brigitte to deduce, like him, the triumph of the soul and its supernatural destiny. But no: Brigitte had spontaneously deduced the universal corruption of the flesh and that death is the inevitable and malicious companion of life.

The words of the preacher did not enter into her mind, which was full of funereal thoughts.

From that day on, Brigitte seemed entirely consecrated to a melancholy dream. Her impulse of delight did not last, and returned her to a dolorous silence. The idea of death was resident within her.

She knew the refinements of an anxious sensitivity. She no longer squandered the minutes; their number, henceforth limited, did not permit prodigality or distraction. She estimated the probabilities of the hours and days that the future retained for her; she calculated and recalculated their sum in her mind, without even thinking of desiring that they might be more abundant. Resigned, she witnessed with a pathetic wonderment the play of duration, like ripples in water.

Sometimes, after long mental wanderings that had strayed into the distresses of mortal anticipation, sudden rebellions gripped her and threw her into an imprudent gaiety. Then she ran and skipped exuberantly, her eyes sparkling, her plait swinging on her back, her apron lifting up and allowing the sight of her little legs, excited by the joy of dancing.

At fifteen, she was a beautiful young woman.

One morning in that year, at the beginning of a bright spring, she was in the house, as usual. She went to the window. The air was calm, a trifle lukewarm, still mingled with a delightful freshness. On the horizon, the snow on the mountains was melting, allowing the foliage of trees that the winter had not afflicted to appear: blue or green firs and black cypresses. At intervals, the sun illuminated admirable reflections, principally on the lake, where the little waves were a luminous frisson of gems.

The carillon of the convent burst forth and multiplied its prettiness. The shrill or deep notes, some tremulous with child-like joy and others soaring into the sky like rockets, took flight. A flock of doves departed, pell-mell, following their whims so cleverly that their sunlit whiteness was gracefully entangled. Brigitte saw them disperse at the same time as she heard the carillon scatter. It seemed to her that there was a concordance between the two charming phenomena. The doves disappeared in the sky when the carillon fell silent.

The silence that fell then was so beautiful that Brigitte, without being aware of it and without wanting to, sang. She had not sung again since the stammered rhymes of her early childhood. Suddenly, her voice, which had just been born, intoxicated her.

Her father was at church. She sang recklessly. She did not pronounce phrases or words; she sang, expanding her voice in fervent and hazardous melodies. The housewives who were passing by stopped in surprise, their baskets balanced against their hips, their heads raised to look upwards beneath their headscarves, their mouths pouted critically. Men stood still, listening. Young people were subject to the singular alarm of that music.

Brigitte sang all morning, surprised herself by her voice and her delight. When her father came home, she did not stop singing. He closed the windows, but she kept on singing, and she was still audible in the street.

On the following says, she sang in the same way.

From the day the songs began, a folly animated the people of the little town. By means of her victorious voice, Brigitte had awakened in them a need for delight that they had never known before. She was their innocent prophetess. She did not perceive the great tumult that she had awakened in their souls, previously somnolent and dismal.

That spring, everyone decided to lead another existence. The existence that they had led until then came to appear paltry, miserable and humiliating. Other towns on the shores on the lake, they knew, had been boldly transformed into luxurious summer resorts to which foreigners flocked, squanderers of gold and joy. They decided to follow that example. The collaboration of rich and audacious companies that provided investment capital was sought; engineers and architects were summoned, with stone, iron, materials and workmen.

The religious old man went to reside elsewhere in the neighborhood, far enough away not to see or hear a new town being built on the ruins of the town where he had gown old. Brigitte refused to go with him; it was necessary for her to witness the triumph of her adolescent frenzy.

Throughout the time the works lasted, she was the extravagant and joyful soul of that dream of a new life. From dawn till dusk, she came and went among the stones that were being carved and piled up, growing from the ground into hotels, casinos, modern houses, municipal palaces, and theaters. She sang; her voice exalted the labor of the masons and carpenters—and one might have thought that her voice was giving life to that valiant architecture.

At dusk, she watched the two electric lamps in front of the telegraph office light up. Those small lights, in the gathering gloom, charmed her heart, where similar gleams had appeared.

In the morning, she was seen more than once going up to the telegraph poles of the roads, placing her ear to the wood and listening for a long time to their strange song, a complex metallic sonority measured by the rhythm of the wind—a song that seemed to her to come from unknown lands. And at sunset, she gazed at the shining wires, mysterious and gilded, through which she knew that news, advertisements and speech from elsewhere was passing.

She thought about those countries, whose names and distances she did not know. She believed that she could hear the noise they made, the echo of their lives and their persuasive counsel of joy. They told her that brief destiny is a magnificent fever; they told her to be docile to the burning desire of earthly life; they told her that even pain enters into the delight of life.

Thus, the vast world concurred with her ardor—but it did not summon her outside the place where she was exalted. It came to her; all the amplitude of kingdoms and oceans converged, to exalt her further, toward autonomic felicity.

Her most beautiful day was the one when the Bridge of Death was demolished.

The local inhabitants, out of superstitious dread, were of the opinion that it should be spared. There were discussions; the engineers demanded its destruction. Brigitte sided with them, arguing eloquently, determinedly and ferociously against the symbol of sadness. She carried away, if not all scruples, at least all uncertainties; the Bridge of Death would be demolished.

The convent claimed the painted wooden panels; it obtained them without difficulty. The nuns came, with the prior, to collect them, and carried them in procession to the convent, in order to avoid the sacrilege and ornament the cloister. They accompanied then with *misereres.*

When the bridge was rid of its images, Brigitte went on to it and, with puerile mockery, utterly excited by her victory over death, started singing, in her marvelous voice:

> *Sur le pont d'Avignon,*
> *L'on y danse, l'on y danse....*

For popular songs travel, far and wide, all the way to countries where no one knows what their original significance was.

Brigitte did not sing *Le Pont d'Avignon* as little girls sing it, but added to the naïve rhyme trills and tender roulades, vocal gaieties, ironic flourishes, mischievous graces and warm resonances. She did not dance—but, with her dress slightly uplifted, her arms scarcely moving, she sketched out the rhythm of a round dance.

A crowd gathered, and danced truly—danced without singing. Brigitte sang. The steps of the dancers resounded on the planking of the bridge.

Then the carpenters set to work. They extracted nails, tore up beam after beam. Pieces of wood and nails fell into the water; the entire skeleton of the bridge went to form a heap of debris on the bank. Soon, nothing remained but the piles, which emerged from the lake like arms sending signals of distress.

The new town was built. By the second year, it was ready to receive visitors. Large houses of white stone awaited them.

They waited in vain. The other towns on the shores of the lake prevented their unexpected rival from prospering. The hotels remained empty. The casino sacked its unnecessary musicians. The rails of the tramways were buried by dust. It was a disaster; there were bankruptcies, lawsuits, miseries. Many of the inhabitants left.

Day after day, Brigitte watched that failure of her young apostolate. She no longer dared sing. Her voice, resounding strangely amid the new and deserted architecture, seemed absurd. The religious old man died. First she saw solitude form around her;

then people detested her, insulted her, branded her with the shame of the defeat, as they had once glorified her for the hope. Was it not she, with her deliriant songs, who had unleashed the madness whose punishment it was now necessary to endure? She was threatened with brutal vengeance.

The nuns offered her the sanctuary of the convent; she would adopt the customs of women who renounce life; she would move silently beneath the arches of the cloister where the images of victorious death had taken refuge before her; she would slowly accustom her eyes and her soul to them; and if she sang again, she would sing, in a modest and constrained voice, the canticles of spiritual life and abnegation.

But she refused, saying that she ought to redeem her sin, and, since she had harmed the people of the town, would now devote her zeal and her strength to serving them.

Thus it was that Brigitte, after having counted on the beautiful ardors of life, had become that poor girl dressed in black who toiled at her task, recited her prayers of contrition, made humble reverences and asked for forgiveness. She never said a word except to indicate her repentance and implore mercy. As the Bridge of Death had disappeared, demolished by her song— as a town in the Bible had collapsed to the sound of trumpets— she no longer spoke except in whispers, and she took from one bank to the other, with her heavy boat, the people who no longer had the route of the bridge. She distributed her petty fortune and for her nourishment she abandoned herself to the aleatory charity of a few good people who thanked her, confusedly.

Michel saw her, and loved her.

He loved her for having wanted to live, and for having renounced it. He loved her soul and her face, because her soul had followed the route that leads from fervor to despair, and her face was as beautiful as a faithful mirror that had retained, and united with delicacy, the two images of delight and grief.

Michel watched her from the bank, inattentive to him, entirely devoted alternately to the task of Martha and the dream of Mary: she realized the most beautiful gospel. And he dared not call her, and climb into the boat she manned.

One day, he did dare. She made him the reverence, begged his pardon and applied herself to the oars. He dared not say anything to her—and when he had arrived at the other bank, he went away, timidly, and wandered around the village that the mountains covered with shadow. He wandered there, not knowing how to occupy himself.

He climbed a mountain path and, from an eminence, gazed at the lake where Brigitte was maneuvering her boat. The day was gray and overcast. On the lake, which was the color of slate, the black-clad Brigitte seemed to be the daughter of the funeral ferryman who carried the living to the realm of the dead; she seemed to be death herself, who had taken the place of Charon, a young death, slightly affected and very gentle.

Michel loved Brigitte, and death.

He went back down to the lake and climbed into the boat. Brigitte did not appear to recognize him, and was not embarrassed by his gaze. He said to her: "You're tired, Brigitte. Give me the oars."

She took advantage of the gesture that bent her over the oars to bow profoundly, and replied: "I beg your pardon."

She continued to row as if Michel had not said anything at all.

Michel went on: "You've renounced life, after having loved life more than anyone, Brigitte. I'm the brother of your mourning."

She did not reply.

He added: "Teach me your despairing wisdom."

She remained obstinately silent. When the boat reached the bank, she made the same invariable salutation, begged the same pardon, kissed the wood of the pile with the same pious humility as usual and ran back to her boat, where she recited her rosary.

Michel loved her amorously, and did not obtain a single word from her. But he thought about her incessantly and wanted to combine his bewildered melancholy with the calm melancholy of Brigitte. He loved her enough to be egotistical and to disdain as a vain scruple the dread of alarming Brigitte, quiet at last, with the company of his unreason. At any rate, she did not seem to notice him. Not once did she raise her eyes toward him.

Every morning, Michel came to the lake. He only went away when his awkwardness and the occasional mocking smiles of passers by commanded him to, but he went away with difficulty and came back in haste, in order to watch Brigitte again, in order to believe that he was near her.

Silence, however, separated them.

That damp region softened Michel, disposed him to the mildness of renunciation. At the edge of the lake, he savored a kind of languid peace. There was an entire week of clouds and mist; the mountains were veiled by them. One could no longer make out the trees except as motionless phantoms in the mist. The old and recent buildings became confused therein and formed vast masses scarcely darker than the air. And on the lake, heavy vapors spread out like long, trailing scarves that would flutter in a slight breeze. The landscape was simplified; forms and colors lost their angles, their bright ridges and their reflections.

Michel became slowly accustomed to that sojourn, the horizon as bleak as if it were that of life itself, the environment of perpetual twilight like the one in which he felt his life draining away.

If the clouds occasionally parted, allowing the sun's rays to fall and uncovering the mountain, he no longer looked at anything but the lake. He feared the rest; he could only tolerate the water where Brigitte had her path.

The water had become his scenery. He loved the stream and the eddies; he loved to imagine it, depending on the weather, heavier or lighter; sometimes cheerful, when the breeze pleated little hasty waves thereon, sometimes overwhelmed by an infinite lassitude, and more often still abandoned indifferently to incomprehensible fatalities.

His eye learned to be content with the frail hazards that changed the aspect of the water. He did not ask for anything more.

And as he became enamored of spiritual poverty, he also became more intimately enamored of Brigitte, who was the soul of that resigned scenery. He spoke to her silently, saying to her: "Brigitte, you pray, and God probably doesn't hear you; but you pray, and that's sufficient."

Or: "Brigitte, you work with your arms and you exhaust yourself, and no one thanks you for it; but you work, and that's sufficient."

And: "Brigitte, you're going to die, and then it will be as if you had never prayed, and never worked. The people you take from one bank to the other will die, and then it will be as if you had left those on the other bank there, and those on this bank here. But all of that is only waiting for death and pretending not to think about it. Unless you're death yourself, gentle death, Brigitte who does not speak and does not smile, the death that summons us: and here we are."

He had acquired the habit of talking to Brigitte like that, without her hearing his words, without the words even being pronounced. Brigitte's silence did not embarrass him; he believed that he was conversing with her, so mysteriously certain was he of the communion of their souls. He was the lover of everything he knew about her, of everything he could divine and everything he could imagine. He was the lover of her silence. He loved her as a singular mute, whose gaze might have more significance than words; he loved her as a shadow that might be realized beneath the appearances on an intangible body; and he loved her as a dead woman whose body and soul might strangely endure, the body attenuated, the soul taciturn; and he loved her as the death that had taken on the aspect of a grim young woman, obliging and beautiful.

"Unless you are the gentle death that awaits us, Brigitte: and here we are...Brigitte, here I am!"

And he climbed into the boat, saluted by gentle death. Gentle death plied the oars and rowed toward the other bank. Michel, in that company, sensed his will dissolve and his individuality vanish; he experienced a kind of joy in that, analogous to the sentiment recluses call by the bizarre name of "jubilation," which is the rhapsody of their piety.

When the boat had reached the middle of the lake, gentle death suddenly swerved, entered the current of the river and followed it, leaving the banks, drawing away.

Michel looked at her; he did not see any change in her face; the rhythm of the oars was the same, and there was absolutely nothing to indicate a sudden resolution, desire or caprice. There was nothing but the abrupt and new direction of the boat. Michel did not make a gesture or say a word. The unexpected voyage enchanted him, and he abandoned himself to the desire of gentle death. Soon, he stopped wondering where he was going; he ceased to be astonished; such was, he thought, the road of his destiny, which Brigitte was guiding.

The scenery was gradually transformed. There were no villages on the banks. The lake shrank. There was the river, framed between mountains and bordered by shady trees. The town was far away; Michel forgot it, as Brigitte seemed to have forgotten it. He believed that he was being taken by gentle death to her own home, in the distant abode of sleep.

Suddenly the boat swerved, as before; it came about. Brigitte was troubled then. She blushed, and seemed to be having difficulty collecting herself.

"I beg your pardon," she said—and she forced the pace of the oars, heading toward the town.

"Why go back to the town?" Michel asked.

But she said nothing, and the vigorous regularity of the thrusts of the oars testified to a decision that Michel had to accept.

Afterwards, he thought that death had wanted to take him, but had rejected him—and he was saddened by that.

* * * * * * *

The next day, as dusk approached, he was on the shore of the lake. Dusk was aflame in the clouds; the blaze was coming closer and closer, launching red, pink and yellow fire, calcinating the profound masses from which it emerged in vivid splendor, leaving nothing but ashes, which it scattered. There were collapses; the rubble turned violet before fading away into the nocturnal gloom.

From the other bank, already dark, Michel saw Brigitte's boat set off. In the bow, Brigitte was rowing; her black form was heaped over the water. Then, in the middle of the boat, a woman was standing: a tall woman, clad in a red cloak; a long golden veil hung over her head; she was wearing the colors of the sun. When she passed into the reflection of the crepuscular flames, she seemed to ignite like the clouds—and Brigitte, beside her, was the night, the gentle night.

The passenger was not looking at Brigitte. She was examining the scenery, manifestly pleased to find it worthy of her. Brigitte did not raise her eyes.

The passenger was beautiful and richly dressed. Soon, Michel was able to make out her pearl necklace, her golden chains and, even brighter, the whiteness of her cheerful face. With her fist on her hip, she stood tall, advancing like a conqueror. She resembled one of those figureheads that ancient mariners set on the prows of their ships and painted in bright colors, boldly cleaving the waves.

In the boat of gentle death, however, she was an image of life, or life itself.

Thus death brought life to Michel, who loved one and began to admire the other.

When the passenger got out of the boat, Brigitte made her reverence, as she did to everyone. In order not to be lacking in courtesy and because she was joyful, the passenger replied with another reverence; with the tips of her gloved fingers she picked up the hem of her red cloak, but while Brigitte bowed her head profoundly she kept her head high, laughing with brilliant teeth.

And thus, on the shore of a defunct town where the setting sun was lavishing its phantasmagorias, with attentive ceremony, those two strangers, life and death saluted one another.

After that, the passenger wanted to give the ferrywoman a

coin, but Brigittie, with a polite gesture, turned away. And thus death refused life's gift.

Michel followed the double performance. He loved Brigitte and was touched to see her so humble, so poor; he pitied the little black heap that was Brigitte, returned to her prayers in the boat—but when the traveler departed in the direction of the village it seemed to him than an unaccustomed solitude descended upon the edge of the lake. When night fell, it fell upon a desert that the lantern in Brigitte's boat hardly illuminated. And Michel could no longer succeed in confining himself in the silence that the passage of life had left in drawing away; in the penumbra that the brightness of life had left, in drawing away; in the bleak reverie in which death had installed him.

He said, silently: "Adieu, Brigitte—and until tomorrow! I'll come back tomorrow, at daybreak, in order to see you and be near you, in the shadow of your quietude, Brigitte."

And he was sincere, with a hint of hypocrisy. He went away hoping to meet the passenger who had the face of life again.

\* \* \* \* \* \* \*

The traveler had booked a room in the same hotel—or, rather, inn—as him, where a great racket was made by her automobile, which had come by another route, with her chauffeur, her footman, her chambermaid, a dog as big as a bear and another dog as small as a rat.

After spending a few minutes in his room Michel went down to the dining-room and found the usual guests there: tradesmen, petty clerks, people who talked loudly. A little later, the traveler arrived—and in her company there was a wonderment, mingled with mockery and concupiscence. She was dressed in white, with her neck uncovered and her arms bare, all the way from the hands, sparkling with rings, to the rounded plump elbows. She was a brunette and wore a large hat analogous to those worn by shepherds in pastoral allegories; her hair had beautiful waves and hid the tops of her ears. Her skin was so white that the contrast between her face and her hair resembled that between ivory and jet. She was so supple that every one of her movements animated her entire body and her corsage outlined the grace of her throat. She was so cheerful that she amused herself by unfolding a napkin as thick as cardboard, and had such an easy familiarity that she was soon chatting with her neighbor, who, in everyday life, was a commercial representative for a chocolate manufacturer.

She asked him: "I believe that there are pleasant walks in the vicinity?"

The other said no, that it was a dirty place. She burst out laughing. Her laughter was like an avalanche of roses. Michel savored her voice, like a surprising sensuality: its crystal sonorities, its twittering; its sudden outburst; its numerous and varied musical notes. He savored it like a delicacy—and if the words were sometimes trivial, he only heard their magnificent sound, their delightful song.

He also noticed that the stranger had a peculiar accent, which emphasized words and gave sentences a poetic rhythm, often concluding them in a confused, pretty, half-stammered melody. Often, laughter accompanied a sentence from beginning to end, and then one might have thought that a garland of roses was unfurling along a motto of levity.

When the diners had retired, one after another, the stranger, who was drinking coffee, remained, and Michel, who had no pretext for remaining, stayed nevertheless. He had placed himself facing the stranger and was contemplating her indiscreetly.

"You don't drink coffee?" she asked him.

He said no, and she replied: "I always do, in order not to sleep. Sleep kills half of life, and I like to live every hour."

"You don't sleep at all?" he said.

"As little as I can. Sleep is death, and I'm life."

He already knew that—that she was life itself. The statement did not astonish him; he merely admired the fact that life had come to him, in that inn in a mountain village, when he was near to dying.

"Who are you?" she asked him.

He did not reply straight away; he experienced a veritable difficulty in remembering what he was, the name he bore—everything that composes and distinguishes a person.

He hesitated, and the stranger said: "Me, I'm La Métienka."

The syllables were not unknown to Michel, but he no longer knew to what memory they were connected.

"La Métienka, the dancer," she added. "And you?"

With ridiculous timidity, he said: "Michel Bedée."

It seemed to him that the syllables of his own name were less familiar than the dancer's name; it seemed to him that they fell into the silence like stones into water—but La Métienka opened her eyes wide and clapped her hands.

"Michel Bedée? Sirium?"

He confessed that he was Michel Bedée, and that he had once discovered sirium—yes, yes, undoubtedly, but long ago! He scarcely remembered sirium and was no longer anything but a vagabond wandering at random....

"At random," he repeated, "at random!"

La Métienka was delighted. "Come to my room," she said. "We'll talk."

She led him away. He followed her willingly.

La Métienka's room was not the kind of inn room that Michel had. When he went into it, Michel marveled at the perfumes the light, the fabrics that ornamented the walls, the picture-frames, the large white fur carpeting the floor and an entire décor of luxurious living.

"There!" said La Métienka. "I travel with my manias. Like a gipsy, I take everything I need with me through the world—except that I don't need much, to be content." She added: "I can't travel any other way. It's because of the evening. In the afternoon, with the sun, everything is beautiful and joyful, but in the evening, if there is nothing to do but shut myself in with poor things, I become sad and nostalgic. Nostalgia is a sadness too, and sadness is death. La Métienka refuses death."

They sat down in armchairs, the silk cushions of which underwent metamorphoses.

"You dance, then?" asked Michel.

"Yes, I dance!" And she laughed because Michel Bedée did not know that. "You haven't seen me!"

He confessed that he had not—but he went out so rarely.

"That's true," she said, "you're a scientist! Although scientists are wrong not to go out, I assure you. They're supposed to explain life, and they're unfamiliar with it. Then, very often, their philosophies have something enclosed and desiccated about them. It's not life, in truth, it's nothing."

Michel agreed with her. For a moment, he remembered the tower that he had once built for his ideas. His ideas were lodged there, in the tall and narrow tower, but La Métienka had not danced there.

"Yes," she related, "I dance wherever I'm summoned, in music-halls or elsewhere, but for money. I need money; poverty is death. What I dance, people don't know. They don't understand it—but they feel it, all the same."

"What do you dance?"

"I dance the will to live, and the negation of the will to live. I'm a disciple of Schopenhauer. Look, he's my master; he never leaves me."

From a table within arm's reach she picked up three red-bound volumes.

"Here he is. My lovers leave me; my master, no. You know how he defined music: 'the immediate objectification of the will.' He would have defined dancing in the same way, if he had seen La Métienka dance. He's dead, poor man."

She had a momentary hint of chagrin—but she continued: "The will to live is not immobile, nor does it make the grand gestures that accompany speech: the words come after or not at all. Nor does it make disorder; there is a rhythm in nature, which is its work. Then it dances—and I imitate its dance. Or rather, when I dance, I am the will to live that is dancing."

Michel listened with surprise.

"You understand, don't you? Another time, I'll explain to you why I also dance the negation of the will to live. It's not death. I'll explain it to you...if you like."

Certainly! But La Métienka went on, swiftly: "Your turn! Tell me about sirium."

Michel felt an immediate annoyance. What did he still know about sirium? Must he dig into the rubble of his memory to search for the shreds of that old story?

"Oh no!" he said. "Please!"

She laughed—but she insisted. She was teasing, gracefully demanding. And Michel was obliged, in the end, to list the properties of sirium. That intimidated him too; the technical terminology embarrassed him.

"Have no fear," said La Métienka. "I understand."

When he had related the principal facts, with a bleak slowness, La Métienka was enchanted.

She concluded: "Sirium is evidently the will to live. Or, if you prefer, sirium is the manifest objectification of the will to live, like my dancing, like me. I shall dance sirium."

Michel had not expected that adventure at all. He laughed at it.

"Don't laugh," said La Metineka. "You'll see. If the dance grips me, if I'm possessed by the will to live, my legs, my arms and my entire body are animated by a movement born of itself, which has no resource but within itself and which multiples by itself; and it is not energy that is lost or squandered or transformed but energy that spreads out and retains its plenitude. The eyes that watch me are avid to receive it; and the bodies that feel me close by quiver; and the souls flourish."

Michel yielded to the ardor of these promises. All the same, he objected: "Except that you get tired?"

"Oh, you haven't seen La Métienka dance!" she cried.

Immediately, she was on her feet. She called out; the chambermaid and the footman came in. The furniture was moved back to the walls or carried into the next room, along with the white fur that served as a carpet. That clearance left a fairly large space, which La Métienka measured, pacing back and forth.

"Remove this too," she said, "and this. No, put that armchair over there is the corner, for Monsieur Bedée. There—that's good."

The chambermaid and the footman left. Michel was alarmed by these preparations, and was even more to when La Métienka unfastened her dress and corsage and appeared in a fine lace underskirt, her arms bare and her cleavage half-uncovered.

"Watch me!" she said.

She extended her arms, stood up on the points of her feet. And, without moving, she began to sing a sort of bizarre cantilena, the words of which he did not understand and the harmony of which had the appearance of ponderously lifting up the masses of primal chaos. Then her arms moved, as if, during the primary animation, elementary confusions were being detached.

The dancer's eyes were closed; they gradually opened. Her lips were only slightly parted to let out the breath of the monot-onous cantilena; the cantilena was exalted, and the beautiful mouth quivered in a joyful smile. Her body escaped the ground, took flight, and, if it fell back, it was only to rebound. It ran and it galloped; it evoked the running of maenads, the fury of bacchantes, the fearful and furtive coquetry of nymphs; it evoked the universal joy of animals that indulge their savage velocities in the forests, the lightness of young women parading their farandoles on beaches.

La Métienka danced with her entire body. She had no more need of song to accompany the mime, the prodigious music of her dance. She arched herself and outlined the forms of moun-tains. She undulated and had the tidal ebb and flow of the sea. She floated and had the marvelous lightness of the air.

She spun on her axis and the light posed vivid reflections and the fluttering of her layers of lace; they seemed to rise up to her raised arms, to her agitating hands, on which the rings shone like flames, after having multiplied the prowess of her ardor; but then one might have thought that her languor was even more ardent, as if everything around her were following her rhythm, the appearance of her repose indicating the paroxysm of the general frenzy. And she set off again, as if, around her, the things were slowing down, and it was necessary to shake them up again.

The tresses of her hair came undone, and danced with her, long and supple; sometimes they leapt, sometimes they followed her like a scarf of darkness. And her breasts were palpitating passionately, white and proud, in the gestures of the dance.

Toward the end of the dance, La Métienka sang again, and it was a great melodious clamor that ended by fading away into silence when the dance had already faded into immobility.

La Métienka came to Michel, and he looked at her avidly; he was subject to a fascination of his senses and his mind. His entire being had participated in the crazed exuberance of that young woman, who enlivened ideas with a fine enthusiasm; and he surrendered himself to her.

She said: "La Métienka is not tired. She is not even warm. Touch her hands, touch her arms."

And Michel touched her, with his tremulous fingers; he obeyed her, and the contact of the white, cool skin frightened him.

She went on: "La Métienka would dance again, if she had not preferred to come to say to you: 'Tire La Métienka, then, if you are brave enough!'"

Then, all thought capsized within Michel's head, and such was the tumult of the blood in his veins that he heard a loud ringing of bells in his ears. He took La Métienka in his arms and, falling into the hollow of an armchair, he felt her, utterly amorous, on his knees, against his breast, against his cheek. He marveled that she was so light to carry, so soft to hold.

And he recited deliriant litanies to her: "La Métienka is the sun that warms me...La Métienka is a spring where I shall drink...La Métienka is a flower whose perfume intoxicates me. Métienka, you are life!"

She poured into him all the delights of sensuality. For the

first time since he had become a man, he knew the pleasure of collective ecstasy; for the first time, love did not appear to him as the fraternal companion of death.

He said to La Métienka: "Métienka, I love you!"

She replied: "Don't love me. Love is the fraternal companion of death. La Métienka is life. Don't love me; profit from the life that is given to you. All that is but pleasure—and love would kill the pleasure."

But he forgot, amid the kisses, the prudence of refraining from love. He confused love and sensuality.

\* \* \* \* \* \*

Michel had beautiful days with La Métienka. He spent them in joyful lust.

They went for walks—and the landscape seemed completely different to Michel. An extraordinary festival had been installed there, a festival of trees, mountains, air and water. If he had loved nature before, it had been to borrow a melancholy sentiment therefrom, compounded of subtle memories and savant delicacies of sorrow—but now nature was no longer anything but joy.

La Métienka celebrated, in philosophy, the will to live, which she was also able to dance. Thus she celebrated sirium, the primary emanation of the will to live—and Michel consented to it. He made sparse utterances in that regard, and La Métienka laughed at the disorder of his ideas. He laughed with her.

But one day, La Métienka said to him: "We're leaving tomorrow."

He did not want to go, and he wept like a child whose caprice has been frustrated. "Why not stay?" he asked.

"Forever?"

"Yes, forever! If happiness is here, we won't find it elsewhere."

She replied: "The will to live doesn't settle; it is movement." She added: "And then, you know, the Baron's demanding me;

I have no desire to lose him. He has a heart of gold!" She burst out laughing. "Gold, you hear? And gold is necessary to life!"

She had not yet mentioned the Baron to him in such a peremptory fashion. Michel protested; he made a scene. La Métienka treated him like a little boy who is saying nothing but stupid things—and then she took pity on him, and gently told him the most consoling things she could contrive.

When he resisted such persuasive remonstrations, she became impatient. "I told you not to love me. I thought you were more intelligent. And in that case, goodbye—I'm leaving on my own."

But at the idea of letting her leave without him, his rebellion was such that he soon accepted whatever La Métienka wished. He even begged her to forgive his violence; he repented of it and promised to be good from now on.

She was able to soothe Michel and divert his bitterness.

They left the next day. They were going to Paris, Michel with chagrin, La Métienka without regret.

Michel was still afraid of the passing time; by virtue of scarcely moving and staying in the same environment of joy or sadness, he forgot that the hours were hurrying madly, but whenever a episode in his life came to an end—and this one was the only one that had satisfied him completely!—he saw the end of everything and despaired.

La Métienka, for her part, counted on the inexhaustible resources of life, on the abundance of chance; she had no sentiment of the past. In short, their imaginations did not inhabit the same portion of time. They had met one another, momentarily, at the point where the domains of their souls were adjacent, and then—now—they were drawing apart.

La Métienka had a whim; to go away, they would cross the lake. The road that they had selected for the journey began on the other shore. The automobile made a long detour and would wait for them over there.

They crossed the lake in Brigitte's boat.

Michel experienced the double attraction of his two companions, life and death. It as life that was leading him; it was death that, docile to the desires of life, was transporting them both—but he did not know whether death would abandon him completely or retain him.

He observed that, while rowing, Brigitte was watching him, and that she was also watching the beautiful, triumphant Métienka amused by the promise of tomorrows. La Métienka did not neglect him, however. She said to him: "Look how the clouds are racing. That one, hemmed with sunlight, is going more rapidly than the others. The others are trying to catch up with it; they're hurrying. One of them is going to fall upon the mountain; it's dead; the others are hurrying. It's a superb folly that exalts them, the folly of the one that had stolen the fragments of the sun and decorated itself with them. It's drawing them all along. How beautiful it is, Michel! It's necessary, therefore, that you kiss me."

Michel kissed her lips, red with life. It seemed to him that gentle death leaned more profoundly over her oars, and, chastely, avoided seeing the ardent conduct of the lovers.

They got out of the boat. Brigitte made the reverence. La Métienka paid no heed to it; the journey was calling to her.

Michel said to Brigitte: "Adieu, Brigitte. I don't know why I'm going, but I'm going; it's a fact that I observe with astonishment."

Brigitte said nothing. She stayed to hear Michel out, though, and Michel said to her then: "I'll never forget you, Brigitte; and when I die, I shall believe that your boat is carrying me away, and that you are at the oars. Adieu; and since you pray, pray for me."

Brigitte listened in silence.

But La Métienka, in the automobile, shouted for Michel. "Well, Michel, come on!"

He came. And when he arrived, La Métienka, laughing, asked him: "Are you not in love with that girl, my dear?"

He did not know what to say. She added: "That girl who is pretty and who has the face of death. I detest her. I don't want the face of death to be pretty."

And Michel said: "Are you jealous?"

"Oh," she said, "you annoy me!"

And they left.

Brigitte, in her boat, prayed.

* * * * * * *

In Paris, Michel initially had the impression of no longer being anything but a stranger in the city that was familiar to him and the appearance of whose streets and houses he recognized. He had no domicile, and took a room in a hotel, like a traveler passing through. He did not know, in any case, whether he would be living in Paris henceforth; he did not think about it. On the first day, he was rather surprised to be there.

Principally, however, he thought about La Métienka, and he suffered because of her, no longer having her. At the railway station he had been obliged, by her order, to pretend not to know her; the Baron was waiting. He saw the Baron, a fat blond man with curly hair. Even his beard was golden. He watched La Métienka, very seductive in his presence. And he had gone away, as La Métienka wished.

In his room, now, he belonged to his jealousy; he could imagine only too clearly the Baron's pleasure, La Métienka's complaisance.

She had said: "I'll try to come to see you tomorrow."

"Today!"

"No, not today. What do you expect?"

Then he understood that she had reserved the entire day and night for her lover—and he was annoyed, with the result that, in her turn, she was annoyed too. And then, he had been so tormented, with such sincere pain that, in order not to see his tears, she had promised to come to see him the same day.

He waited for her, and she did not come. But as she might have come, he dared not go out, and waited, absurdly, until nightfall for the faintest noise in the corridor, the rolling of carriage-wheels in the street, the purr of automobiles. His fingers quivered and the joints of his knuckles ached. He looked at the time and marched back and forth, counting on the duration of those short trajectories to occupy the series of minutes.

His night was weighed down by fever and disturbed by insomnia.

La Métienka did not come the next day, and Michel wrote to her. She arrived, furious: "The Baron might have seen that letter—and what then?"

"Then," said Michel, "that's what I want."

Passion drove him crazy.

She arrived furious, but even more charmed by that love, which she ignited by desire as much as by joy. She intoxicated Michel with the magnificent gift of her ingenious fervor—but when she announced that she was going home, to the Baron's house, Michel argued and protested.

She ran away, and Michel was not quick enough to run after her. He called to her from the window. In order not to howl, he stuck his fist between his teeth.

Afterwards, La Métienka became skillful in taming that fury. With lies and calculated promises, with jokes, with sensuality, with cynicism, she exhausted an inconvenient jealousy, and debased Michel to the extent that she obtained his patience.

She even introduced him to the Baron, and Michel accepted his dinner invitations, evenings at the theater and cabarets. He made the decision not to be foolish, and to allow people to laugh at him because he was a dreamer, a simpleton, and taciturn.

La Métienka called him "her philosopher"—and, in fact, he was no longer Michel Bedée, but La Métienka's philosopher and the lover of her heart. He was also the Baron's parasite—one of his parasites, for the fat fellow had a court, an entourage of flunkeys, which cost him dear.

One evening, La Métienka made her debut in a concert hall. Michel was in front of the stage, with the Baron. As people were looking at the Baron, the enormous ruby on his chest, his exceedingly "Parisian" face, they also saw Michel, and he was recognized; the newspapers and magazines had published his portrait when he had discovered sirium. Michel noticed that people were talking about him; he sensed that they were scornful of him, or believed that they were, and he was momentarily ashamed; then he pretended to think that he provoked those multitudes, and was scornful of them. Then he repeated desperately to himself that "there is nothing vile in the house of Jupiter, in the house of Unity." What did that crowd of imbeciles matter? And why should he blush and tremble?

The Baron said to him: "You know, Bedée, you're having a little too much success—you're going to spoil La Métienka's entrance. Kindly slip behind me into the back of the box."

Michel was glad to hide, but when La Métienka appeared on the stage, he forgot everything else. The applause that burst out resounded in his ears like the sound of glory and made him want to cry, so involved was he in that triumph.

Modestly, the Baron did not applaud.

And when La Métienka danced, Michel watched her, curious to know whether she would smile at him or the Baron, whom he detested at that moment. She did not smile at the Baron or at him; she did not even glance at them—but she surrendered herself to the anonymous crowd, carried it away with her in her movement, threw it from one extreme of the stage to the other at a run, causing it to dread her departure and animating it with the delight of her returns.

Michel was jealous of the crowd, but then he melted into the vehement crowd, and, in its midst, received the prodigality of smiles, gestures, swoons and graces that La Métienka distributed generously.

Afterwards, there as a splendid supper at La Métienka's home, with the Baron's friends, their mistresses—people who wanted to laugh. The Baron did things well, and they supped amid a profusion of flowers.

La Métienka was drunk, on the wine, the flowers and the success. She sang in Russian, turbulent songs whose pantomime indicated obscenity. She became sleepy and recited phrases from Schopenhauer, which, thus presented, seemed a trifle equivocal. And the Baron, with a jesting eye and innocent soul, affirmed that he did not understand; then people searched for hidden meanings.

La Métienka declared: "Don't you think they're stupid, my little Michel?" And she begged Michel to come and undress her, because she was tired—but the Baron protested, and there were offensive remarks, ridiculous remarks.

Michel left, and outside, in the fresh air, he felt that he was as drunk as La Métienka. He wanted her; his concupiscent hands wanted her, and searched in front of him as he walked. He retraced his steps and slyly hid himself as best he could at the corner of the house next door, to wait stupidly. He did not go home until dawn, and then went to the window; the day had a difficult genesis, amid a confusion of gray and yellow vapors. Michel was sickened by the wretched aspect of the pregnant sky, giving birth in a sickly dawn.

And he went to bed. He slept heavily, as if exhausted.

He slept late into the afternoon, but someone knocked on his door. He woke up, shouted "Come in"—and saw, fresh and radiant, La Métienka.

"No, no, you're not dreaming," she said, "it's me."

And she had come running, because the Baron had forbidden her to see Michel again.

"Oh, oh, I shall still see you!" she affirmed. "Except, my dear Michel, let's be prudent!"

And she only had two minutes, All the same, yes, all the same, she couldn't go like that, no, no. She had wanted Michel since the night before...no, since the morning...one no longer knew, with these nocturnal follies...and so much the worse for the Baron!

She had, indeed, wanted Michel since the morning, and it was her morning desire that she contented. When she had gone, still cheerful out of habit, she was no longer launched into the future by a new desire—and Michel did not retain her. They had arrived together at full satiation and separated indifferently.

"I'll come again next week," said La Métienka.

"Yes."

"Adieu, my darling!"

"Adieu, my beauty!"

And Michel was disgusted by those words, which were nothing but polite hypocrisy; he wiped the lamentable kiss of their farewell from his lips. Then he did not miss La Métienka at all—but for want of diversion, he missed the occupation of his days and his heart by the mad love of that woman.

* * * * * * *

Henceforth, there was nothing for him to do but wander through the streets of the city like a lost dog. He knew the horrible ennui of afternoons that drag on and on, the distress of metropolitan dusks, the desolate gleam of the first lights that star the half-light of the declining day; he knew the fatigue of vain walking.

More than once, passers-by greeted him; he did not try to remember their names or faces. Unknown to him, the newspapers had announced his return. He was hardly alive, but the little that he lived did not place him in reality; he belonged neither to time nor space. He endured, and drifted at random.

One evening, however, the whim took him to go and see his house, out there in Auteuil. By the time he arrived there it was dark, and he walked alongside the walls like a thief. That house, however, which was no longer his own, he distinguished from the others with a singular emotion. It was not only his eyes that found it again; an extraordinary movement of his heart identified it to him—and he looked at it for a long time.

It was exactly as he had left it, in the midst of clumps of trees. Since his departure, however, the trees had shed their dead leaves; now, in spring, their new verdure was forming large bouquets.

There was light in all the windows of the house. Genevieve was there, watching over the patients: Genevieve and Pierre

Dauzanne.

"Genevieve Dauzanne." Michel repeated that name, which astonished him. He half-expected the garden gate to open, and that Genevieve Dauzanne would come out; she would not see him but he would see her.

Genevieve did not come out. After a few minutes, Michel left. He was not devastated, but he had sensed the continuation of life without him.

Life had forgotten him; and he also forgot it.

The next morning, led by hazard, he went into a church. The organ was playing and the choir singing, for a funeral. There were black drapes and candles around a catafalque, forming a kind of fragment of nocturnal sky, fallen upon the dead man to reclaim him from the earth.

Michel sat down among the people who were paying amicable tribute to the dead man. The church pleased him. He recognized its atmosphere, its odor; he felt that he was surrounded by memories; he thought that after strange adventures, he had returned to Brittany, and that the lumber of his childhood was welcoming him kindly. He experienced a sort of gratitude, a kind of soft tenderness, and yielded to its charm.

Once, when he had quit the vicinity of the church, when he had left the gentle shadow that it spread over his mother's garden, he had been languishing for a long time in the midst of holy customs and their sadness; they were like a heavy cloak upon him. Young, and counting on marvels, he had thrown away that cloak and had departed, curious and full of hope—but here he was, back again, his soul bare and shivering; the mantle of mourning made him envious.

In the same way that he had once diverted himself from a poignant ennui by squandering himself among the perpetual novelties of ideology and nature, now it was the past that astonished him and tempted him with a bizarre attraction. The episodes of the liturgy led him through the paths of his memory. He followed the course of the Latin phrases; sometimes he anticipated the words and the tune, and was content when the words arrived in the places assigned to them.

When the *Dies irae* burst forth, he submitted to the grim declamation of the psalm as to a tempestuous fatality. He surrendered passionately to the universal death that was passing, the storm that kills, that hastens to kill, to kill everything, since everything is nothing but pain.

> *Dies irae, dies illa*
> *Solvet saeclum in favilla!*

Ashes! Final ashes, scattered in the wind of the supreme cyclone: ashes in which the residue of beings and things is annihilated; the ashes of peoples and individuals, the ashes of monuments and dwellings; the ashes of thought and its inventions; the ashes of effort and its works; the ashes of hope and its deceptions; the ashes of barbaric or ingenious frenzy; the ashes of the general devastation, the dissolution of the All and its miseries, the final and ultimately sterile ashes!

That tragic malediction of life did not frighten Michel. His mind accepted it easily. He had always heard it proffered, in churches, with the vehemence of the spiritualism that bloodies the flesh in order to disengage the soul. And this time, the fury of the cantors shook him more profoundly; but the paradoxical doctrine of the life that the living blaspheme found him ready for persuasion.

The infinite plaint, the desolate appeal, the tremulous prayer of the *Requiem* went, beyond his present soul, to search for his erstwhile soul. *Lamb of God, who bears the sins of the world, grant him eternal rest.*

*Lamb of God, who bears the sins of the world*, Michel thought. *The sins of the world—that's life. Lamb of God, give us eternal rest. Eternal rest—that's death. Lamb of God, let us die.*

Michel's reverie calmed him, as if he were lulled by a tender and continual nursery song, a song to induce sleep—rest and sleep, death and darkness.

He remembered his mother, whom he had forgotten. He

remembered her with no more sorrow that one experiences with regard to the distant past. He remembered that she was dead, and asleep in eternal rest.

He also remembered his sister, whom he had forgotten, and who was dead to the world, to the sins of life, and who was participating, in a distant convent, in eternal rest.

And he remembered himself, as if he were dead too, and dead long enough for even his regret to have died.

All those dead people, the song of eternal rest prayed for, and with its prayer, lulled them, sent them to sleep.

Michel continued thinking about them, candidly and softly, until the end of the mass. Then he went out. On the parvis, he waited, not knowing what he was waiting for. He was no longer thinking about anything precisely; his thoughts had gradually dispersed into a singular lethargy.

When the coffin was carried to the hearse he thought that it was his own coffin, and when the hearse moved off, he accompanied the cortege; and he thought that he was following his own funeral procession.

He thought about himself for some time, as people who were following the funeral procession devoted the initial chatter of the route to the dead man.

"He was a jolly good fellow," someone said.

And Michel began to feel kindly toward the jolly good fellow who was himself, now.

"He didn't have much luck," added another friend.

"No," murmured Michel, "he didn't have much luck; but he was a jolly good fellow, very simple, very kind."

And he would gladly have exchanged a few memories of the jolly good fellow, very simple and very kind, with his neighbors in the cortege—except that they were already talking about something else. Then Michel, too, stopped thinking about the dead man, the dead man who was himself.

Afterwards, he abandoned the cortege.

* * * * * * *

He ate lunch in a little restaurant in an outlying district. He ordered his meal, as if he were not dead, and ate very attentively. Then he resumed walking, aimlessly, his arms swinging.

He encountered a crowd that was gathering at a narrow doorway and not getting through easily. He joined the queue. When people jostled him, he jostled back, jogged elbows, was artful, disdained insults and went in.

He perceived that he was in a large malodorous hall, where people were smoking and shouting, and he missed the open air— but there was no possibility of getting out; the crowd continued to flow in and it was impossible to go against the current.

Michel saw a stage in front of him covered in red twill, decorated with red flags; a kind of theater, rather wretched; a puppet-show of unaccustomed dimensions.

Two memories mingled in Michel's confused mind: the memory of the puerile Punch-and-Judy show in which his childhood had loved to see the policeman thrashed—and what joy when that policeman died, head hanging down, over the edge of the little stage!—and the memory of that other, enticing marionette, the pink and white Métienka, who exerted herself and fluttered. Michel fused them willingly!

He did not know and scarcely wondered what was going to be performed—the polemic of the puppet-show and the policeman or La Métienka's dance. He did not distinguish between the two spectacles clearly enough for it to be necessary to choose.

A poster he perceived, however, changed the course of his ideas. That poster was, like all the rest, red—the red of ox-blood. And in black letters, it advertised a great social gathering, entitled *Science and the Revolution.*

Michel looked around. The hall, broad and deep, was packed with men and women, pell-mell. There were even children, several at the teat.

One of Michel's neighbors annoyed him, because he spat a little too frequently; he spat after each of the puffs he took on his short pipe. Michel remembered very exactly that he had never bee able to abide contact with the so-called "working class" and he regretted being a virtual prisoner of badly-dressed and violent people.

He read the names of the listed orators. They were: Citizen Lourdelot, député; Citizen Lionel Dupont "of the Society of Painters"; and Citizen Flandreau, "astronomer." Michel remembered Flandreau, who had once been a fellow student; he remembered him, and he did not want to see him—but he would see him, among others, and that was that.

There was a movement of enthusiasm in the audience when the dignitaries of science and the revolution appeared on the stage. Lourdelot was in the lead. He had a coarse face, black-haired and bearded; he was corpulent; if he represented the starving in Parliament, he evidently did not let himself go hungry—but he had a rather timid, not to say pusillanimous, air about him. His small eyes, which did not sparkle overmuch between thick eyelids, consulted the audience anxiously. There was applause, and he was satisfied. Then, in a corner of the room, someone whistled; he became uneasy. The whistler, however, having received convincing digs in the ribs, fell silent, and Lourdelot, reassured, was triumphant.

Citizen Lionel Dupont, very tall and long-legged, slim-waisted and broad-shouldered, neatly dressed, tried to smile with jovial bonhomie that was neither in his character nor within reach of his talent. He had devoted the greater part of his existence to painting portraits of rich ladies; for imitating furs and fabrics he had no rival, and he had been in favor in the salons when he had suddenly been seized by the desire to change his clientele for another: the State. The lovely women of Paris, London, New York and Chicago had enriched him; the State would give him honors, the presidency of committees, influence and medals. So, he had applied himself to decorative painting; for the walls of national monuments he composed many republican panels, in which the people sympathize with a black-and-red-striped president, with députés of the left, with naked symbols of truth, justice and progress, and he spoke out rudely against bourgeois capitalism. He did not do it easily; involuntarily, his language conserved a singular subtlety. When he announced the coming of the Great Day, he sounded like a fop prattling about a great party. He perceived that; it embarrassed him. However, he experienced a perverse and delicious satisfaction in associating with the workers and paining the bosses, for the salons did not hold it against him; indeed, they welcomed him with more enthusiasm, as a more singular individual, very dangerous, whom they put on a semblance of domesticating.

And Flandreau, a small, brisk and wiry man, going gray, insinuated himself. He came in third, but was the foremost among the orators of the red table. As Lourdelot was applauded, Flandreau bowed, and people then applauded the smiling fellow's advanced politeness.

After the orators came a dozen hearty fellows: former workers who no longer worked, having found good sinecures in syndical politics. They sat down, framing the orators, like a benevolent guard.

Lourdelot got up and proposed the singing of the *Internationale*. Everyone stood up. Michel, remaining seated, received sharp admonitions in his arms and back. He obeyed. And they sang.

The song dragged on, like a mediocre litany. Flandreau's shrill voice passed through it like an odd thread in a weave. Lourdelot went at it wholeheartedly. Lionel Dupont, a trifle disorientated, contented himself with beating time, sometimes out of step.

Michel listened to that bleak canticle with astonishment. He was unmoved by it. He had the vague impression of being present at the celebration of a strange religion, a new religion whose rites did not concern him. The church, in any case, shocked him by its ugliness, and the sight of the officiants displeased him.

After the song, when the time came for the speeches, he did not think he was hearing a sermon; the puppet-theater was substituted for the church, and Lourdelot's pantomime seemed droll to him. The enormous fellow did not have the room to fling his arms around as he wished. Lionel Dupont, who was to his right, and Flandreau, to his left, realized that and did their best to move away, making signs to their neighbors to move along, taking their chairs in both hands and hopping like fleas. They became tightly-packed, but Lourdelot seemed to swell up as he obtained more space, with the result that he bumped into them several times.

Now that he was speaking he no longer seemed timid. He spoke loudly, as fearful children sing in the dark; the formidable sound of his voice tranquilized him. What he said was of no importance, but he said it with so much zeal that one would not have believed that he was repeating himself mechanically for the hundredth time. He rolled out romantic metaphors, which floated over his speech like banners, and the banners were soon so numerous that they became confused, like flags with which a façade has been excessively decorated: the façade can no longer be seen and the colors of the flags mingle.

Michel did not try to make sense of it; he submitted to Lourdelot's verbal flux; when people applauded, he applauded too, having no reason to protest against the overabundant, inno-cent words that he did not understand. A sudden contradictor surprised him; he even wondered what the man could have to complain about. The polemicist was silenced, and Michel thought that quite right.

After half an hour, Lourdelot shut up. Michel counted that to his credit; Lourdelot's silence was a gift that cost the benefactor; besides which, there was no reason why a Lourdelot speech should terminate at one point rather than another; the orator had plenty of breath, and what he had repeated he could repeat endlessly. Michel appreciated the good manners; if the rain stops when the sky is still cloudy, one is pleased. One would be even more pleased if the clouds had disappeared, because one fears that the rain might start again. Michel could see that Lourdelot was still charged with eloquence; he suspected a further down-pour.

In fact, Lourdelot got up again. He seemed to be struggling with difficulty against the din of applause. He swayed backwards and forwards, his belly posed on the red table. Michel applauded in order that he would remain silent.

He spoke, but it was only to hand the floor to Citizen Lionel Dupont, "the great and generous artist, the superb thinker."

Citizen Dupont was not an improviser. He took a sheet of paper from his pocket, covered with scribbling in pencil, and read it awkwardly. The little phrases flowed as best they could. After Lourdelot's muddy and violent torrent, it was a rather pure, gracious stream, but which ran over pebbles.

As the speech was having no success, Dupont experienced a need to change direction. He screwed up his text, stuffed it in his trouser pocket, altered his voice and cried: "Hurrah for revolution by science! Hurrah for science for humanity! Hurrah for humanity for itself!"

Michel excused him. Truly, an orator cannot push abnegation to the point of refusing all assent.

And the floor was Citizen Flandreau's.

He was not hampered by literature, but he claimed a long tradition of dissipated scientists, the anticlerical and unfortunate Galileo and the democratic republican Arago, whom he outbid. His eloquence consisted of talking loudly and rapidly. He was not timid, and he addressed himself to the crowd as if to an audience of schoolchildren, except that she stammered slightly.

Michel had always thought him loquacious, but he admired the casual manner of the astronomer, who emerged from his astronomy so easily. First, Flandreau put religion on trial. He was blunt, condemning Catholic priests as sorcerers, accusing them of spreading lies that profited their cupidity and oppressed the people. Michel did not like that at all. Flandreau drew a picture of the Court of Rome that excited the enthusiastic and sympathetic hilarity of the audience. Michel was offended by it; he became impatient.

Flandreau began mocking the ceremonies of the Church—mass, communion, candles and incense. He recounted anecdotes that delighted his public, who stamped their feet in satisfaction.

Michel restrained himself from shouting at Flandreau that he was an imbecile. Beside him, the pipe-smoker was no longer spitting; he was listening, open-mouthed, and sometimes wiped the back of his hand over his lips, which drooled slightly as he laughed.

Secondly—for the astronomer's speech developed like a gross theorem—Flandreau sang the praises of science. He opposed to the absurd mummery of the Roman sorcerers the serene activity of scientists, their perfect disinterest, their studious thought. And while religion speculated cynically upon the naivety of multitudes, science cared for them; the discoveries of scientists became the remedies that human infirmity demands. Here was placed, willy-nilly, a digression on the "infamous comedy" of Lourdes; that was indispensable to animate an audience that was becoming less amused. Its amusement was renewed. Then Flandreau, who had not forgotten his theme, came back to science, the incomparable healer of all ills

"Two years ago," he announced, "a man of genius found a new substance, sirium...."

Michel shivered.

"Sirium has, since then, cured dozens of sick people who would otherwise have died...."

"They'll die all the same," Michel muttered.

His neighbor gave him a dirty look. "What! They'll die?" he said.

"Yes, they'll die!" Michel replied.

The other gave the impression of getting a joke. "Ah! For sure!" And he laughed.

Michel was listening to Flandreau, who was prophesying without precaution the miracles of sirium.

"Dozens of sick people have been cured; hundreds will be cured; thousands will be cured; millions will be cured. And then all the sick will be cured. There will be no more disease. And what will have done that? Science. Who will it harm? Priests, because priests are the parasites of disease and death; they live on it. Sirium will have killed those two scourges of humankind, disease and religion."

Michel felt provoked. All the stupidities that Flandreau was spreading offended him. He stood up and said: "I request to speak."

He was booed—but Flandreau recognized him. "Citizens," he declared, "citizens...."

As Michel remained standing, cries for him to sit down came from every direction. The tumult was such that Lourdelot intervened—but Flandreau claimed supremacy. He shouted: "Citizens, we have the great honor of counting among us the man of genius that I cited just now, Citizen Michel Bedée, the inventor of sirium, the savior of those unfortunate hosts...."

Michel protested, but his denial was lost in the din of unleashed enthusiasm.

Flandreau went on: "Citizen Bedée, do us the honor of coming to sit with us on the podium; your place is here."

Then, speaking while standing up, he grabbed the back of his chair and, with a forceful gesture and planted it between Citizen Lourdelot and himself. Lourdelot, who had nothing to say, shrank.

Michel had no desire to go up on stage, but the favor of the audience carried him there. When he was there, Lourdelot congratulated him and Lionel Dupont immediately wanted to be introduced to him. Michel bowed. He was angry; he was impatient to say why. He began: "Citizens...."

He regretted the word when Flandreau interrupted him. "I request Citizen Bedée's permission to finish my speech. Afterwards, we will gladly give him the floor."

In the audience people were shouting "Bedée!" and "Flandreau!"

Loudelot rose to his feet. "Citizen Flandreau has the floor, for the continuation of his admirable discourse." He knew how much one suffers from not speaking, and came to the aid of his comrade; the few words he spoke did him good.

Flandreau reached his third point: the substitution of scientific morality for religious morality.

Michel had difficulty restraining himself, and when Flandreau paused for breath, he said to him: "There is no scientific morality."

Flandreau was bewildered. "Not yet!" he said. And he developed his idea of a morality founded on the integral truth. It was not humorous. He had intended to extract jokes from that philosophy—but Michel was inhibiting him. Because of Michel, he dared not give in to his broad comedy. He was torn between the demands of the crowd and the fear of a contradiction that he divined—with the result that he became tedious. Then the audience, curious about Michel, stopped listening. Michel was the only one listening to what he was saying, and Michel was exasperated by it. It was necessary for Lourdelot to intervene several times to calm him down.

Michel wanted to respond to every statement; he was agitated. Lourdelot, becoming anxious, would gladly have closed the session when Flandreau fell silent amid the general indifference—but the audience demanded Citizen Bedée.

Michel cried, brutally: "Messieurs, you are being deceived!"

Flandreau, who was expecting it, attempted to laugh, but Lourdelot was annoyed. He tried to express his annoyance, but someone shouted: "Let Citizen Bedée speak."

"You are being deceived," Michel went on. "Science is not that at all, not at all! There are some here who are talking to you about science as something that exists. That's not true. Science does not exist!"

Flandreau continued smiling, but his mouth was strangely contracted and his hands were trembling so much that, in order to occupy them with some movement that seemed voluntary, he tapped his fingertips against one another. He smiled, but he was not amused. Lionel Dupont was the one who was amused; he was secretly amused, with a slightly epicurean expression. His recent mania for brazen anarchism found a more malign pleasure in that swift demolition of science than the facile ideative edifices of a Lourdelot, let alone a Flandreau. Michel's words procured him a kind of quasi-sensual joy.

Lourdelot, however, was bewildered. He examined the audience with a genuine anguish. It was not yet certain how it would react to this bizarre incident. It was hesitant. It seemed very cheerful, for the time being. But if it admitted Michel Bedée's statements, the meeting would turn against the organizers, and if it evicted the killjoy, there would at least be a row, perhaps a brawl. The good Lourdelot did not like that. He leaned over behind Michel Bedée toward his comrade Flandreau and consulted him with a glance. Flandreau pulled a disdainful face.

Lourdelot, whom anxiety made decisive, rose to his feet. "Citizens!" he cried.

But in the first row of the audience, a pale and furious individual shouted, energetically: "Let Citizen Bedée speak!"

Lourdelot started again: "Citizens!"

"Let Citizen Bedée speak!" repeated the other, which an obstinacy that evidently would not yield.

Lourdelot argued: "I have the responsibility for this meeting. Citizen Bedée is not on the list of speakers. I do not have the right...."

Someone in the distance shouted: "Shut up!"

And the fanatic in the first row repeated: "Let Citizen Bedée speak!"

"Yes! Yes! Yes!" was shouted on all sides.

Lourdelot wondered whether he ought not to close the session. People thought that he was backing down. Already, there was laughter in the auditorium. Besides which, Flandreau was unflinching, and Lionel Dupont had no intention of renouncing such a diversion. Crestfallen, Lourdelot fell back into his seat, with an expression of reluctant patience.

And Michel went on: "No, science does not exist. If it existed, with the evidence that is its very character, there would be no skeptics, there would be no infidels; it would impose itself. What they are calling science is merely a petty labor scarcely begun, which does not advance and which is always beginning over. You have heard my sirium praised. Well, here is the truth. My sirium demonstrates that the scientific hypothesis most assured thus far, is unsustainable, and worthless. Everything has to be remade. Yes, it will be remade, and perhaps I have remade it. I have my hypothesis; one of these days, another discovery will demolish it; I expect that; I desire it."

He seemed brave. People applauded, and someone shouted: "Bravo! Bravo, Bedée!"

Lourdelot was at a loss; he no longer knew where things were headed.

And Michel, hitting his stride, did not stop. "Now, I ask you," he continued, "What good can it be to you—to you—that sirium produces heat and electricity without diminishing its mass or its volume? What can it matter to you—to you—whether the law of conservation of energy is exact or false? It's a conversation for the astronomer Flandreau and me...and then again, no, it's none of his business!"

There was an outburst of laughter, because Flandreau scowled.

"You've been told that sirium cures sick people. I don't deny it. I don't say anything—it's not my business. But because physicians and pharmacists sometimes utilize the discoveries of scientists, that's no reason for anyone to excite you in the name of a science that doesn't exist. There is no connection whatsoever between science and politics, between science and social life, between science and your labor as workers. There is no connection whatsoever between science and your pains, between science and your joys. There is no connection whatsoever between science and you."

That offended several vanities in the audience. There were protests in places. Lourdelot, who sensed support, said: "I reject energetically that entirely aristocratic notion of science. The people will approve."

"Let Citizen Bedée speak!" shouted the petty fanatic.

"You're being duped!" Michel went on. "I know where science is, and I swear to you that it has found nothing—nothing at all, absolutely nothing—that engages you to live from now on otherwise than you have been living. Science isn't much, but in any case, it's something other than life. If someone tells you that in Peking, some mandarin had had his fingernails cut, you wouldn't get excited about that. When someone tells you that I've discovered sirium, it's of no greater importance for you. It's something else. I tell you that it's something else!"

He became animated, and took on the tone of an impetuous prophet. "Science...science is inhuman. It would be the unique marvel, if it existed and if we were pure intelligences to contemplate it. Science is the eternal diversion of God."

"Down with the clergy!" someone bellowed.

"Look, I wanted to devote all my thought to science. Look at me—pity me. I'll tell you what I've done, in order to devote all my thought to science. I've left my mother's house, the cathedral of my childhood, the comfortable life that my parents and grandparents had carefully prepared for me. I've left my house, my homeland, my wife. I've left my memories, my affections, my loves. I've left everything. I've left myself. I locked myself away in a place that had no pleasures to distract me. I offered my head to ideas. They took up residence there as if they were at home; and they threw me out. I've become this: a man who has lost myself. I'm no longer anything but a vagabond, because I've left my location to ideas. Logically, it would have been necessary to die, but the body continued to live after I had lost myself, and it's the body that is wandering, in search of myself."

They thought he was mad; it seemed obvious.

"When I tell you that I'm searching for it, no—I don't want it any longer. Alas, where could I lodge it, now that ideas have taken complete possession of my head? I know full well where it is; it's where everyone's self is: in the shadow of a church, in the maternal house. So I'm warning you: science is inhuman; humanity has nothing to do with science. Don't you be fooled! Remain in the shadow of a church, in the house of memory and habit where you were born. Cultivate your god."

"Down with the clergy!"

"You've been told that religions are nothing but lies. Don't believe it. You've been deceived. Religions, I tell you, are human truths, just as science is inhuman."

The audience was restless. There were shouts, but Michel paid no heed to them.

"The ingenious religions, which have lived and suffered in the course of the centuries with humankind, which have amused themselves with it, the good and beautiful religions, invite you. Don't venture beyond their holy bounds; don't emerge from their walls, papered with ex-votos. Beware of committing the folly of which I repent: don't be men who have lost themselves. I say to you, I tell you this: say your prayers, in imitation of the ones your old mother said."

There was whistling; there was howling—and when Michel tried to continue speaking, he was shouted down. His arms beat the air; he sketched grand gestures and, without being aware of it, without thinking about it, he slowly and broadly made the sign of the cross, crying: "In the name of the Father, the Son and the Holy Spirit, so let it be"

The crowd rushed upon him. The first to arrive grabbed him. Lourdelot abandoned him to them. Dupont was not a fighting man and Flandreau soon gave up on defending him. Michel was abused and shaken. He was thrown outside.

He was left there, more dead than alive.

* * * * * * *

He was there, standing up, his legs like jelly, leaning back against a wall, his clothing ripped, his hands bloody, shivering and weeping, when a strange face appeared that he had difficulty recognizing at first.

"Michel!"

It was the Alchemist.

"Michel! My little Michel! Come on!"

But Michel could not move; he feared that he might fall if he moved. A policeman helped the old man to hold him up; they took him under the arms and led him to a fiacre.

The Alchemist sat down beside Michel, the policeman next

to the coachman. In a pharmacist's shop, Michel fainted. While the pharmacist laid him on the ground, fanned him and took care of him, the policeman questioned the witness, for his report.

"Monsieur Bedée," the Alchemist replied. "Yes, Monsieur Bedée the scientist.... I was there by chance.... No, I don't know where he lives. I came to Paris to see him six days ago, but it was impossible to discover his address. He's been traveling for several months.... Then, in passing, I went into that lecture hall.... I don't know what happened.... That's all I can tell you. The rest has nothing to do with me."

The policeman persisted,

"I tell you that the rest has nothing to do with me. It wasn't me who mistreated Monsieur Bedée. I came to his aid, as best I could, through a furious crowd."

Michel came round. He was asked for his address; he gave it. The pharmacist certified that he was not seriously injured—just bruises. A little rest, calm....

It was four o'clock in the afternoon. Sunday strollers were out and about. There was a crowd at the door of the pharmacy that scarcely parted as the Alchemist and Michel went through. Hatless and in rags, Michel advanced like a drunken man. The Alchemist had the roof of the cab raised. The adventure put him to the torture; he, who had once stood up so bravely to the wrath of an entire town, was ashamed of his tatterdemalion companion. More than anything else, he was tormented by the frightful anxiety that Michel might heave gone mad.

They remained silent all the way back to the hotel and went up to Michel's room amid the mocking gazes of waiters and maids.

"Go to bed," said the Alchemist. "I'll help you."

Like a sick child, Michel allowed him to do it. When he was in bed, he closed his eyes. Ideas came and went in his mind, not pausing. And he went to sleep.

The Alchemist sat in an armchair and watched him sleep, mouth open, like an abandoned corpse: Michel Bedée, his pupil, the mid of genius whose science he had awakened, the mind of genius, who had gone mad.

The minutes dragged like hours; the Alchemist filled them with his chagrin.

He consulted himself as to whether he ought to call a doctor; the old hatred he had for men of that profession restrained him. Then again, if Michel had gone mad, was he to be locked up like a vulgar lunatic in a padded cell? Were the death-throes of that admirable brain to be prolonged? What was the point?

Besides, Michel was not mad. The speech he had given, his odious speech, did not reveal mental alienation; the ideas followed one another rigorously. No, Michel had not gone mad. But in that case, he had, while fully lucid, blasphemed science. The Alchemist did not know whether he pitied Michel or whether, on principle, he hated him. In a state of uncertainty he watched over him, monitored his respiration, and observed the movement of his muscles, which contracted at times.

He would have liked to interrogate him, to ask him, gently: "What's wrong, Michel? What's wrong with your thinking? Tell me what has happened to your mind, to the most beautiful, strong and subtle mind of the epoch? If something has frightened you, tell me. Perhaps it's something simple that has frightened you; I'll explain it to you...."

Michel's sleep irritated him. It seemed to him that if he could talk to Michel for a little while he could bring him back to a true sense of reality. He coughed—but was immediately fearful of the sight of Michel sitting up in bed and talking nonsense. He remained silent, avoiding movement. Except that he feared that, in that strange sleep, so sudden and so absolute, Michel might sink, as a man fallen into water might drown.

He waited—and he thought about Michel's work, the manuscript from Rijnsburg of which he was the custodian. It was, in the clearest form, the most powerful effort of reasoning furnished by a human mind since Leibniz. It was a prodigious monadology, taken further than any other, founded on the most rich and new experience, rich in unexpected facts and surprising promises.

*Michel, Michel*, the Alchemist said to himself, *you were the great honor of science. Your genius was radiant. You were our enlightenment!*

There were two brief raps at the door. The Alchemist dared not respond. He got up without making a noise, and carefully opened the door.

"Monsieur Bedée? Have I made a mistake?"

"Come in," said Michel's voice.

La Métienka came in, astonished to find Michel in such a posture. Michel looked at her, and made no reply.

"Monsieur Bedée is ill," said the Alchemist. "I hope that it's nothing, but he needs rest."

La Métienka had a thousand questions.

"He needs rest," replied the Alchemist—and he indicated well enough that he had no comment to make other than that affirmation. La Métienka put her gloves, her umbrella and her feather boa down on a table, and sat down next to the bed on a chair.

Michel closed his eyes. Then, suddenly, he raised his head, sat up on his elbow and, looking at La Métienka, he said: "Go away, my beautiful Métienka, go away!"

"No," she said.

"Yes, yes. Go away. I no longer want you. It's necessary that you go away. Your place isn't with me. Go away, be kind. Go where I tell you to go. Go back, quickly, to where we were. Go to the lake. Call Brigitte. Tell her to come, and to hurry, because I'm waiting for her."

La Métienka listened in amazement. She did not reply. Michel saw her embarrassment, and saw her consult the old man with her eyes. The latter was pale, his jaws clenched, and he was trembling.

Michel was speaking as if in a kind of dream. He smiled slightly, to say to La Métienka: "You won't go to fetch Brigitte for me? Are you jealous, my beautiful Métienka?"

She too tried to smile, but she could not; her painted lips made a grimace of dolor over her pretty teeth.

"Adieu," said Michel, then. "Adieu, my beautiful Métienka. And enjoy yourself, out there. You need to enjoy yourself, or what would you do?"

She did not go away. She wanted to away, but she was held back by a sentiment of politeness. Her head was thrown back, her nostrils pinched with horror, as if she feared an odor of death and was avoiding it.

"Go away! Go away! Go away!" Michel shouted.

He was beginning to get angry.

"Go away, Métienka, if you don't want me to throw you out. Go away—and if you refuse to go in search of Brigitte for me, well, Brigitte will come of her own accord. I'm not worried about Brigitte; she'll come when you're gone. But go!"

La Métienka stood up. She held out her hand to Michel.

"No, no, go away!"

Michel let himself fall back on the pillow. He hid his face there and breathed deeply.

The Alchemist accompanied La Métienka to the door. He bowed to her, and she disappeared.

"Has she gone?" Michel asked.

"Yes," the Alchemist replied. "Who is she?"

"Didn't you recognize her? Oh, that's true—you don't know her! No, no. How could you know her? An old scientist, always enclosed by the thick walls of his laboratory. It's true, its true— you don't know her, my poor old master!" He burst out laughing and said: "That's funny!"

"Who is she?" asked the Alchemist.

"Well, she's life!"

"Ah!" said the Alchemist, with an expression of good faith. "And this Brigitte you were asking for, who's she?"

"You know her. She's coming. She's not far away. You'll see her. She's charming. She's death."

The Alchemist said nothing. Michel's mind was wandering.

"You see," Michel continued. "In a country—I don't know which—I encountered life and death. I hesitated between those two women, who both tempted me. I took life first; she was less patient. Now I'm waiting for the other. You'll see her. She's a strange girl, all dressed in black, with a black hood. She has a rosary in her hands. She makes reverences to you and begs your pardon. I've loved her for a long time. She's blonde. The tresses of her blonde hair, beside her black hood, make a delightful contrast. And her voice! It's a voice that speaks to souls, in a whisper."

"Get some rest!" said the Alchemist.

Michel rested for some time. He was lying on his back, and looking straight ahead, vaguely. The Alchemist drew away slightly, and read the papers that he took out of his pocket, making no noise, so as to leave Michel in the solitude in which he was languishing.

Suddenly, however, Michel asked him: "Did you understand?"

"What?"

"What I said to you just now?"

"Yes!"

"I don't believe it. That would astonish me, because all that is no business of a scientist. What I said to you is, however, the main thing—but it's exactly what you've neglected during your entire life. What an adventure!"

A little later, he added: "There's something I don't understand, though—which is what you're doing here, with me?"

The Alchemist was pleased by the surprise that Michel exhibited: a judicious surprise. It seemed to him that the sick man was returning to a true sentiment of reality; it was a good sign.

Then, in short sentences, easy to understand, he recounted how he had come to Paris because of the article in the newspapers that had announced the return of the illustrious scientist. And then....

But Michel interrupted him.

"I don't say no. Anyway, what does it matter? Except, when Brigitte comes, you'll go away?"

The Alchemist, disconcerted, had no response.

"Before then, however," Michel said, "I have a few things to say to you. Firstly, I have to forgive you. You've done me a great deal of harm. Yes, all the harm, it's you who've done it. I didn't ask you for anything. I was a child, like the others. I had my mother and my sister. I was a good child, who liked to stay close to his mother's dress. And you called me outside. I came. Oh, you didn't seem like a siren, to look at you!"

Michel laughed, almost mechanically."

"It wasn't you who were calling me; it was your mistress, science! Oh, she's pretty, your mistress!"

The Alchemist shivered. Michel took pity on him. "I forgive you. It isn't your fault. You were an old man who had a very demanding mistress, who wasn't sufficient to satisfy her. For that mistress, science, you procured a young man—and that was me, unfortunately. We left, she and I. The most cynical thing, of course, is that you protected our amours, and you accompanied us; you installed us together, out there, in a solitude in which she would have me all to herself, to slake her avid ardor. I was married, but so what? The demoiselle had need of my services. Anyway, don't distress yourself, since I forgive you."

Evening was approaching. The Alchemist switched on the electric lights. Then he closed the curtains at the window. There was a small chandelier in the ceiling, and a lamp on the nightstand.

Michel, his eyes bright with fever, spoke without pause. One idea led to another, often a long way, and there was an uninterrupted procession.

"Brigitte does better. She too was expelled, wounded; no one loves her, no one talks to her, no one thanks her, everyone scorns her. And it's she who, instead of forgiving, asks forgiveness. Me, I forgive you, that's all. But when Brigitte comes I shall say to her: 'Brigitte, give me your hands, let me mingle my fingers with yours, and we'll both recite the same rosary....' To begin with, she'll move away, because she's a little skittish. That's quite natural: she's a young woman! But I'll be able to convince her. And we'll go together through the streets of the city, reciting our rosary, in order that the people of the city might learn from us that they should do it like that, and not otherwise. We'll go everywhere, into the outlying districts, into the public meetings. We'll be threatened. And Brigitte, with her reverences, will mollify the most ferocious. But beside her, I shall say: 'In he name of the Father, the Son and the Holy Spirit, I assure you that there is no other science than reciting, in a modest voice, one's rosary in the presence of Brigitte, who is death. Science is an inhuman lie....'"

"No!" cried the Alchemist, involuntarily.

"If you prefer," Michel went on, "I'll say: 'Science is an inhuman truth....' Oh no, that's too much! Master, you're putting words in my mouth. I'll say: 'Science is a small scrap of inhuman truth; but here, in the rosary, is all human hope. Scorn science, and say your rosary, in the name of the Father, the Son and the Holy Spirit, so let it be!' That's what I shall do. I forgive you, yes, but it's necessary, all the same, that others shouldn't be duped by you, as I was. I'll be an apostle of repentance, against science."

"Shut up, Michel," said the Alchemist. "That's blasphemy."

"No, no."

"Yes, it's blasphemy! It's you, however, who wrote these sublime pages...."

"Oh, let's talk about them!"

"Yes, these pages where there is a summation of truth—the most powerful that ever emerged from a human brain...."

"Tear them up; I repent. Give them to me, so that I can tear them up. Give them to me, give them to me!"

He escaped from the bed, furious—but he was so weak that the Alchemist was able to reckon with him and lie him down. He said to him: "Come on, Michel, my little Michel, try to sleep. It's late and you need rest."

"Yes, I need rest!" Michel confessed, in a weak voice. "I need an immense rest. Only, Brigitte hasn't arrived. What time is it?"

"Sleep, sleep, Close your eyes. Don't think abut anything. Sleep."

Michel complained about the light; the Alchemist switched off the chandelier. The lamp was also irritating Michel; and he promised to go to sleep if the lamp were extinguished.

They were both in the dark, the Alchemist immobile in an armchair, and Michel restless beneath his sheets, the Alchemist devastated, as if in confrontation with a disaster, and Michel sincerely docile, trying to go to sleep.

He did not succeed. After a short time, he declared: "A curse upon science! Get her out of here; she's torturing me."

"Be quiet and go to sleep," replied the Alchemist.

"I tell you she's torturing me. Save me from science. A curse on her!"

"Be quiet and go to sleep," repeated the Alchemist, brutally this time.

"A curse on her! A curse on her!"

"Shut up! Shut up! Shut up!"

Thus their vehement contradiction alternated in the gloom. Now the Alchemist was no longer looking after Michel. He renounced him, and, in the final analysis, was defending insulted science against him.

He renounced Michel, because, all things considered, what else could he do? Michel—the real Michel—was dead. What was left of Michel was worthless.

And the two voices of the two men who could not see one another disputed violently for and against science, with mystical and hateful phrases.

Michel no longer forgave the Alchemist; and the Alchemist no longer spared Michel; he reproached him for his apostasy, the shameful discourse at the public meeting and that girl, La Métienka, and that other girl, Brigitte—in brief, all the debauchery in which the genius of the scientist been besmirched, debased. And Michel replied with sarcasm, imprecations and prayers.

Afterwards, he went to sleep, exhausted.

The Alchemist heard him breathing strongly and steadily. When he was certain that Michel was asleep, he got up from his armchair, walking on tiptoe, picked up his hat and went out.

* * * * * *

He came back some time afterwards.

He opened the door with infinite precaution, approached the bed and listened. Michel was asleep.

He took a candle from the mantelpiece, put it on the floor and placed his hat in front of it like a screen, so that the light would not wake Michel. He knelt down and began to maneuver various small objects, including a hypodermic syringe and a bottle, without making a noise. He filled the syringe with potassium cyanide, He stood up and approached Michel.

Michel was asleep. His neck was free and his arms were outside the covers, limply stretched out.

The Alchemist looked at him and thought: *He won't even know that he's dying. He'll continue to sleep. You won't wake up again, Michel!*

He gazed at the delicate features, the high forehead where the unkempt hair outlined a fringe. He gazed at the little moustache, the thin lips quivering in the breath of respiration, the palpitating nostrils. He gazed at the face that he loved, the face that remained so young and had not been spoiled either by hard work, or the rude alarms of thought, or the vicissitudes of existence. He murmured: "Poor little Michel, my child!"

And tears came to his eyes.

However, he was afraid of abandoning himself to more emotion than he needed to do what he had resolved to do.

*It's necessary*, he thought.

With a rapid gesture, he passed his fingers over his eyes; he stiffened himself; he waited a second for his will to obtain sovereignty over his entire body; he braced himself firmly on his legs; he leaned over Michel, and pushed back the sleeper's sleeve. The sleeper moved. Immediately, with a curt thrust, the Alchemist plunged the sharp point of the syringe into the flesh of the arm. The sleeper started slightly—and that was all.

The act accomplished, the Alchemist pulled Michel's sleeve down. He buttoned the cuff. He parted the hair that was hiding the beautiful amplitude of the forehead. He arranged the head in such a way that it was not tilted toward either shoulder, and he said, in a tremulous voice: "Like that, you're handsome!"

Then he fell into the armchair and sobbed.

Then he spoke, aloud: "Poor child, who didn't have the strength of your genius. Poor child, who had, with that genius, all the weakness of humanity! Science will never be done if human heads are too weak too bear its admirable commencements. Adieu, Michel, man of genius and poor child!"

The Alchemist took a pen and paper. He wrote:

*I have killed Michel Bedée, who was a genius, with an injection of potassium cyanide. The work of his genius will be found in my laboratory. I have killed him because he went mad and blasphemed science; he would have dishonored it, after having honored it. It was necessary that the madman not be able to debase the work and memory of the sublime scientist.*

He added:

*I loved him; he had been my pupil.*

He signed it. He placed the edge of the candlestick on the top of the sheet that he had covered with his attentive handwriting. He reread the lines. Then he wrote:

*And I am killing myself likewise.*

He lay down on a chaise-longue, pricked himself, and died. And in the chamber poorly lit by candlelight, the terrible master and his extraordinary pupil began to sleep their eternal slumber.

# ABOUT THE TRANSLATOR

**BRIAN STABLEFORD** has translated more than a hundred volumes of French prose into English. His principal interests are the French Romantic Movement and its Decadent/Symbolist aftermath, with particular reference to the evolution of the *conte cruel*, and the evolution of the *roman scientifique* from its origins in the eighteen-century *conte philosophique* to the aftermath of the Great War of 1914-18.

www.ingramcontent.com/pod-product-compliance
Lightning Source LLC
Chambersburg PA
CBHW020312260626
47156CB00004B/1194